Gallagher sta
*as she lay unc***

Not once since he'd
the two men at the s
that the nun in captivity was the woman who
he had suspected of being behind the
kidnapping. Yet here she was, a victim herself.

He hesitated a moment, then lifted the hem of
her robe and smoothed it up her calf. He
stopped and stared. There was a gun strapped
low on her hips. He smoothed the robe farther
up her leg and followed the narrow belt holding
the holster to one irresistibly sexy pair of
bikini pants.

A nun who wore X-rated underwear and topped
it off with a .38.

A nun who obviously wasn't.

Gallagher forced his jaw back into place. He
felt glad that question had been cleared up. He
really did. He finally knew something for sure.
There was just one thing he didn't know.

Who the hell was she?

Dear Reader,

When two people fall in love, the world is suddenly new and exciting, and it's that same excitement we bring to you in Silhouette Intimate Moments. These are stories with scope and grandeur. The characters lead lives we all dream of, and everything they do reflects the wonder of being in love.

Longer and more sensuous than most romances, Silhouette Intimate Moments novels take you away from everyday life and let you share the magic of love. Adventure, glamour, drama, even suspense—these are the passwords that let you into a world where love has a power beyond the ordinary, where the best authors in the field today create stories of love and commitment that will stay with you always.

In coming months, look for novels by your favorite authors: Kathleen Eagle, Marilyn Pappano, Emilie Richards, Heather Graham Pozzessere and Kathleen Korbel, to name only a few. And whenever—and wherever—you buy books, look for all the Silhouette Intimate Moments, love stories with that extra something, books written especially for you by today's top authors.

Leslie J. Wainger
Senior Editor and Editorial Coordinator

EMILIE RICHARDS

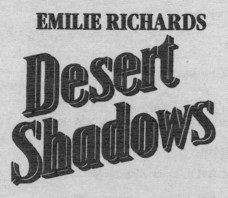

Desert Shadows

SILHOUETTE·INTIMATE·MOMENTS®

Published by Silhouette Books New York

America's Publisher of Contemporary Romance

SILHOUETTE BOOKS
300 East 42nd St., New York, N.Y. 10017

DESERT SHADOWS

Copyright © 1991 by Emilie Richards McGee

All rights reserved. Except for use in any review,
the reproduction or utilization of this work in
whole or in part in any form by any electronic,
mechanical or other means, now known or
hereafter invented, including xerography,
photocopying and recording, or in any information
storage or retrieval system, is forbidden without
the permission of the publisher, Silhouette Books,
300 E. 42nd St., New York, N.Y. 10017

ISBN: 0-373-07401-8

First Silhouette Books printing October 1991

All the characters in this book have no existence
outside the imagination of the author and have
no relation whatsoever to anyone bearing the same
name or names. They are not even distantly
inspired by any individual known or unknown
to the author, and all incidents are pure invention.

®: Trademark used under license and
registered in the United States Patent and
Trademark Office and in other countries.

Printed in the U.S.A.

EMILIE RICHARDS

believes that opposites attract, and her marriage is vivid proof. "When we met," the author says, "the only thing my husband and I could agree on was that we were very much in love. Fortunately, we haven't changed our minds about that in all the years we've been together."

The couple live in Ohio with their four children. Emilie has put her master's degree in family development to good use—raising her own brood, working for Head Start, counseling in a mental health clinic and serving in VISTA.

Though her first book was written in snatches with an infant on her lap, Emilie now writes five hours a day and "rejoices in the opportunity to create, to grow and to have such a good time."

Chapter 1

As far as Sister Felicia was concerned, there were two kinds of goats: those that smelled bad and those that smelled worse. Without exception, the goats at the Blessed Garden Convent fell into the latter category.

Then there was the goat shed.

Sister Felicia looked up and realized Sister Madeline was trying to tell her something. She schooled herself not to let her dislike of the goats show. Her sister nuns might not speak to each other except in the evening hours, but nowhere else was there a group of human beings who read facial expressions more adeptly.

She still hadn't accustomed herself to the Blessed Garden's unique sign language. She wasn't the first to be a slow learner, and the sisters for whom the Blessed Garden was a permanent home were used to patiently teaching the nuns from other orders who came to the convent for a year's retreat. Sister Madeline, however, was not a patient person.

The wrinkled nun made the swift downward jab of her thumb once again. If Sister Felicia hadn't known better, she would have bet that Sister Madeline was telling her where to go.

The thumb whizzed through the air and pointed toward the open goat-shed door. Sister Felicia finally understood. She nodded—a nearly universal symbol with which the Sisters of the Garden had thoughtfully not tampered—and threw her shovel to the side. Then, warning herself not to show disgust as she picked her way across the straw-strewn floor, she grasped the worn wooden handles of the wheelbarrow and trundled it past Sister Madeline to freedom.

Outside the desert morning was clear and cool, no forecast of the day to come. Stars still littered the black velvet sky. Only a thin border of gray along the horizon warned of the eventual onslaught of sunshine that would suck all the water from her slender body until her loose cotton habit was damp with it. For a moment she reveled in the fantasy of removing the veil that covered her cropped black hair and baring her head to the light breeze sweeping in from the west.

There were so many simple pleasures she was no longer allowed. Somewhere she'd heard that it took deprivation to develop appreciation. She wondered if the words had come from the nineteenth-century theological text that Mother Jeanne had droned aloud last night during supper.

As if the other nun had heard her thoughts, Sister Madeline appeared beside her and hiked her thumb toward the expansive vegetable garden five hundred yards away. Sister Felicia nodded and started in that direction. To her relief the other nun turned and limped back toward the house, her job completed. There were probably fifty wheelbarrow loads of straw and manure for Sister Felicia to haul and dump between rows. She wouldn't need supervision for quite some time.

Sister Felicia watched her wrinkled supervisor go, pleased that she would be alone for a while. At the exact moment Sister Madeline disappeared from view, Sister Felicia practiced her sign language again.

The flip of her fingers would have been understood on any urban street corner.

"You kin bunk here." Ralph flipped his hand in one of the spare, expressive gestures that Gallagher had already come to expect from him.

"You won't mind if I clean it up a bit, will you?" Gallagher looked around the six-by-eight room with distaste. There were no windows, and the stucco walls were cobweb-encrusted. An inch-thick layer of dust carpeted the floor and adorned the single bed and dresser.

"Don't care what you do, 'cept talk. I don't hold no store with talkin'. Leave me be, and we'll get along fine."

"If I leave you be, we won't have to get along." Gallagher walked across the room as he spoke and rested one booted foot on the bed, bouncing it up and down. When it didn't collapse, he nodded. "This'll do."

"You want better, you kin go somewheres else."

Gallagher could think of lots of better places. A prison cell. A migrant camp. A Bangladesh flood plain. But the subtleties of that would be lost on Ralph. The old man had apparently been left alone with his own thoughts for too many years. The desert sun had worn away his smarts before it had started on his health.

Gallagher faced him. "I'll scrub the place down this morning. Then you can show me my chores."

"Don't want no help," Ralph said churlishly. "Didn't ask you to come."

"I know." Despite his lack of enthusiasm for this setup, Gallagher felt a glimmer of empathy. The old man possessed so little, and now he felt that was being taken from him. "Look, I'm just here until you're feeling better. Father Melrose and Mother Jeanne want you to get well quickly. Just rest and enjoy having someone else do the heavy work for a while. You deserve a vacation."

"Don't want no vacation." Ralph turned and left the room.

Gallagher squelched the desire to follow him. If he followed the handyman he might just keep going, and he couldn't do that. He'd given his word to see this through. Besides, how often could a man afford a stay at a Palm Springs resort? Maybe the Blessed Garden wasn't exactly Palm Springs, and maybe it wasn't exactly a resort, but it was close. This convent of the Sisters of the Garden was only eighty miles as the crow flies from the posh California desert town, and it had some of the same attributes. Sand. Palm trees. Wells to turn the desert into verdant meadows.

And it had females galore, although admittedly his taste didn't normally run to nuns.

A noise in the doorway yanked him to attention. Ralph stood there with a broom and a mop. Wordlessly he handed them to Gallagher, then disappeared from sight once more. Gallagher assessed his chances of removing cobwebs without removing stucco. Since the odds seemed about even, he set to work.

Since arriving at the Blessed Garden, Sister Felicia had spent more time prostrate on the floor than a temperamental two-year-old. Mother Jeanne was a strict believer in total obedience, and what better way was there to prove obedience than to lie facedown on the tile floor of the chapel until a nun's penance had been accepted?

Actually, Sister Felicia decided, there were worse places at the Blessed Garden to be. Take the goat shed, for instance. And there were worse positions to be in, like stooping to shovel goat berries into a wheelbarrow. The tile floor was deliciously cool, and lying on her stomach eased the nagging pain in her back. It did nothing, however, for the relentless craving that was worming its way through her self-control.

Cigarettes.

As her sister nuns piously offered their hearts and minds to God, Sister Felicia contemplated the beauties of tobacco. Strangely, in her life before the convent, she had not been a heavy smoker. She had rarely smoked as many as a half-dozen cigarettes a day, although if she had counted the secondhand smoke she'd inhaled, the daily total would have soared.

But smoking had been just one of the earthly pleasures she had reveled in, and a minor one at that. Why was it eating away at her now? Was it sensory deprivation? Was the dry desert air so like a beloved blast of tobacco smoke to a parched throat? Was it the same personality quirk that had always made her want anything she couldn't have?

The last seemed a fitting question to contemplate; in fact, that train of thought would probably even be heartily approved by the women surrounding her. She *had* always wanted the things she couldn't have, and of course Felice Cristy, the child and woman she had been before donning the robes of a nun, had often been faced with things she wasn't allowed.

It hadn't mattered that her parents were wealthy enough to own a sizable chunk of the world and had, in fact, done just that. Felice had been raised in a cloistered atmosphere that made the Blessed Garden convent seem liberated in contrast. She had attended strict Catholic schools, suffered chaperons—a genteel word for bodyguards—everywhere she went and watched from the sidelines as the little girls who had thrown parties she couldn't attend had become big girls going out on dates she wasn't allowed on, either.

Her parents had loved her—still did, in fact—although her vocation was the cause of a grim-lipped silence between them. But as a child they had helped her, just as they had been protected, out of generations of tradition and fear. She was a direct descendant of two of the first Spanish landowners in California, and, as such, her wealth and status had been a weight around her Castilian neck. The expectations she had been forced to live up to had been a mile high, and when she had abandoned them she had abandoned them but good.

Which was one of the reasons she was prostrate on a cool tile floor at the moment.

The soft swish of cotton alerted her that noon prayer had ended. She waited impatiently for the tap on her shoulder that finally came. Then, with everyone watching, she slunk up to the front and knelt in front of Mother Jeanne, waiting for her nod. She could almost have sworn there was a twinkle in the eye of the stern-faced old nun. "You are not improving," Mother Jeanne said quietly.

Sister Felicia tried to look contrite.

"You will take dinner to Ralph and the new man as penance."

"New man?" As soon as she'd spoken, Sister Felicia knew she'd made another mistake. She had just spent half an hour on the floor for being caught talking to herself in the vegetable garden.

If there had been a twinkle in Mother Jeanne's eye, it disappeared. She waved her hands, and two dozen nuns vanished on cue. "You are *not* improving," she repeated when they were gone.

Sister Felicia's chin dropped to her chest—or as close as it could come with the high white collar of her habit blocking its descent.

"Silence must be observed at all times except when clarifying your tasks or during the brief period between the end of supper time and darkness."

Sister Felicia nodded.

"Do you want to leave, child? Our regimen isn't for everyone. I'll call your Mother Superior myself and tell her you tried."

Sister Felicia shook her head.

"Look at me."

Sister Felicia schooled herself to an unwavering stare.

"Perhaps I'll call your Mother Superior anyway."

Sister Felicia didn't, couldn't, answer, although she had volumes to say about that.

Mother Jeanne sighed. "Go on. Take two dinners to Ralph's quarters. Then eat yours in the kitchen, where you won't be tempted to speak to anyone."

Sister Felicia rose and bowed low, then turned and started down the aisle.

"And since you weren't listening last night at supper during announcements," Mother Jeanne said when Sister Felicia reached the doorway, "I'll repeat what I said then. Father Melrose has sent us a man to help Ralph for the next month or so, until he's feeling better. You're to ignore him, just as you ignore Ralph."

Sister Felicia thought that Mother Jeanne would be surprised at how little she had ignored Ralph—or anyone else at the convent, for that matter. There was no sign language to convey that thought, however, even if she had wanted to. She bowed again at the doorway, then started toward the kitchen.

The Blessed Garden Convent of the Sisters of the Garden was a cool, utterly peaceful house perfectly suited to its desert environment. Built more than a century before of cream-colored adobe around a Spanish-style courtyard, the convent was spacious and simple. One wing, the largest and most elaborate, held the chapel, where worship was conducted three times daily. Another wing held the parlor, where visitors were received, and, behind a heavily barred door separating the parlor from the rest of the wing, the convent living area and Mother Jeanne's office. The third and final wing was a series of individual cells separately housing the nuns, each with a narrow bed, bookshelf and stool. Like the sisters themselves, the cells were subtly individual, some austere and prim, others surprisingly cozy, decorated with brightly bound books and colorful pictures of saints.

Sister Felicia crossed the courtyard to take a shortcut to the kitchen. Marigolds and passion pink petunias flirted with her from the garden surrounding the perpetually flowing marble fountain. Her leather sandals slapped the bricks beneath her feet, accompaniment for the bees buzzing merrily in the garden. The bees weren't keeping silence, and she for one was glad.

In the kitchen nuns bustled from sink to counter, finishing preparations for the day's meal. Breakfast was always a simple affair of homemade muffins and fresh goat's milk. Dinner, the noon meal, was as elaborate as breakfast was not. There were always at least three different vegetables from the convent garden or freezer, creamy goat cheese and dark whole-grain bread still warm from the oven. Sometimes there was meat, if it had been a bad day for an unsuspecting kid or chicken, or if Father Melrose had come that morning with gifts from his congregation. Always there was fresh fruit and dessert, a goat's milk pudding or frozen yogurt, which the Sisters of the Garden had been eating long before the secular public discovered it.

Today there was meat. Sister Felicia stood to one side and watched Sister Althea pull one crusty chicken pie after another out of the commercial-size stove that had been a recent legacy from the parents of one of the sisters. She struggled not to swallow noticeably or look particularly interested. She knew she'd failed when Sister Mary Grace winked at her.

She smiled her thanks. Sister Mary Grace took down two heavy crockery plates and cut one of the pies, dishing out large portions on each. She set them on a wooden tray and added two bowls of salad and a smaller plate with bread, butter and cheese. Then she gestured for Sister Felicia to get the tray.

She smiled her thanks again. If she'd had to wait until all the sisters had been served, her own meal would have been delayed until it was cold and tasteless. Now, with the tray prepared for her, she could deliver it to the caretaker's house, return and eat before she was expected back in the goat shed.

Sister Mary Grace, with her fine-boned features and ready helping hand, was her favorite sister at the convent. Her gray eyes were often sad, but she didn't stint on warmth toward the other sisters. There were those who said that Sister Mary Grace was too warm, too giving. But Sister Felicia wasn't at the Blessed Garden to make value judgments.

The walk to Ralph's palm-shaded house took several minutes. A roadrunner crossed her path, and she half expected to see his coyote adversary following behind, but the rest of the trip was uneventful.

Ralph's house—or, more honestly, his shack—had once been a stable. Thick adobe walls and a high roof kept it cool enough for habitation in the summer, with the addition of an air conditioner and ceiling fans. Twenty years before, Ralph had come to the Blessed Garden and claimed the space as his own. The nuns, younger and more self-sufficient then, hadn't wanted him, but he had stayed anyway. Eventually they had learned to coexist with him, and then they had learned to rely on him.

From the beginning, Ralph had taken on the jobs the sisters could not do themselves. He had never asked for a salary, but every day a sister delivered three good meals, and every week his laundry disappeared, to be replaced with clean or new clothes, whichever were needed. Spending money magically appeared in his mailbox monthly, and any gifts to the convent that could be shared with him were. After his recent heart attack the Sisters of the Garden had quietly picked up the hospital bill, as well as instructions for taking care of a proud old man who wanted to pretend he had never been stricken.

Sister Felicia knew more about Ralph than some of the other sisters did. She knew that he had once been a successful Oklahoma farmer who had lost his land after two years of drought, then lost his bitter wife as a consequence. Afterwards he had wandered the country, swilling whiskey and harvesting the crops of other farmers until the day he had seen the Blessed Garden and decided to call it home. He hadn't had a drop of liquor since coming to live on the convent grounds, and his loyalty to the sisters who lived there couldn't be questioned.

Except by someone who questioned everything.

Sister Felicia lifted the hem of her robe around her trim ankles and took the two steps up to Ralph's porch. She knew that now he sometimes napped in the hottest part of the day, and she wondered if she should jangle the old cowbell hanging from a string beside the door to summon him.

She was saved the trouble by a man. And not an ordinary one. Her lips clamped together to ward off a grunt of surprise.

"What's this?" Gallagher pushed the screen door open as Sister Felicia took an unconscious step backward.

She considered him as she considered the rule of silence. She decided that in this instance she was perfectly within her rights to answer him. "I've brought Ralph's dinner. Are you his new helper?"

Gallagher took his time answering. He wasn't sure which was more surprising, to find a nun delivering lunch to his doorstep or to find this nun anywhere. She was an angelic vision, a Madonna in repose. Her face, outlined by a stark white wimple and veil, was oval and her creamy young skin flawless. Her eyes, heavily lashed and faintly almond-shaped, were the green of an island lagoon, and her lips were full and sensual, an odd twist in a face that El Greco would have wept over.

There wasn't much he could tell about her body under the shapeless monk-style robe belted around her waist with a braided rope, but everything he could see added up to a crying shame. The thought was sacrilegious and sexist, and didn't surprise him at all. Despite knowing better, he was perfectly capable of being both.

"I'm Ralph's helper," he said, when he realized she was staring back at him, assessing him, too. He reached for the tray, and her fingertips brushed his arm as she transferred it to him. He saw that her hands, unlike her face, were old before their time. He was staring at them when he spoke. "It looks like you could use a handyman. Someone's been working you pretty hard.''

Humiliated, Sister Felicia tucked her hands into the wide pocket made for that purpose in the front of her robe. "We will appreciate your help.''

She took another step backward before turning to go. All her senses were acutely alert, and everything visible about the man was now committed to memory. He was tall, with a wide chest and a rock-hard longshoreman's physique clothed in low-riding patched jeans and a faded T-shirt with a picture of the San Francisco skyline. He sported a three-day growth of auburn whiskers, and his hair was a darker, curling whiskey brown that needed a good trim. His down-and-out appearance suggested drifters, sailors' bars and a chest covered with tattoos.

More arresting were his eyes. They were the identical shade of his hair, and admiring, but even as he looked his fill, she sensed he was also perfectly aware of everything else around him. Like a man waiting for something to happen.

Her alarm system screamed a warning.

"I'm afraid Ralph is less than thrilled I'm here," he said. "By the way, my name's Gallagher. Josiah Gallagher."

She nodded. "I'm Sister Felicia."

He thought the name was perfect, except for the Sister part. What this woman had run from or to by becoming a nun was a mystery he would like to solve. But solving Sister Felicia's mystery was not his purpose for being at the Blessed Garden. At least, he didn't think so.

"I must go. We—we're not allowed to speak, you know."

He had known this was a cloistered convent, but hadn't fully realized everything that meant. His last experience with nuns had been in sixth grade, when a sister a foot shorter than his then five foot eleven had slapped his knuckles with a ruler. He had gently pried the offending weapon from her fingers and snapped it in two. And the next day he'd become a connoisseur of public-school education.

"I didn't know," he said. "I'll remember."

She nodded again, glad for once to hide behind silence. She lifted her robe and quickly took the steps. Then she started down the path back to the convent house.

She was sure that Josiah Gallagher watched her go, and she hurried, to give him as limited a view as possible.

The view she gave him was extraordinary, though. Gallagher assessed the sway of her hips and the proud set of her head as she fled down the path. He remembered the mesmerizing glide of the nuns in his elementary school. During their novitiate, someone had apparently taught them to walk as if they were floating on a heavenly cloud. No one had taught Sister Felicia to float, but someone had certainly taught her how to catch a man's attention.

She had definitely succeeded in catching his.

Chapter 2

The convent's herd of goats was comprised of two breeds. The Nubians were raised for meat and milk. The Angoras were raised for their mohair wool, which the sisters spun, dyed and wove into altar vestments, which they sold through the mail.

Sister Felicia had no favorite between them, although in the goat world, both breeds were beauty queens. The Nubians were large and loppy-eared, with short glossy hair. The Angoras had long, curly white fleece and a sheeplike demeanor that did nothing to endear them to Sister Felicia.

Before coming to the Blessed Garden, she had never seen a goat, at least, not one that she hadn't exorcised from her mind. Perhaps somewhere in her extensive genealogy was a Basque herdsman, but she rather doubted it. There was no enlightened ripple in her gene pool when she looked at the convent goats. They were smelly, noisy and uncooperative. She, who had never even wanted a kitten, was the least likely person to be sitting on a stool stripping the teats of a recalcitrant doe.

"Kick me again and you're barbecue," she muttered to the bad-tempered nanny. Muttering wasn't forbidden now that vespers were over and darkness hadn't yet descended, and Sister Felicia had been taking full advantage since entering the goat shed.

As if to test her words, Mary Poppins threw her full weight onto her front legs and let fly with her back ones. One hoof grazed Sister Felicia's shoulder, and she winced and jerked backward, simultaneously reaching for the milk pail so as not to lose the quart she'd already gained.

"Aren't you finished, Sister?"

Sister Felicia mentally counted to ten, then repeated the numbers backward in Spanish. "I'm sorry," she said to the voice from the shadows, "but Mary Poppins is giving me trouble."

"You don't seem to have the touch." Sister Madeline walked across the shed and peered into the milk bucket. "She knows you don't like her."

"Then she's more intelligent than I thought."

"Goats are like people, Sister. They respond to love and kindness. I often repeat a prayer when I milk. It soothes them, and they stand quietly for me, as if they're listening."

"I'm certain that's just the thing," Sister Felicia said. "Why don't you show me? Mary Poppins has more to give, I'm sure."

"By the time I washed and prepared myself for milking, it would be dark."

Sister Felicia wasn't surprised that she wasn't going to get any help. "Then I'd better continue quickly, or the rest of the goats will bust an udder."

"Sister!"

"I'm sorry. Is 'udder' one of those words the Sisters of the Garden don't say?" Sister Felicia wiped her forehead along the length of her long white sleeve. From the gasp beside her, she imagined she had just done something else forbidden, but she had rapidly moved past caring. The goat shed was fearfully hot, and the smell was stifling. Sweat trickled along her spine and pooled at her cinched waist, and under her veil her sadly shorn hair was sticking in clumps to her scalp. Worse than the heat, the smell and her antipathy for both Mary Poppins and Sister Madeline, was her mushrooming desire for a cigarette.

"Perhaps your community is more liberal than ours," Sister Madeline said primly, "but for the next months, you are a guest of the Sisters of the Garden. You'll obey our rules and respect our feelings, or you'll find yourself back in Los Angeles standing before your own Mother Superior."

"I find it easy to respect the feelings of almost every sister here, particularly those who do their share of the work." Sister Felicia leaned forward and angrily grabbed a goat teat. Mary Poppins kicked out in surprise and this time sent the milk pail flying. In a second the contents dripped from the skirt of Sister Madeline's habit.

"I'll speak to Mother about your behavior." Sister Madeline turned and stomped from the goat shed, her departure mourned by the bleating of ten sympathetic Nubians.

"Quiet, girls, while I sing a hymn!" Sister Felicia stood and grabbed the overturned milk bucket, then headed for the hand pump to sanitize it all over again. Over the cacophony of goat music, she made good her threat and started the only song that came to mind.

It had been some time since Gallagher had been to church, and he knew that things had changed since then. Mass was no longer in Latin; a kiss of peace was often exchanged between church members who years before had never even looked each other in the eye. But nowhere had he heard that Spanish love songs had become the hymns of choice.

His Spanish was elementary, but he could swear the song Sister Felicia was singing to the goats—if you could call the shrill noise echoing from her throat singing—was decidedly erotic. Weren't nuns supposed to have the voices of angels? And weren't they supposed to sing praises to God? In Latin?

"That's one of the new nuns," Ralph said, in one of his longer sentences. "Came just before I went away."

The song stopped abruptly at Ralph's words. Sister Felicia whirled and looked at the two men. The goats began to bleat their disappointment.

"Ceiling's gotta be fixed. Showin' him." Ralph jerked his thumb at Gallagher. Gallagher thought the picture-pretty young nun looked distinctly guilty.

"I'm not done with the milking," she said.

In Gallagher's judgment, Sister Felicia was probably worn to a frazzle. The evening breeze was just beginning to cool the interior of the shed, but the temperature inside was still above eighty. Her habit was loose, similar in style to an Arab's *thwab*, but Gallagher knew it must still hold the heat. He wondered if desert nuns ever had the desire to strip down and expose their skin to the cooling effect of the evening air. Then he wondered why the possibility of Sister Felicia stripping interested him so much.

"I'll give you a hand with the milking after Ralph shows me what I have to do tomorrow," he said.

"She won't let you help," Ralph said. "Do it themselves."

"You *can* help," Sister Felicia said, ignoring Ralph. "Getting this done is more important than who does it."

Ralph grunted.

"The Lord loves a willing helper," she added piously, and wondered if that, too, had come from supper-time reading.

"Show you the roof now." Ralph wandered off in search of a stepladder.

Out of the corner of her eye Sister Felicia watched the two men leave. She had panicked for a moment when she realized that they might have heard her singing, but luck seemed to be with her. And what could they have done, anyway? Report her to Mother Jeanne? They would have had to stand in line.

She was just glad that she hadn't been overheard by another sister. Singing the provocative little ditty had been silly and willful, not to mention unprofessional. If she wasn't careful, she would be back inside the blue-and-white habit in which she had arrived, heading out the Blessed Garden's forbidding iron gate.

She stood to empty her bucket into the sanitized milk can. There were four goats left to milk and Mary Poppins to finish. She had relegated Mary P. to the end, hoping the goat's temper would cool by then. Now she led the goat she had just emptied back to her stall and brought another one back with her to the milking stand, locking her in with a crossbar. She put the required grain bribe by the goat's broad lips and settled herself at her side.

She dipped each teat in a diluted iodine mixture to carefully sanitize it, then started to strip out the milk.

Would anyone who had known her before believe that now she spent her days shoveling goat berries and pulling teats? Would they believe that she washed her face with the convent's homemade soap and helped sew by hand everything she wore? Was there anyone, anywhere, who would believe that she, Felice Cristy, who at eighteen had rebelled so violently against authority, was now a nun?

She was locked in contemplation when the two men returned. She didn't hear them, but over the standard goat-shed odors she smelled the fragrance of tobacco. At first she thought it was just her vibrant fantasy life. Since coming to the Blessed Garden she had sometimes awakened at night with the sharp tang of smoke hovering in the air. Then, as she'd come fully awake, she'd realized the smoke had been a glorious dream.

She wasn't asleep now, though. She was wide-awake, and she smelled tobacco smoke. It took her a minute to realize that the smell emanated from Ralph—the only pleasant one that did— and that he was up on a stepladder six yards away. More important was the pack of cigarettes lying on the supply shelf six feet behind him, almost as if the devil himself were tempting her.

She pieced together the scenario. Ralph was still smoking, although his doctor had strictly forbidden it. Ralph had just had a cigarette while outside on his stepladder search. Ralph had thoughtlessly—or thoughtfully, depending on perspective—set the cigarette pack on the shelf when he'd come back in with the ladder. Why he hadn't stuffed it back in his shirt pocket was obvious. The pocket now bulged with something else—nails, from the look of it. Perhaps he intended to do something temporary to the roof; she didn't know.

But she did know something more important. Ralph's cigarettes were staring at her from the supply shelf, begging her to liberate them. Weighing the lungs of the sick old man against those of a deprived young nun, she made the chivalrous choice.

She would not take them all. Ralph wasn't stupid, although a stranger might have thought so, but he was said to have grown absentminded since his heart attack. It was doubtful he would notice the loss of a few cigarettes, and if he did, he would just assume he hadn't paid attention to how much he was smoking.

She could take three. No, four. Maybe even five, if the pack was nearly full.

She said a short, silent prayer that the pack had just been opened. Then she prepared her strategy.

The nanny on the milking stand moved restlessly. Sister Felicia snapped to attention and finished quickly. Her hands weren't quite steady as she carried the milk to the can to empty it, and a thin stream trickled down the stainless steel side. St. Michael, the resident barn cat made a dash for the can, almost knocking her off her feet, but she shooed him away and polished the can with a towel. The Saint would get his share when she was finished, but he, like the goats, had to be taught some manners.

Back at the milking stand she unhooked the crossbar and led the goat back to her stall. Then, with carefully plotted cunning, she went for Mary Poppins.

Mary P. was no more malleable than she had been half an hour before. She planted her feet in the straw of her stall and refused to move. Then, with calculated finesse, she sat.

Sister Felicia dropped the rope and slapped her hands on her hips. "Is this any way for a convent goat to act?" she wheedled, hoping that in moments Mary P. would act much worse.

"Having trouble, Sister?" Gallagher asked from behind her.

"Thank you, Mr. Gallagher, but I can handle her." She moved just far enough to the side to be sure that he knew she didn't mean it.

"She needs a lesson in manners."

"She's one of God's own creatures. I couldn't abuse her."

Gallagher had the distinct impression that Sister Felicia would like nothing better than to string the goat up by its stubby tail, but he had no way to test his theory. "Would you like me to get her for you?"

"I should do it myself."

He reached for the goat's rope. "But this way I get the blessings of being a willing helper."

Sister Felicia took several steps backward, as if to move out of the goat's way. A quick glance behind her showed that she was less than four yards from the supply shelf. Ralph, on the top step of the ladder, was busily nailing something back in place.

The goat was no more enthusiastic about Gallagher's tugs than she had been about Sister Felicia's. Gallagher moved closer; Sister Felicia inched backward.

"Come on, nanny. Let's get you out of here." Gallagher tugged again. Mary P. made a suitable bleating response.

"Perhaps if you pushed her from behind?" Sister Felicia suggested.

Gallagher grunted and dropped the rope to take her suggestion. Sister Felicia watched, her hands folded piously in her pocket.

As soon as Mary P. felt the man behind her, she leapt to her feet, performed her familiar bucking-back-leg kick, then headed for freedom. She was a stubborn goat, but not a stupid one. She was through the shed aisle and out the open door to the yard before Gallagher, who had leaped backward into a pile of straw, was steady on his feet again.

"Oh, no!" Sister Felicia started after the goat, tripping conveniently on the hem of her robe.

"I'll get her." Gallagher's masculinity was in disarray. He wasn't immune to mistakes, but he couldn't remember ever being bested by any four-legged beast smaller than a bronco. And somewhere, too deep in his consciousness to examine at the moment, he was sure that Sister Felicia was laughing at him.

"You're so kind." Sister Felicia was an arm's length from the supply shelf now, and Ralph was still on the ladder hammering, as if nothing had happened. She watched Gallagher's six foot three bend to accommodate the doorway; then he was gone.

With her eyes glued to Ralph, she made her final move. The shelf was at her fingertips, then the pack of cigarettes. To the reassuring rhythm of the hammer, she lifted the pack, judging from weight alone that her prayers had been answered. In a moment the pack was in front of her, and with her eyes still on Ralph, she was shaking out cigarettes.

Overwhelmed by temptation, she took six. Five would have been safer, four safest, but six meant six whole nights of earthly pleasure.

Starting tonight.

She eased the pack back to the shelf and the cigarettes into her pocket. Ralph had never once looked at her, but her timing couldn't have been better, because now his hammer was silent and his feet were on the top step, as if he intended to climb down. She had moved around the base of the ladder toward the doorway when she realized a man was blocking her route to the outside.

A man and one docile nanny goat.

Gallagher held out the rope. Only a slight narrowing of his whiskey-colored eyes warned her that he knew what she'd done.

Maybe he hadn't seen her. Sister Felicia knelt in the chapel for compline, the last prayers before bedtime, and considered the events of the evening. Maybe Gallagher hadn't seen her steal Ralph's cigarettes, and if Ralph questioned him—as he might, since she had stolen so many—Gallagher wouldn't finger her as the culprit.

Besides, even if he'd seen her and he squealed, who would believe it? The cigarettes were safely folded in a scrap of tarp from the goat shed and hidden in a crevice between two rocks by the bubbling spring that gave the Blessed Garden life. She could easily admit to lifting the pack from the shelf. "I was so surprised to see that Ralph was still smoking, I just picked up the pack and stared at it," she would say.

And who would believe that a nun who had taken her final vows would still crave tobacco, anyway?

Mother Jeanne would. Particularly if it was this nun. Sister Felicia made the sign of the cross on cue with the other nuns. She would just have to hope that either Gallagher hadn't seen her or he wouldn't tell if he had.

He was a strange man. He looked like a drifter, with his three-day-old beard and his worn clothing. But with a good haircut, a shave and a three-piece suit, he would look like... Making the sign of the cross once more, she tried to imagine. He would look like... a politician? No. He looked more intelligent than that. She couldn't see his wide, cynical mouth making promises he couldn't keep.

A banker. Definitely not. A CEO? The thought gave her pause. There was something calculating, crafty, about him. She imagined that Donald Trump or Adnan Khashoggi wore the same expression when they made million-dollar deals. But somehow she couldn't imagine Gallagher at home in a boardroom.

A hit man.

God help them all, that was exactly what he looked like. A hit man or an IRA terrorist. "June" on an "Assassins of the Month" calendar, posed with an Uzi propped on his knee and the green hills of Ireland stretching out behind him.

But, of course, it wasn't Ireland or the IRA she was worried about. Her fears were closer to home.

She stood with the other sisters and stepped into line to file quietly out of the chapel. There would be no speaking for the rest of the night. Even Mother Jeanne kept silence now, so she was in no danger of a summons to Mother's office tonight. Each nun would go to her cell and prepare herself for bed. They could read or continue their prayers for half an hour; then a bell would signal lights out.

And she would wait fifteen minutes before sneaking out to the spring.

Dozens of sandals slapped the courtyard cobblestones as the nuns crossed to their wing. Inside they dropped off, one by one. Sister Felicia saw Sister Madeline enter her cell, then Sister Mary Grace. The cells were surprisingly private, each with a heavy door that was kept closed, except in summer, when it was left open to take advantage of the antiquated air-conditioning system.

Sister Althea had told her that the nuns at the Blessed Garden considered air-conditioning to be an awful luxury, but that without it they could not live in the desert and continue their work. The day that the goats were taken up into the San Jacinto mountains for the summer, the air conditioner was turned on. The air-conditioning was compensation for the sad absence of fresh goat's milk in their diet for those months.

Sister Felicia closed the door of her cell behind her and undressed quickly. Compared to the habits of many traditional orders, the Sisters of the Garden's habit was blessedly simple and lightweight. Sister Felicia unpinned her veil, then unwrapped the utilitarian cotton wimple until her head was bare. Dipping her cupped hands into the crockery bowl at her bedside, she bent low and spilled water over her hair until it was thoroughly wet. Then she washed her face and hands before she removed her wooden cross and the rosary looped at her belt.

The robe was held together by the seeds of a desert plant that one of the nuns made into buttons. She unfastened one loop below the high collar and two more tucked inside the front placket; then she untied the heavy rope belt and shrugged the robe off her shoulders. Convent undergarments, like the rest of the dress, were utilitarian and nothing else. Woven of coarse cotton, the short-sleeved undershirt and knee-length pants were changed daily. Each nun set hers outside her door to be picked up for the daily laundry in the morning. Sister Felicia was never convinced that the garments that came back to her were the same ones she had worn two days before.

Happily naked at last, she sponged her body with a washcloth until she was four degrees cooler. Sponge baths were allowed whenever necessary, but showers were only allowed in the morning. They were brief, spartan affairs, but they were still Sister Felicia's favorite part of the day.

Dressed in her cotton nightgown, she lay down on her bed. There was a tiny window in all the doors, and she knew that sometime in the next few minutes a sister would peek inside to be sure she was there. Then, at the sound of the bell, lights would go off simultaneously and the same sister would walk down the hallway to be sure no light streamed through a cell window. Sister Felicia wanted to be the model of propriety when her cell was checked.

Half an hour later, she got up quietly in the darkness and pulled her robe from its wooden peg. She didn't bother to remove her nightgown. Instead she pulled the robe over it, then hastily wrapped her wimple and pinned her veil. If she was caught outside her cell, explanations would be difficult at best.

If she was caught outside her cell without her habit, explanations would be impossible.

Her door didn't creak when she opened it, a detail she and a little chicken fat had seen to on her first day at the convent. No one was in sight. All too aware that her white robe was a beacon in the darkness, she crept to the door that sealed the wing of cells from the courtyard. That door didn't creak, either—and for the same reason. When she was in the courtyard she crept around the perimeter, blending as best she could with the adobe.

A goat was bleating when she passed the shed. The aroma of freshly spread goat manure greeted her as she passed the vegetable garden. Beyond the garden, at a fork in the path, she hesitated. To the right lay the spring, a true oasis in a barren stretch of desert. At the spring were her precious stolen cigarettes. To the left lay Ralph's house, now Gallagher's, too. Gallagher, who all instincts told her was not whom he seemed.

She turned left. The path was lined with native vegetation, burro bush and other desert plants whose names she had never learned. Closer to the house was a palm grove, testifying to an underground spring. She glided in and out of the palm trees until she came to rest against a likely clump. Then she settled herself to wait.

She didn't have to wait long. Abruptly from inside the house the sound of a country-and-western radio station wailed heartbreak into the night silence. Moments later Ralph appeared on the porch for a smoke. He stared at the sliver of moon overhead, blowing smoke toward the star-studded sky. Sister Felicia could almost taste each puff.

She'd been watching—and coveting—while he smoked two more cigarettes, when another figure joined him on the porch. Gallagher's wide shoulders and narrow jean-clad hips would have been hard to mistake for anyone else's. He leaned against the porch railing and said something she couldn't discern. Ralph dropped his cigarette butt to the floor and ground it out with the sole of his shoe. Then, as if he couldn't tolerate Gallagher's company, he went back inside.

Gallagher didn't act like a man rebuffed. He folded his arms and stared at the same sliver of moon that had fascinated

Ralph. She had never seen a man stand so still. She had never stood so still herself.

Just when she was beginning to think that he would never go back inside, he did. The door closed behind him; the radio went off, and minutes later the house was plunged into darkness.

She waited some more. Ten minutes went by, then another five. Finally convinced that Gallagher was in bed for the night, Sister Felicia crept back the way she had come until she turned onto the long-awaited right fork in the path.

She stole cigarettes and stood perfectly still, like a pool of moonlight in the darkness, spying on Ralph's house.

Who was Sister Felicia, the Madonna with the provocatively swaying hips and the erotic croaking songs?

For the fourth time Gallagher went over the possible reasons for Sister Felicia's actions. There was the faintest possibility that she had taken Ralph's cigarettes to keep him from smoking them. There was the faintest possibility that, in a fit of guilt, she had come to the house to return them and changed her mind when she saw him on the porch.

There was a far greater possibility that she wasn't whom she seemed.

Trailing a white-robed nun in the darkness was as easy as catching fireflies. But Gallagher didn't intend to catch Sister Felicia. He intended to watch her. What would she tell him if he questioned her and what would his questioning tell her about him? No, he'd discovered long ago that watching and waiting got more information in the long run. And right now he didn't have enough information to consider her dangerous. Just rebellious.

That much was absolutely certain. Not another nun was in sight on the grounds anywhere. Obviously everyone else had retired for the night, because all the lights at the house were off. The nuns rose early and worked hard. Sister Felicia worked particularly hard, because she was young and strong and able to do chores the older nuns couldn't handle. So why wasn't she in bed getting the sleep she desperately needed?

Gallagher knew the setup at the Blessed Garden in detail. Father Melrose had explained it to him so he would know just what he was getting himself into. The Sisters of the Garden was an old, respected community of nuns, a cloistered order, which meant that they were shut away from the rest of the world to meditate and pray without benefit of many of society's advantages.

Once communities such as this one had drawn their share of the women seeking convent life. Now, along with every other order, the Sisters of the Garden drew far fewer recruits. Their youngest member was fifty; two younger women who had come to them last year had left within six months to join less restrictive orders.

Times had changed. With more opportunities open to women who didn't opt for the traditional roles of wife and mother, thousands of starry-eyed Catholic girls no longer flocked to convents. By the same token, orders were now more selective. Much had been learned through the years about what made a good nun. Highly educated administrators counseled and tested to be sure that the women asking admittance were suited to the life they would lead.

Gallagher wondered if anyone had counseled and tested Sister Felicia. Was she more at home in her own order? He knew from Father Melrose that eight of the women living at the Blessed Garden right now were here as guests. When a long retreat was needed, nuns from more worldly orders came to the Blessed Garden for a year to think and pray and to assist the Sisters of the Garden in their difficult labor. The system was mutually beneficial, although it certainly wasn't tension-free. Sometimes the guest nuns had problems adapting to the spartan life and backbreaking work.

He guessed that sometimes adapting took every ounce of inner strength a nun possessed. Take the woman dancing her way around the tree-lined spring, for instance.

Something moved inside Gallagher at the sight of Sister Felicia swaying sensually to her own inner music. She had the sexiest walk he ever remembered seeing. It was an energetic, bouncing, jitterbugging stride that signaled a tremendous inner vitality.

In days of yore women had often been banished to convents as punishment or simply for political convenience. He couldn't imagine that happening now, but watching Sister Felicia made him wonder.

She seemed to know exactly where she was going. He had no trouble following her. The spring was an oasis within an oasis, a desert developer's fondest dream. It was surrounded by lush tropical plantings, and he used a row of blooming hibiscus for cover as he skirted the edge. Sister Felicia used nothing. She obviously believed she was alone as she made her way to the rock-lined pool.

Gallagher had expected almost anything, but even he was surprised. Sister Felicia sat down on a large rock and reached below it, pulling something out of a crevice. Then, her booty on her lap, she propped her feet on the rock beside her and hiked her robe halfway up her thighs, revealing a pair of long, shapely legs. As he watched at full attention, she took off her veil and unwrapped the cloth surrounding her face.

Her hair was dark and boyishly short, emphasizing an elegantly shaped head and graceful neck. She ruffled her hair with her fingers, and he could almost hear her purr of pleasure. Her walk was no mistake; this was a highly sensual woman, and he was a man fast being turned on by a nun.

Mentally he pulled himself up short. He wasn't here to salivate over forbidden flesh. He was here to watch, to assess, to decide if this woman was dangerous. She didn't look dangerous, though. She looked like a normal young woman stealing a few moments of pleasure for herself. She wasn't asking for much. The sound of a bubbling spring. Tropical fragrances on a spring night. A star-studded sky. The feel of cool air on her head and legs.

And tobacco smoke in her lungs.

For a moment Gallagher wasn't sure he had really seen the flare of a match, the glowing tip of a cigarette. Then he knew he wasn't mistaken. Her hidden treasure had been cigarettes, probably Ralph's cigarettes, and now she was smoking one like an addict with her favorite fix. Never had he seen such a look of unadulterated pleasure. It was hard to miss, even by the dim light of a thin crescent moon.

Sister Felicia had not been protecting Ralph from himself. She had stolen the cigarettes because she had needed, wanted, craved them for herself.

He discarded the possibility that she had come from an order so liberal its nuns smoked. If such an order existed, they didn't send nuns to the Blessed Garden on retreat. He discarded the possibility that this was just a petty rebellion aimed at the nuns who were working her so hard. If Sister Felicia was feeling rebellious, he suspected her retaliation would have been more open, and probably more spiteful.

She smoked the cigarette like a pro, drawing the smoke deeply into her lungs, exhaling it as if she were caressing each puff with the muscles of her throat. When she finally ground it out, he knew there was nothing left but the filter—and she'd probably smoked some of that.

When she was done she looked distinctly dejected. He knew she'd stolen more than one cigarette, but she was apparently saving the rest for another time. She regretfully fingered the tiny package on her lap, then wrapped it up and stuck it back in the crevice, along with the stub of the cigarette she'd just smoked.

Gallagher would have expected almost anything next. Cartwheels and somersaults. Gorging on the fresh figs interplanted among the palms. What happened instead was something he would never have suspected. Sister Felicia rose and wrapped her face and covered her head once more. Then, as he safely trailed yards behind her, she took him on a tour of the convent grounds. By the time she picked the lock and reentered the house, he knew that every gate was safely fastened, every foot of the high stone walls unbreached.

More interesting was the fact that she knew it, too. And that she cared.

Chapter 3

A self-appointed night watchwoman? Or something more insidious?

At breakfast the next morning Gallagher was still mulling over Sister Felicia's behavior. Another nun delivered the morning tray of muffins and boiled eggs, and he ate his share without paying much attention to taste. Ralph was sleeping in, complete with raucous snores edging through the crack under his bedroom door.

Ralph, who appeared to be trying to scare him away, had given him a list of chores nearly a mile long. Gallagher didn't waste time after breakfast, only lingering extra seconds over the second cup of coffee from a pot he'd brewed himself. Ralph's coffee, he'd discovered, tasted like the goat shed smelled. Clad in the same jeans he'd worn yesterday and a clean T-shirt, he set out.

His plan was simple. The roof in the goat shed needed more repair than Ralph had managed, but since no rain was forecast for the next four months, he knew he could safely put off that job until it suited him. And it would suit him to do it while Sister Felicia was there, perhaps tonight, when she was milking.

Of course, that was unfair to her. Anyone knew that loud hammering made the goats nervous and milking more difficult, but being fair was way down on his list of things to worry about. Sister Felicia was up at the top.

He passed three nuns working silently in the vegetable garden. He knew they did most of their work while it was still cool and used the hottest hours of the day to pray and contemplate. All three smiled at him as he passed, surprising him a little. He wasn't sure what he had expected, gloomy, forbidding faces, perhaps, but these women looked remarkably content and peaceful, and their smiles shared those feelings with him.

He hadn't given much thought to what went on here, but now he did. The Blessed Garden was twenty acres of land, some lush, irrigated oasis, some desert vegetation and sand. The gardens were beautifully tended, the house in excellent repair. The goats were fat and healthy, the chickens perky-eyed and amazingly fertile, as if the nuns coaxed eggs out of them by prayer.

All this was accomplished by one handyman and several dozen older women—some in their seventies. The Blessed Garden had to flourish on love or it wouldn't flourish at all. Love, obedience and discipline were absolutely required.

Sister Felicia lacked obedience and discipline. That Gallagher was sure of. Love was something he didn't know about. Perhaps she was struggling with herself, trying to fit in. Perhaps last night had been a temporary lapse. Of course, that didn't explain her professional patrol of the grounds, or the skill with which she had picked the lock on the west-wing door of the house.

He passed other nuns performing morning chores before he finally spotted Sister Felicia. His pulse sped up a little when he recognized the nun walking beside her. They were heading to the Angora pasture—if the mess of brambles and weeds growing there could be called anything so poetic—and they were chatting as they went.

Item thirteen on Ralph's list was fencing around that pasture that needed to be mended. Gallagher headed that way. He only hoped the nuns would keep talking if he was nearby.

* * *

"I feel like I'm committing a sin."

"You're not." Sister Mary Grace linked her arm through Sister Felicia's as they walked toward the pasture. "We have permission to talk this morning and discuss this. Reverend Mother is worried about you."

"I don't mean to worry anyone."

"Dear, it's obvious to everyone that you're not having an easy time of it here."

"Maybe I'm just not used to it yet."

"I'm not familiar with your order."

Sister Felicia could hardly admit she wasn't familiar with it, either. "Well, we're not as strict, certainly, as the Sisters of the Garden."

"There's a certain beauty in the regimen here, though, don't you think?"

Sister Felicia swallowed. "I suppose I'm spending too much time with the goats to think about beauty," she said at last.

Sister Mary Grace's laughter pealed merrily through the morning air.

"And too much time with Sister Madeline," Sister Felicia added.

"That won't be happening anymore. Reverend Mother has assigned her elsewhere, I believe. Somewhere she can't foist her jobs off on anyone else."

"I didn't know anyone else had noticed."

"Surely you know by now that nuns aren't perfect. Had you expected cloistered nuns to be angels?"

"Maybe."

"Whatever veil we wear, we struggle together. We all want things we can't have. Leisure. Lovers. Children. And we all reach for the thing we can, God's love."

Sister Felicia felt a pang of pure, unadulterated guilt. Sister Mary Grace was sharing her heart with the wrong woman, and that woman was about to compound her sins. "Are you finding God's love here, Sister?" she asked, as humbly as she knew how.

Sister Mary Grace was silent for a while. They were almost to the pasture when she spoke. "I found His love more easily

on Isla Tesoro, where I was a teaching sister. I saw it in the faces
of the children who came to the mission, and in the awful af-
termath of the revolution. I saw it in the faces of the men who
wanted me dead for speaking the truth about what the people
of the island needed.''

"I'm sorry. I didn't mean to—"

"You didn't. I have my own struggles. But to answer your
question, yes, I'm finding God's love here. Like you, I'm just
having to look under every loaf of bread I bake and every to-
mato I pick."

"Then I'll have to look under every goat berry I shovel."

Sister Mary Grace laughed again. "If it helps you to talk out
your feelings, ask Mother Jeanne for permission. She only
wants the best for you."

"Does she? My nose is growing flat from the hours I'm
spending on the chapel floor."

"You have a lovely nose, dear. Not a nun's nose at all."

"And what is a nun's nose?"

"One permanently flared from trying not to poke it into
everyone else's business."

They were both laughing when they reached the pasture gate.
To an untrained eye, the fenced-in acre would have seemed
nothing more than a thicket of noxious weeds and wildflowers. To the goats, it was goat heaven, and that was how the sisters referred to it.

Goats, Sister Felicia had learned unwillingly, actually did
deserve a place in the universal scheme of things. Unlike their
rivals, the cow and the sheep, they dined happily on a gardener's worst nightmares, the thornier, scrubbier and weedier the
better. Lovely green grass lacked the nutrition their bodies
craved, and they could pick their way through an overgrown
field like the happiest gourmet.

Goat Heaven was crowded with blackberry brambles and
jerusalem artichokes, the rabbit-like multipliers of the plant
world. There was a much-nibbled comfrey patch, too, but most
of the plants growing in Goat Heaven were wild. Unfortunately, some of those plants were toxic. Sister Felicia and Sister Mary Grace were on a search this morning because one of
the other sisters had spotted climbing milkweed in an isolated

corner. Most of the goats seemed to sense what they shouldn't eat, but since there were new kids in the pasture, the nuns weren't taking chances.

"Shall we spread out?" Sister Mary Grace asked.

"I warn you, if I find milkweed, I'll be tempted to fertilize it, make a novena to it, even."

"If you were transferred to other work, you'd miss the goats."

"I could pray for acceptance."

Sister Mary Grace shot her a smile. In a moment both women, heads down, were inching their way around the fence.

Despite her words, Sister Felicia wasn't trying to miss the milkweed, but neither was she concentrating on her task. She slapped two fleecy white rumps and sent a group of Angoras to the other end of the pasture, but even that was halfhearted. The other nun's words were nagging at her.

Sister Mary Grace was not a member of the community of the Sisters of the Garden. She was part of a teaching order that worked in the trouble spots of the world, bringing education to people who wouldn't have been offered any otherwise. As a young nun she had been sent to Isla Tesoro, a self-governed island off the coast of Honduras in the Caribbean. She had stayed for twenty-five years to become a powerful voice for change. Her outspoken opinions had almost gotten her killed.

Sister Felicia knew the story well—better, perhaps, than Sister Mary Grace herself. She knew, for instance, that even though Sister Mary Grace was no longer on Tesoro, her life was still in danger. She had been sent to the Blessed Garden for exactly that reason. An independent, spirited woman with seemingly no fear of death, she had refused the church's protection, just as she had refused to promise not to return to Tesoro someday. She had agreed, however, to spend an undetermined number of months at the Blessed Garden on retreat to contemplate her future.

It was believed that there was little threat to her life at the Blessed Garden. The church had been careful to spirit her here without anyone's knowledge. The Blessed Garden, miles from anywhere and so strictly enclosed that visitors were initially re-

ceived through a door with a thick iron grille, was uninten-
tionally a perfect hiding place.

The church, of course, hadn't bargained with Luis Cortez, a
man who had known Sister Mary Grace's whereabouts from the
day she'd stepped into the private plane that had flown her
away from her island mission.

"Watch out!"

Sister Felicia didn't think. She dropped to one knee, and her
hand slid inside the side pocket of her robe. Her head whirled
toward the source of the shout.

"What in hell?" Gallagher started toward her, even though
the fence with its thin strand of barbed wire was between them.

Sister Felicia took in everything in a split second. Gallagher's low-riding jeans and the snug gray T-shirt advertising a
popular brand of motor oil. The dangerous glitter of amber
brown eyes in a rugged, unshaven face. One masculine dimple
accenting an assessing frown.

"You scared the . . . bejeepers out of me." She started to get
to her feet.

He stepped forward, as if to stop her, but the fence was between them, and he was too late, anyway. She felt the impact
of a two-ton truck explode against her backside. In a moment
she was sprawled face down in jerusalem artichokes.

Something whizzed over her head, words, profane and to the
point, as well as a barrage of sticks to scare away her attacker.
From behind her she heard the scurry of retreating hooves.

"I . . . detest . . . goats!" Painfully she rolled to one side and
peered over her shoulder. The Angora billy, christened Bulldozer by a sister who had since moved to a convent in Mis-
souri that tended apple orchards, was strutting back to an
admiring crowd of young does.

"I'd help you up, but that's probably not allowed."

Sister Felicia looked up at the man who was politely trying
not to smile. "You've already done your part. You *almost*
warned me."

"Anyone else would have looked behind them." His face
settled back into a frown. "For a minute there I thought you

were afraid of something different. Something other than the goats."

Sister Felicia stood, hopelessly trying to brush pieces of the desert off her robe. "Lightning. I'm always sure I'm about to be struck by lightning," she muttered.

"You almost looked like a cop going for his gun."

"Why do men always assume that cop's a masculine term?" She disciplined herself not to continue that strain of conversation. "Let me assure you, Mr. Gallagher, if I was going for anything, as you put it, it was my rosary. Besides, I didn't drop to the ground. I tripped."

"Are you all right?" Sister Mary Grace, who could glide effortlessly even in a goat pasture, reached Sister Felicia's side.

"My pride is damaged, which is probably all for the good." Sister Felicia gave a rueful smile.

Sister Mary Grace's eyes twinkled. "Bulldozer was showing off."

"I'm sure he impressed all his little friends. There'll probably be a record number of kids this year."

"Someday, Sister, I have to hear the story of why *you* became a nun."

Gallagher couldn't echo Sister Mary Grace's words out loud, but he echoed them silently. Someday he wanted to hear the same story; in fact, he was determined to hear it. He watched the two nuns start back around the pasture, this time together. One glided, one swung her hips. With a shake of his head, he went back to mending the fence. But at no time, did he take his eyes off the two sisters for more than a second or two.

There was justice in the convent. Sister Madeline *had* been taken off goat duty and set to work scrubbing pots and pans under the watchful eye of Sister Althea. She had even made a proper apology to Sister Felicia, one that had sounded remarkably sincere.

Unfortunately no one else had been assigned to take her place. Since the vegetable garden was at its peak, every hand that could be spared was needed for picking produce and canning or freezing it. Mother Jeanne explained to Sister Felicia that she would have to feed and milk the goats by herself in the

evening until most of the vegetables had been taken care of. She
had even sympathized a little, a fact that so astounded Sister
Felicia that she had assured the Mother Superior that she understood completely and would find the task strengthening.

But what it was going to strengthen remained a mystery to
her that evening as she milked her sixth nanny. Surely her arms
were stronger, and her fingers. Possibly even the muscles in her
lower back had grown stronger and more supple from the endless bending and lifting of a Blessed Garden day. As far as she
could see, however, nothing internal was one ounce, inch or
iota stronger than it had been when she arrived. Spiritually she
was still the Felice Cristy who had always been skipped when
the nuns at her school asked if her fellow students had ever
considered a religious vocation.

And what goats had to do with God was still beyond her.

By the time she got to Mary Poppins, she had milked two
more nannies, calming them with a yodeled rendition of "Old
MacDonald." Mary P. looked distinctly belligerent this evening, as if she had spent the last twenty-four hours plotting di-
abolical tricks. Sister Corinne, the nun who had done the
morning milking, had assured Sister Felicia that Mary P. had
behaved like a lamb and had most certainly learned her lesson.
Sister Felicia—who not only saw a glass as half-empty but who
wanted the contents tested before she drank it—knew Mary P.
had just been saving up her mischief.

"Mary, babe," she said, as she tied a rope to Mary's collar,
"you and I are going to come to an understanding."

Mary Poppins followed her to the milking stand, taking the
steps up without hesitation. Her shining black coat looked as
if it had just been freshly groomed. Her long, snowy ears
framed a face of great goat beauty. Only her eyes, narrowed in
contemplation like those of the woman about to milk her, gave
any indication of her true personality.

Sister Felicia scooped grain into the bucket and set it on the
other side of the crossbar. Then, as Mary Poppins leaned forward, she lowered the bar. "What'll it be Mary? A bow-wow
here and a bow-wow there, or a moo-moo and a quack-
quack?"

Mary munched quietly. Sister Felicia was almost fooled. She began to hum "Old MacDonald," not yet secure enough for a more high-powered version. Mary stood absolutely still. Not a muscle rippled as Sister Felicia got herself into position. She didn't move as Sister Felicia smoothed her hands gently over the goat's satin sides. She didn't move as Sister Felicia performed the sanitation ritual. She didn't move as Sister Felicia began to milk her.

She moved when the pail was half-full. At the precise moment when Sister Felicia relaxed.

"Damn!" Sister Felicia leaned backward as goat hooves flew out at random angles. Mary Poppins bucked twice. The first time she had managed a solid kick to Sister Felicia's arm. The second time she caught the milk bucket. Sister Felicia watched the sisters' fresh milk, their cheese and pudding, soak into the straw-covered floor.

Tears of pain sprang to her eyes, and she covered her throbbing arm with her hand as if to protect it from more blows.

"Get out of the way!"

She hadn't realized that Gallagher had come into the shed, but now his command came from right behind her. She obeyed without hesitation. Mary Poppins's side was the last place she wanted to be.

The next seconds passed in a blur. The goat bucked again and got a pail of water thrown over her head before her feet were firmly on the ground. Once they were, her tail got a good hard yank. The goat sputtered in protest, but locked in by the crossbar, there was little else she could do.

And when the sputtering was done, she stood as still as a statue.

"This is how it works," Gallagher said, in kindergarten-teacher tones. "The goat does something you don't like, you do something she doesn't like. The goat kicks you, you throw water over her head or pull her tail or both. This goat, being God's own creation, has been endowed with a brain. I'm sure God won't mind you exercising it now and again."

Sister Felicia rubbed her arm and bit her lip.

"Are you all right?"

She nodded.

"Then shall I finish milking her, or shall you?"

"I'll do it." Her arm was fast growing numb, which was both welcome and worrisome. But Gallagher was right. The time had come to stop letting the goat get the better of her. She lifted the bucket with her uninjured arm and carried it to the pump to sanitize it all over again.

Gallagher was still standing beside the goat when she returned. "I'll be all right," she assured him. "Thank you for trying to teach her some manners."

"I'm staying right here. If she kicks again, I'll be ready for her."

She situated herself at Mary Poppins's side again, wincing as she reached out to start milking her. She forced herself to continue, even though her arm didn't want to respond.

Gallagher saw the wince and realized the goat had kicked her harder than he'd thought. Despite his doubts about Sister Felicia, he felt a stab of sympathy. "It looks like she's making up for kicking you."

Milk poured into the bucket as if Mary Poppins *were* apologizing. The goat herself didn't do so much as swish her tail. "How do you know so much about animals?" she asked.

"I was raised on a ranch."

"You just happened to have a bucket of water handy?"

"I saw who you were working on when I walked in. I scooped the water out of the trough, just in case."

"Well, thank you. It seems to have helped."

"Hopefully it'll be the end of your problems." He waited until enough time had passed to make his next comment seem conversational. "You didn't grow up on a ranch, I take it."

She thought about the thousand-acre spread near Santa Barbara that was her birthright. She supposed it was a ranch, although there had rarely been animals in sight of the house. She had been driven down the road to the stables to ride, and she'd learned on an English saddle, from a prim little man who dressed like a ringmaster.

"When we come here," she said, "we forsake our pasts. They are no longer a topic for conversation."

"Do you choose to come here, Sister, or are you sent?"

She wondered how a Sister of the Garden would answer that. "God chooses us," she said, proud of herself.

Frustrated, Gallagher realized he couldn't keep up this line of questioning. Casual conversation was obviously frowned upon, and casual conversation between the handyman and a nun was probably forbidden. He watched as Sister Felicia stripped the last drops of milk from a docile Mary Poppins. Then he stood back as she rose and reached to lift the bucket. He was close enough to hear the moan deep in her throat as the bucket clattered back to the floor.

Before she could reach for it with her other hand, he took it and carried it to the milk pail to empty it. Then he returned for the goat and led her back to her stall. He shook his head as Sister Felicia started for the next goat. "Let me see that arm."

"I don't think—"

"Then go back up to the house and let somebody there treat it."

"I can't do that. By the time I get there and have it seen to, it will be time for prayers. There are still goats to milk."

"Then let me see it."

Sister Felicia contemplated her choices. Certainly nuns didn't bare any part of their bodies to men. Somewhere there was probably a rule made just for this occasion. She could almost hear Mother Jeanne. *Right there on page one thousand and seventeen, Sister Felicia. Sisters who are victims of nasty-tempered nanny goats may not have their wounds treated by ruggedly sexy handymen in snug T-shirts.*

She couldn't suppress a smile.

"I take it that means I can," Gallagher said.

She struggled to sound pious. "I suppose it's for the good of the community."

"No question." He beckoned her to the door leading out to the goat yard, where no one would see them. "Push up your sleeve."

The feat was easier said than done. First there was the small matter of a looped cord to loosen. Even wrists weren't bared to the world at the Blessed Garden. Awkwardly she managed to untwist the cord, suddenly all thumbs. As she pushed up her sleeve she felt herself growing warm with embarrassment. She, who at age nine had escaped her pack of chaperons to go skinny-dipping in a mountain creek with a ranch hand's son.

"Looks like she got you good." Gallagher gently took her wrist and eased his hands up her soft flesh to her upper arm, where the goat's hoof had caught her. It was swollen and red, but the skin wasn't torn, and the arm didn't look misshapen, as it probably would have if the bone had been broken. He realized her gaze was lowered to her sandals.

He was curiously reluctant to drop her arm. He had certainly touched more provocative parts of a woman. Had lifetime celibacy been a requirement of the job here, he would have had to go elsewhere. But usually he had bypassed arms and gone for softer, warmer parts of a woman. Now he was fast becoming an arm connoisseur, or maybe it was just that this particular arm belonged to the same nun who had stretched and sensuously preened at the spring last night like a sleek female leopard performing for her mate.

"What do you think?" she asked softly.

What he was thinking would make a movie X-rated. He dropped her arm as if he'd been burned. "Lift it," he said, through a throat suddenly thick. "Lift it above your head."

She grimaced, but made herself do it. Her arm hovered there, a slender creamy arc, a ballet dancer's perfect accompaniment to a *pirouette*. Then it dropped to her side. "I suppose that's a good sign," she said.

"Is there a first-aid kit out here?"

"There's one on the shelf."

He couldn't resist. "The shelf where Ralph always lays his cigarettes?"

She didn't blink. "There's only one shelf."

He left her in the doorway to get the kit. She watched him go and wondered if she was losing her mind. His fingers against her skin had been like the first puff of tobacco smoke filling her lungs last night. She had missed more than cigarettes and long showers. She had missed a man's touch, and the unshaven drifter with the penetrating whiskey eyes had just brought that home with a thud.

"Surprisingly well equipped." Gallagher was beside her again before she'd had time to do more than recognize what had just happened to her. For a moment she wasn't sure *what* he thought was well equipped. Then she realized he meant the first-aid kit.

"Doctors are expensive," she murmured. "We treat everything we can ourselves."

"Someone thought to include a cold pack." He twisted the pack to trigger the chemical inside it to action. "Let me see your arm again."

She almost refused, but that would have drawn attention to her reaction, and she didn't need that. Gallagher might know about the cigarettes, but he didn't need to know he had turned her insides into steaming chicken soup just by stroking his hand up her arm. There was no telling who the man was or why he was here, and no matter who he was she didn't want him to be suspicious of her.

She held out her arm, and to distract herself she thought about all the deprivations of life at the Blessed Garden. The simple, nearly meatless diet. The lack of alcohol and tobacco. The hours on her knees. The hours with the goats. The silence. The hard cot in her bare-walled cell. The scrape of roughly woven cotton against her skin. Her cropped hair and ruined hands.

She concentrated on the last as she felt him wrap his fingers around her arm. Not so long ago her hair had fallen well past her shoulders, straight and silky, and her fingernails had been long scarlet crescents. She had cut both before becoming a sister, but the sacrificial chin-length bob she'd chosen for her hair hadn't been short enough for Mother Jeanne. "You'll find we don't have time or water enough for vanity," she had observed. "And short hair's more practical under our veil, besides."

Obviously a failed barber in her former life, the Reverend Mother had briskly sheared away all but random tufts and wisps before giving Sister Felicia the temporary habit of the Sisters of the Garden. Without having seen a mirror during or after, she could only guess how she looked.

"Hold this in place."

Sister Felicia realized Gallagher was finished. Her hand trembled slightly as she reached for the ice pack. Gallagher, who didn't seem to miss anything, noticed immediately.

"You'd better sit down. You're shaking."

"I'll be fine. My arm feels better already."

"I'll finish the milking."

She started to protest.

"You can't milk without hands, Sister. Stay and supervise, if you feel you have to."

She weighed what she might find out about him if she stayed against what he might find out about her. Despite her own abilities, she had a feeling she was well matched.

"There are only three more to go," she said. "Then, if you can lift the pail into the wagon for me, I can pull it up to the house with my good arm."

"I'll do it quickly."

He was half finished with the second goat when he spoke again. "What are you allowed to talk about?"

"Our work."

"Do you enjoy your work? I believe you said you detest goats."

Sister Felicia knew that if she could see his face, it would be lit with a one-dimpled smile. "I pray to enjoy it and to learn from it."

Gallagher knew when he was being handed a crock. "I hope your prayers are answered, Sister."

She wondered if she'd imagined that "Sister" had been stressed. "Do you enjoy your work, Mr. Gallagher?"

"I move on when I get bored."

"What other sorts of things have you done?"

He sensed they weren't having just any old conversation. "A little of this and a lot of that."

"A lot of what?"

"Drifting."

"It must be nice to see the world."

"If you'd thought the world was nice to see, why did you end up in a place like this?"

"No one can have everything they want." Sister Felicia stopped and wondered where that particular piece of theology had come from. She didn't think it was something Mother Jeanne had intoned during a meal. Was the Blessed Garden actually having an effect on her personal philosophy after all? Certainly Felice Cristy had always believed she could have everything she wanted, if she just tried hard enough.

"So you chose the convent over travel?"

"This . . . this is only my temporary home. I belong to a different order. I could be sent anywhere when I leave here."

"And what does your order do?" he probed. "Teach? Nurse? Hold out hands to the heathen?"

"We . . . do a number of things." She cast around for something he would believe. "I teach little children. Poor children, actually." She liked the noble sound of that. "Human kids are a million miles from the goat kind. And being in the world is a bit different from being here."

"What do you teach your human kids?"

She tried to remember twenty-one years before, when she had been in kindergarten. Of course that had been a class of ten, and there had been thousands of dollars worth of Montessori equipment lining the walls. "How to live," she said, when nothing better came to mind.

"I imagine most poor kids could teach you and me a thing or two about that."

"How to live as God's children."

If any of this was true, and he was more and more convinced it wasn't, Gallagher pitied the children in Sister Felicia's care. He wondered if she sang to them. They would be dropouts before first grade.

He stood and carried the bucket to the milk pail and exchanged the goat for the last to be milked. He had almost finished when she spoke again. "How did you come upon this job, Mr. Gallagher? It certainly can't be every man's dream to be doing chores in a convent."

He wondered if she wanted his whole life history and references to boot. He decided to give her a good scare and assess the results. He hated to frighten an innocent sister, but he hated more not knowing if she *was* innocent. "Oh, I just drifted into Our Lady of Mercy one day and asked Father Melrose for a handout. He seems to be a trusting soul. He asked me if I wanted this job, and I said I did. He didn't even ask where I'd been or where I was going.''

He smiled up at her.

The dimple didn't fool her. One deep dent at the right corner of his mouth didn't make him look innocent. ''How lucky you were to be in the right place at the right time,'' she murmured. She stepped back as he carried the last of the milk to the pail. He wiped the pail clean, capped it and lifted it to the wagon.

She watched the muscles in his arms tighten as he effortlessly lifted the heavy pail. She abandoned the ice pack and pulled down her sleeve, twisting the cord with a snap. She said a polite thank you and grasped the wagon handle in her hand. His eyes bored through her back as she hauled the wagon toward the convent kitchen.

Halfway up the path she decided the time had come to start wearing her gun.

Chapter 4

"You look awful."

"Keep your voice low and spit out your gum. For God's sake, Kell, act like you're visiting a nun." Sister Felicia said the words with a pleasant smile, her eyes fixed demurely on her work-worn hands.

"There's nobody around." Kelley Samuels turned her head slowly, as if admiring the convent parlor's heavy mission oak furniture.

"There are eyes everywhere."

Kelley lowered her voice. "The only eyes I see are Mary's, and she's a picture on the wall. A pretty awful rendition at that."

"We've only got a few minutes." Sister Felicia looked her friend squarely in the eye. "You know, you don't look so good yourself."

"I've quit smoking again." Reluctantly Kelley removed her gum and stuck it under a nineteenth-century chair.

Sister Felicia examined her friend. Her dark red curls, always frazzled, hadn't taken well to Kelley's haphazard taming for this occasion. They stood out from her head like a deranged turban, framing blue eyes in a snub-nosed face. It was an urchin's face, but the woman to whom it belonged had a record at the shooting range that had once been the envy of every male cop in the Los Angeles police department.

Sister Felicia shoved away disappointment that she wouldn't be able to bum a new pack of cigarettes from her friend, but a trace of self-pity showed. "Try giving up cigarettes, liquor, men and most of your hair and see how it feels."

"Poor baby." Kelley leaned forward. "Does her need a little sympathy?" she cooed.

Sister Felicia laughed, but she sobered quickly. "I need whatever you can get on a man named Josiah Gallagher... if that's his real name."

Kelley waited. When no more was forthcoming, she prodded, "What else've you got on him?"

"Not much. He's the temporary handyman here, but he just breezed in from nowhere. Father Melrose over in Smoke Tree sent him. He's about thirty-two, tall, built like a million bucks, brown eyes, reddish-brown curly hair that he wears too long. He claims he's been a drifter, doing a little of this and a little of that."

Kelley didn't write anything down. The perfect aim went with a computer memory. "You suspicious or horny?"

"I'm wearing my gun." Sister Felicia patted her leg.

"How much longer are you going to stay, Felice?"

"I don't make a very good nun." Sister Felicia vanished and Felice Cristy gave up, just for these few minutes with Kelley, even trying to pretend. "I thought I could pull off anything. You know how many surveillances I've done, how many undercover jobs I've taken on. I even studied method acting, for heaven's sake, so I could throw myself more fully into whatever role I had to play."

"You've always been the best."

"Well, I'm not the best here. I feel like such a fake." She was almost whispering. "These women think I'm just a rebellious nun from another order, but they're anything but stupid. They're going to start putting two and two together, and if they find out I'm a private investigator here to spy on them, they're going to feel violated."

"You're not spying on them. You're trying to protect Sister Mary Grace."

"Do you think the distinction's going to matter? These are good women, and God knows they're sincere. They'd have to be." She tried to think of a way to express the essence of the Blessed Garden. "The life here is austere, but there's a sweetness about it . . ."

"This doesn't sound like you."

"Sometimes I get confused about who I am."

"I'll tell you who you are." Kelley leaned farther forward. "You're Felice Cristy. You and I run the best private-investigation agency in Palm Springs, and you're needed at home. We've got cases piling up. I've had to hire two more part-timers to do surveillance—"

"Did you find good people?"

"Yeah. But we're stretched to the limit. I need to know when you're coming back."

"I don't know. We can't exactly send someone in to take my place, can we? And the sisters are even more vulnerable than we believed. Anyone who wanted could be over that wall and inside the grounds without straining a muscle. I stay as close to Sister Mary Grace as I can, and I patrol the grounds every night, but even that's hardly enough."

"Sounds like you're planning to stay a while."

Felice didn't want to say yes. But she realized, glumly, that she couldn't say no, either.

Kelley shook her head. "Maybe I'd better put one of the new guys on full-time."

"Temporarily, maybe."

There was a rustle in the hallway, and both women sat up straight. Kelley pulled her skirt over her knees, or at least she tried.

Sister Faith, the sister who watchdogged visitors, appeared in the doorway. "Sister Felicia, it's almost time for prayer. Would your guest like to join us?"

Kelley rose and primly shook her head. "I'm so sorry, Sister, but I must get back to my children. The twins are such mischief makers, and little Timothy has a cold. I have to be sure he gets his medicine before he goes to bed for the night."

Felice stood. There had been no hint of a brogue in Kelley's voice, but her portrayal of a devoted, Irish-American mother had been award-winning. She was equally good at playing ladies of the night. "I'll say a prayer for him, Kelley."

"Thank you, Sister."

Felice walked Kelley as far as the armored door with the thick wire grille. She watched Sister Faith let Kelley out with the huge set of keys she carried on her belt and thought that if the rest of the Blessed Garden was this secure she could rip off her robe and make a dash for the car along with her friend.

A sinking feeling descended when the door clanked behind Kelley and Sister Faith turned the key in the lock once more.

"Your friend gave you a gift?"

Felice held it out to her. "A book about St. Thomas Aquinas. Will that be all right?"

Sister Faith smiled. "Of course. Some of the rest might like to read it when you've finished."

Only later, alone in her cell, did Felice realize that there was a large part of the book that no one would ever get to read. A four-by-six-inch section had been cut neatly from the center of pages 150 through 450. Nestled inside and taped securely to the back cover were a pack of Winstons and a pair of multi-folded silk-and-lace bikini panties.

The road to the Blessed Garden had started simply enough. Felice had gone into her office as usual one morning to find a message from a Mr. Luis Cortez on the top of her pile. The spring day had been a typical Palm Springs beauty, warm, sunny and dry enough to keep all the surrounding health resorts and salons knee-deep in moisturizers. She'd had to fight the urge to call a friend to make a date for a morning tennis game, but she had known that her desk would be piled with work since she had been out of town for three days visiting her parents.

The office of Cristy and Samuels was in a two-story building tucked between boutiques in a wide courtyard just off Indian Avenue and had nothing in common with the fictional hole-in-the-wall of a paperback private eye. An interior designer with an unfaithful husband had traded her services for theirs, and the office could just as easily have belonged to a plastic surgeon or divorce attorney, two flourishing Palm Springs professions.

The comfortable low-slung furniture in the reception area was southwestern in its functional style and muted desert colors. A soft-sculpture cactus bloomed in the corner, and the landscapes dotting the creamy beige walls were by a Native American artist fast gaining prominence. Both Kelley and Felice had small, pleasant offices lined with files and furnished with simple desks and leather chairs. Another larger office held three desks with telephones that were almost constantly in use. The agency's long-distance bills were more than their substantial rent.

The agency expenses weren't cheap—nothing in Palm Springs came cheaply—but their income astounded even Felice, who'd been more certain than Kelley that the idea of another investigation agency in Palm Springs was a good one. That morning, however, she'd felt vaguely dissatisfied with all they had accomplished in the eighteen months they had been in business. She had hoped that the message to call Luis Cortez might be the key to easing the feeling that she wasn't yet a success.

An hour after returning Luis's call she had climbed in her white MR2 convertible and started down Highway 111, heading for Indio to meet with him.

The MR2 was a compromise, a moderately expensive sports car that blended in with the more expensive cars of the area residents. It wasn't expensive enough or flashy enough to attract attention—or, for that matter, to please Felice—but neither was it a gas-guzzling domestic like Kelley's ten-year-old wagon. They exchanged cars frequently, depending on what kind of job they were on, and Felice could jump start Kelley's car like a pro.

That morning she passed expensive country-club estates and elegant strip malls without giving them much thought. The scenery changed regularly from the lush green of the developed land that was draining away the vast underground water reserve of the desert to the natural landscape of cactus, succulents and wildflowers.

Near Indio she followed Luis's directions until she saw the estate he had described, sitting back on a rise behind acres of date palms. She paused at the entrance to the drive leading up to the house. She had vacationed in Palm Springs every winter of her childhood, and she had lived in the area for almost two years now. Still, despite a lifetime of privilege, she was impressed.

Luis's home was Spanish in style, hardly an anomaly in Southern California, but it was a magnificent prototype for the thousands of inferior imitations that had followed. The stuccoed walls had to be at least a foot thick, the red-tiled roof constructed to last as long as the desert sands. The slag-heap mountains that had captured Felice's heart the first time she'd seen them were a jagged line behind the house, arrowheads taking aim at the bright blue heavens.

She took the palm-lined drive slowly, admiring the well-tended groves fanning out on both sides. Closer to the house the landscaping changed to gardens unrivaled by any she had noted at other lavish estates. Men worked unobtrusively in both the grove and the gardens, and she calculated Luis's labor costs as she pulled up to the iron gate leading to a parking area surrounded by low white stucco walls.

A gardener let her in and waited patiently until she had parked. Then he led her through an arched opening in the wall into the most beautiful courtyard she had ever seen. She straightened the skirt of her Anne Klein suit and checked the silver filigree clip holding her hair back from her face. She was rarely ill at ease, but everything about Luis Cortez's house reminded her of her childhood home. And if she was ill at ease anywhere, it was there.

"Miss Cristy." Luis Cortez came forward to meet her. He didn't shake her hand, as she had expected; instead he rested his hands on her shoulders and bent to kiss her cheek. It was a courtly gesture from a man old enough to be her father, and she was touched. "I know your mother well. You look like her," he said, after she had murmured a greeting. "Even more beautiful, but don't ever tell her I said so."

Felice laughed. "I value my life."

Luis gestured her to a table beside an elaborate waterfall surrounded by tropical foliage that included sweetly blooming gardenias. "And how is Nita?" he asked, when Felice was comfortably seated and iced tea had been poured for her by a maid who vanished back into the shrubbery.

"Well, thank you. I just came back from seeing the family."

"Nita was always a charmer. Men wept when your father captured her heart."

"I believe my father's wept a time or two, himself. His dearest Nita runs his life with military precision."

Luis laughed. "And what do Nita and your father think of your chosen profession, Miss Cristy?"

"Felice." She studied him, aware that the question wasn't as casual as it might seem. He was evaluating her. "They aren't pleased."

"Other aspirations for you?" he asked, lifting one brow.

She thought what a handsome man he was. Never married, Luis Cortez had been considered the best catch in the Coachella Valley for more years than Felice had been alive. He had the olive skin of his Spanish ancestors and their dark eyes. His hair had probably once been dark but was now a distinguished silver. More intriguing was the faintest hint of sadness in his eyes. Dreams unfulfilled, she guessed. Pleasures denied a man who, by appearances, seemed to have everything.

"They had other aspirations for me," she acknowledged. "A degree in classics, maybe, or languages. Marriage to the right man from the right family. I've been a disappointment."

"Their loss could be my gain."

She settled down to do business, now that the pleasantries had ended. People moved into asking for her professional services at their own speed. She never rushed them, although she knew how to act on cue to cut the process shorter.

"Do you need my help, Mr. Cortez?"

"Luis. And I'll have to tell you a story before I can ask you for anything. Do you have time to indulge an old man?"

"I don't see one." She sipped her tea and waited. It only took her a moment to realize that Luis was going to have trouble beginning. "I'd love to see your gardens," she said. "Would you mind showing them to me while we talk?"

"Thank you." Felice knew he was thanking her for more than the opportunity to show her something he obviously loved. He stood, and she joined him. Chatting comfortably, they moved slowly through the gardens, admiring everything from bright splashes of scarlet bougainvillea to monstrous cactus.

At the date grove, Luis halted. "Are you interested in dates, Felice?"

"I was certainly interested in high school." She smiled at his polite laughter. "Will you show me the groves?"

They walked between rows of palms towering high over their heads. "These trees are all offshoots of palms brought in from the Sahara in the early part of the century. There was a time when Highway 111 was lined with date palms from Palm Springs to Mecca."

"Are they easy to grow?"

"Not at all. Everything must be done by hand. We have to protect the young trees from sun and wind. Dates must have one hundred inches of rainfall a year, so we have to irrigate. Even pollination has to be done by hand."

She tried to imagine that. "Sounds kinky."

He chuckled. "You were a trial to your mother, weren't you?"

"No past tense about it."

"My *palmeros* have their work cut out for them."

"Palmeros?"

"The men who work the trees." He pointed above them. "They have to climb the trees to thin and pollinate each inflorescence." He saw that she obviously didn't understand. "Cluster of flowers. Then they have to slip paper bags over each cluster, to protect them. Later, when it's time for harvest, each date of certain varieties has to be picked just at the right moment. So the men are up and down the palms each day."

"Do you climb the palms, too?"

"I do." He took her arm and turned her back toward the house. "Do you like the mountains, Felice?"

"I'm living here because of them. I always loved them as a child. When I had a chance to come back as an adult, I took it."

"The way I understand it, you made your own chance."

"I suppose."

He guided her back the way they had come and through an additional grove, explaining more about the dates as they went. "Would you like to see my favorite view of the mountains?"

She nodded and followed him through the grove that ringed one side of the house.

Behind the house were more gardens and a tile patio roofed with open white slats that let the sun filter gently to the natural wicker furniture clustered in inviting seating arrangements. There were two pools unobtrusively placed and lushly landscaped. One was large and meant for swimming. The other was smaller, bubbling and perfect for romance.

"It's a large house and too much land for a man alone," Luis said.

"You love it." Felice wandered slowly through the garden, aware that Luis was about to tell her why he'd called. "What's this?" she asked, pointing to a small cedar gazebo.

"Go in and see."

She stepped up and saw panels unobtrusively lining the walls below the waist-high ledge, opening the entire gazebo to a spectacular view of the mountains. Luis followed her up and opened one of the panels, showing her an array of switches. "It's command central," he told her. "All the irrigation's done automatically, but any time I want more or less water directed anywhere on the property it can be done from here. Watch." He flipped a switch, and huge spouts of water shot into the air, then washed down into the deep ridges between the closest rows of palms. He indicated other cabinets. "There's an alarm system here. A communication system there."

She gave a low whistle of appreciation. "Very clever. I thought it was a lovers' trysting place."

"This is the view I told you about."

"It's wonderful. But do you always combine the sentimental and the practical?"

"It's funny you should put it that way." Luis crossed his arms and gazed out toward the mountains. "Because I'm about to ask you to help me do just that."

Felice pulled herself up to the ledge and made herself comfortable. But it was Luis she watched, not the glorious view of the Little San Bernardino Mountains.

He started his story. "I was in love once, with a woman named Katherine Phillips. We met in Spain. I was visiting distant relatives, and Katherine was just out of college, touring Europe. She was younger than I by almost ten years, twenty-one to my thirty. I'd been a spoiled playboy and hadn't wanted to settle down. But then I met Katherine."

"And you wanted to marry her."

He nodded. "I had never been in love before—or since, for that matter. Katherine was everything I hadn't even dreamed of in a woman, beautiful, innocent, loving. She loved me, too, I could tell she did, and I was certain that nothing could come between us." He was silent, as if still mystified that something had.

"Were you driven apart?"

"Pulled gently. Katherine had come to Europe to make a decision. She wanted to become a nun, and she had given herself the summer in Europe to change her mind. When it was over, she knew that her mind couldn't be changed. If it could have been, I would have done it."

Felice felt compassion for the proud man beside her. She waited.

"So she went home and became a sister. Two years later, I was there when she took her final vows. We wrote for several years after, but eventually I realized that nothing would change. The letters were too painful for me, and perhaps for her too. We stopped writing, but I kept track of her. She was sent to Isla Tesoro, to teach the poor. Do you know about the revolution there?"

Felice nodded. Isla Tesoro, like many poor Latin American nations, had been in a state of political upheaval for decades. Recently the wealthy landowners had been overthrown, but little good had yet emerged from the revolution. A moderate but weak government controlled the nation now, but both leftist and right-wing rebel groups were struggling to gain control. The struggles had only worsened the lot of the peasants, whose main concern was feeding their children and tending their sick and wounded.

"Katherine became Sister Mary Grace. She was at the forefront of those speaking for the rights of the people. She was jailed twice. Once she almost died in prison. After the revolution she continued to speak out. She was in danger from all sides."

"She must be a very brave woman."

"Brave and powerful. She has a large number of supporters, enough to make a difference in any election. Everyone recognized her potential to cause problems."

"Everyone?"

"Everyone struggling to hold on to or gain control there. The right, the middle, the left. She was constantly under threat, but mostly from the right-wing groups who wanted the old government reinstated. The present government refused to protect her. They're so afraid of offending anyone, they do nothing. Finally the church—some believe at the insistence of our government—ordered her off the island."

"Did she go?"

"She disappeared one day. The church spirited her away, and she's safe not too many miles from here."

"You must be relieved."

"Felice, if I know where she is, who else knows?" he asked.

She was silent, beginning to understand why he was telling her the story.

"I have no more connections than any other wealthy man," he went on. "I knew where she was going before she did." Luis turned to her. "There are many who won't feel safe until Katherine is dead."

"Then you're afraid for her life?"

"She has refused protection from everyone who's offered it. She believes she is safe where she is. I believe she isn't."

"What do you want me to do?"

"I want you to protect her. I know your background and your skills. I think you can do it."

Felice slid down off the ledge to stand beside him. "But why me? You've obviously got people you can trust who've been doing your detective work."

"They are men."

"And that's a problem?"

"Katherine's in a convent in the desert." He smiled a little, almost as if offering his sympathy. "A cloistered convent. There's only one way anyone will be able to get near enough to protect her. I need a woman who can pretend to be a nun."

Was she a nun, or was she just pretending to be one?

The convent pickup truck rattled like a Reno roulette wheel. Gallagher didn't know why Ralph hadn't taken better care of the only vehicle the sisters owned, but once he got to Smoke Tree he intended to have it gone over by the town's only mechanic. Someday he might have to make a quick exit out of the Blessed Garden, and if he did, the truck would have to be his transportation of choice.

He had some questions for Father Melrose, too. Most of them centered around a certain Sister Felicia and how she had gotten inside the thick convent walls. He also had some questions that Father Melrose wouldn't be able to answer, but there were telephones at the presbytery and faceless men at the other end of the line.

Gallagher thought about the five nights since he had first seen Sister Felicia smoking at the spring. Each one had developed exactly the same way, with one notable exception. One extremely notable exception.

Sister Felicia was no longer the only sister visiting the spring when all good nuns were supposed to be in bed dreaming about whatever it was nuns dreamed about. Two nights—and two more clandestine cigarettes—after Gallagher had first followed Sister Felicia, he had followed her again over the same moonlit path. This time, however, she had hidden herself just out of sight of the springs.

He had stood in his own hiding place, wishing he had an aerial photo of the ridiculous tableau. She hid, he hid, like two children in a game of hide-and-seek where no one was "it." A bum and a nun, hiding, pretending, watching, waiting.

He had moved farther into the bushes at the sound of sandaled feet flapping against the path from the springs. As he had watched—and certainly as Sister Felicia had watched, too—Sister Mary Grace had moved into the moonlight, crossing just in front of him. Her steps were unhurried. If she knew she wasn't the only person there, she gave no sign. She glided through the night, a radiant, ethereal vision, not unlike a picture of the Virgin appearing to Bernadette at Lourdes.

There was nothing radiant or ethereal about the woman who followed her. He had admired Sister Felicia's stealth and cunning—not to mention her provocative walk—but she was earth to Sister Mary Grace's heaven. She tailed her fellow nun like a pro, even in flapping sandals and a white robe. His hand had moved to his gun and hovered close by as he followed the two women.

Sister Mary Grace had gone back to the house, letting herself in with ease. Sister Felicia had stood watch for what seemed like hours, then turned, and passing close by him, returned to the spring herself.

He had watched her repeat her nightly ritual, watched as she bared her elegant head to the cool night air and pulled her robe to her knees. Each night the ritual had dug deeper inside him; each night he had asked himself why the sight of a woman's neck and calves was affecting him so. Each night he had reminded himself that she was either a nun or an assassin, and neither was a good choice for a lover.

And each night he had watched with clenched jaw as she drew smoke into her lungs with an easy, unstudied sensuality that made him grow hard and aching.

Then, last night, he had almost given himself away. He had hidden himself and waited in the trees by the spring to watch and wait. Sister Mary Grace had come first, staring into the night beyond the spring as if she could read answers in the distant lights from Smoke Tree.

Then, after she had been gone for some time, Sister Felicia had come. She had stood beside the spring for long minutes, as if considering something. The night had been dark, but she had peered into every corner of it, until he was afraid he had been seen. Then, just as he was certain she was going to confront him, she had turned her back to him and begun to strip off her robe.

As she bent to remove her sandals, he had gone cold, then hot with longing, like an adolescent boy who had never kissed a girl. She had been hidden by shrubbery to her waist, but when she stepped up on the rocks at the edge of the spring-fed pool, she had been a long, slender female form, utterly naked. Utterly perfect.

She had stepped into the water and covered herself in its icy depths, but not before he had almost exploded at the sight. She was as beautiful as he had imagined, long-legged and slender-hipped. Her waist had seemed small enough for him to circle with his hands, her breasts large enough to fill them.

She had only stayed in the water for a few minutes, but for those minutes he had learned some hard truths about himself. He was not the objective, emotionless machine he had been trained to be. He was losing his head over a woman who had to be permanently off-limits for him, no matter who or what she was.

And now he was on his way to Smoke Tree to drive that fact home. He just wondered how he was going to ignore the persistent visions he'd had since that night, of Sister Felicia rising from the spring, water pearling on her breasts and in the dark thatch of hair between her legs. Sister Felicia shaking herself gracefully until drops of water fell like rain to the ground at her feet.

He parked beside the presbytery and went inside to have his questions answered.

Chapter 5

Sister Mary Grace was fearless. She was also almost as sneaky as Felice herself, and in her own serene way almost as rebellious.

Felice had gotten a good scare the first night she'd caught Sister Mary Grace at the spring. She had watched the nun enter her cell not more than forty-five minutes before, yet there she had been when Felice had arrived at the spring for her smoke, sitting and contemplating—well, contemplating something momentous by the look on her face. Felice had felt a simultaneous surge of sympathy and respect. Despite an obviously troubled soul, Sister Mary Grace could pick locks and blend into the shadows like a professional.

Felice knew better than to get involved with her clients or her targets. Whatever empathy she'd been born with had been whittled to strictly manageable proportions in her first year as a rookie cop. The first rule she'd learned had been to forget the golden rule. In police work and in private investigation, you didn't do unto others as you would have them do unto you. You did unto others only what the job required, and you didn't waste time worrying about what that meant or you went crazy.

Maybe she was going a little crazy now. A week after she had first come upon Sister Mary Grace at the spring, Felice crouched in the shrubbery and watched her again. Tonight the nun had barely waited until lights were off in the house to make her way outside. A faint sliver of moonlight bounced off the stark white of her veil like the shimmer of a halo. She looked toward the lights of Smoke Tree, but instinctively Felice knew that she was seeing something else.

She wondered what or whom. At moments such as this, did Sister Mary Grace think of Luís and what she had given up to become a nun? Did she think about the relative futility of her years on Isla Tesoro, about the people she couldn't help and the government she couldn't influence? Did she think about the men who wanted to kill her and ask for mercy on their souls?

Felice could find no echoing prayer for mercy in her own heart. Perhaps Sister Felicia, had she been real, could have drummed up forgiveness, but Felice Cristy wanted nothing more than a chance to wrap her hands around the throats of anyone who threatened the woman in front of her.

She had lost her detachment. Funny how desert days and nights, hard work and enforced silence, could do that to a person.

One leg was asleep, and the other was fading quickly. She was crouched in the midst of the same shrubbery that had hidden her every night that Sister Mary Grace had come to the spring, but tonight the wait seemed agonizing. A branch bit into the small of her back, and the pollen of some night-blooming desert flower tickled her nose and throat until stifling a sneeze was a torment.

Sister Mary Grace stood at last. She stretched and turned slowly, examining the bushes as if she had suddenly developed a passion for oasis horticulture.

Felice made herself as small as possible, but there was no way to escape the other woman's probing gaze. She knew that if she moved, she would surely be seen.

Sister Mary Grace started straight toward her. "It must be terribly uncomfortable in those bushes," she said, pausing at the edge of the shrubbery. "I'll be happy to share my rock with you."

Felice doubted the nun could be speaking to anyone else. It didn't surprise her to be caught. White robes and sparse cover made for rotten surveillance, but her professional pride still smarted. She rose to a stoop with as much dignity as she could muster and limped out of her cover, silently inventing a plausible story as she went.

"You must think I'm awful," she said. "But I was so surprised to find you here that I didn't know what to do."

Sister Mary Grace smiled. "Cut the bull, please."

Felice knew how to take the measure of any situation in an instant. She nodded. "Okay."

Sister Mary Grace turned and went back to the rock where she'd been sitting. Felice followed and sat on another rock beside her.

"You've been following me everywhere," Sister Mary Grace said. "At first I thought maybe you were just lonely and needed a mentor. I thought you might be watching me so that you'd know how to behave here."

"Apparently it didn't help."

Sister Mary Grace smiled. Her hand slid between the two rocks, and she lifted the scrap of tarp with Felice's precious cigarettes rolled inside. "I found this last night."

"I confess."

"Who are you?"

Felice considered all her options. She had already determined that this was a woman to be reckoned with. A host of stories came to mind, some good, some excellent. The best one by far, however, was the truth—and it was the only one, she suspected, that Sister Mary Grace was going to believe.

"I'm a private investigator. Luis Cortez hired me to watch over you."

Sister Mary Grace held the cigarettes out to Felice. She took them, but smoking had lost its appeal.

"How is Luis?"

Felice had expected almost anything but that particular calmly voiced question. "Worried about you," she said, after a moment.

"I think of him often. Did he ever marry?"

Felice shook her head.

"I hoped he would. I wanted that for him."

"So did half the women in the Coachella Valley."

Sister Mary Grace laughed a little. "That's not hard to believe."

"He followed all the events in Isla Tesoro. He knew the moment you came here. He was afraid—"

"Luis never understood that my life must be in God's hands."

"Perhaps not, but he understands what it's like to lose someone he loves to God. I don't think he could bear to lose you to killers, too."

"It's not something I look forward to, either," Sister Mary Grace said dryly.

"Then you'll let me stay and protect you?"

"Absolutely not." She examined Felice unhurriedly. "Being a nun is against all your natural inclinations, isn't it? Luis must be paying you a fortune."

"Close to it."

"Are you even a Catholic, child?"

Felice nodded, although she didn't add that in her first day at the Blessed Garden she had spent more time in the chapel than she'd spent in a church in the last eight years.

"And do you know that you could be excommunicated for coming here and lying about who you are? The Church takes a dim view of outsiders inside convent walls."

"I know."

"The money was more important than that?"

Felice opened her mouth to reply, then closed it again.

"Sounds a little like you sold your immortal soul, doesn't it?"

"It wasn't just the money." Felice felt her cheeks grow warm at the revelation.

"Wasn't it?"

"No."

"And that surprises you, doesn't it?"

"The money was important," Felice said defensively.

"You're poor?"

"No."

Sister Mary Grace shrugged, as if that settled that.

"There's a house," Felice tried to explain. "I wanted to buy it, and I didn't have the down payment." She didn't add any of the reasons why the house had been so important to her. They seemed superficial somehow. "Luis came to me at just the right moment."

"And if Luis had asked you to come here to spy on me so that he could use the information to hurt me?"

"Of course I wouldn't have done it!"

"Wouldn't you?"

"I'm an investigator. I sneak around for a living. I've done lots of things that might not seem moral or right to you, but I have some standards. I wouldn't have come here to hurt you. I took the job because I wanted to protect you, and I was going to be paid damn well to do it."

"And if you hadn't been paid damn well?"

Felice was silent.

"You don't know, do you, child?"

"I know that I'll be paid well. I know that I've done everything I can to make sure you stay safe."

"Did you ever think it was my right to decide if I wanted protection or not?"

"I'm not paid to think that way."

"But you've had lots of time to think since you arrived, I imagine."

Felice was feeling more and more uncomfortable with the direction of the conversation. "I don't want anyone to hurt you."

"But you've hurt me, and Luis has hurt me."

"That's not the same thing."

"All part of the same thing. You want something for me. Luis wants something for me. The men who are trying to grind Isla Tesoro under their heels want something for me. But it's only what God wants that matters."

"I'm sorry, but I'll never understand that."

"That's because God wants something entirely different for you." Sister Mary Grace rested her hand on Felice's knee. "You really did make a lousy nun. Whatever made you think you could pull it off?"

Felice felt like a little girl making her first confession. "Pride and greed, I suppose."

"You *have* done some thinking." Sister Mary Grace stood, smoothing her robe.

"Are you going to tell Mother Jeanne?" Felice asked.

"Shall I?"

"I'd rather you didn't."

"Then I won't."

Felice waited for Sister Mary Grace to ask her to leave the convent on her own, but she said nothing else. Felice stood. "May I walk you back up to the house?"

"I don't think so. I really don't want a bodyguard."

Felice watched Sister Mary Grace disappear up the path and resisted the urge to follow her. The game was over, and Sister Mary Grace had won hands down. Felice couldn't force protection on a woman who didn't want it. If she persisted in staying at the Blessed Garden, Sister Mary Grace would have to report her. And the occasional twinkle in Mother Jeanne's eyes wouldn't extend to a situation as grave as this one.

Felice realized the precious stash of cigarettes was still in her hands. When she unwrapped the tarp, she found that during her conversation with Sister Mary Grace, she had unconsciously twisted them into shreds.

Ralph was surprisingly garrulous tonight. Gallagher peeked at his watch and wished he'd been smart enough to select a model with a display that lit up. He'd been so bent on looking like a proper drifter that he'd settled for the cheapest model he could find. His fieldwork skills were in sad disrepair.

"Don't know why Father Melrose sent you here. Nuthin' you can do I can't do better."

"I'm not looking to take your job away," Gallagher said for the umpteenth time since he'd set foot on the Blessed Garden grounds. "I'm just here till you're feeling better."

"Feelin' fine."

Actually, Gallagher believed him. In the weeks since he had arrived, Ralph had improved steadily every day. It seemed probable that the old man was going to make a good recovery. Gallagher knew that before too long his presence was going to be questionable to the nuns. Either Ralph was going to have to be taken into confidence and told to lie low, or Ralph was going to have to be forced to leave.

The second alternative didn't appeal to Gallagher. He had developed a very unprofessional affection for the old man. Sentiment was frowned upon in his line of work, but then, so were leaves of absence like the one he was supposed to be taking right now.

Supposed to be taking.

"Don't need you here." Ralph snuffed out his cigarette, grinding it into dust under his shoe.

"You know you love my help," Gallagher said, staring off the porch and searching the distant trees for a glimpse of white. "Besides, what did you do for entertainment before you had me to gripe about?"

Ralph harrumphed. Gallagher figured it was as close to a laugh as the old man could get.

The door slammed as Ralph went inside, and the night was finally silent. Gallagher knew better than to make a beeline for the house. If Sister Felicia—or whoever she was, and he still didn't know—was watching, she would expect him to stay on the porch for a little while, as he always did.

He couldn't be certain, but he didn't think she was watching tonight. That troubled him. If she wasn't watching him, who *was* she watching—and why? Since Ralph had stayed on the porch with him longer than usual, it was already late. Was Sister Mary Grace at the spring? Was Sister Felicia there, too?

A man couldn't stay in this profession without developing a sixth sense about trouble. Outsiders thought that men in his position were cold-blooded and calculating, human computers who fed data in and acted only after logical conclusions had been drawn. They didn't know that some of the best work that had ever been done had been based solely on guts and instinct, with nothing logical in the picture at all.

His guts were twined in knots, and his instincts were twanging like guitar strings at a rock concert. Logically he knew he should stay on the porch and look bored for at least another five minutes. Instinctively he headed for the house instead, switching off lights and disappearing out the back door as soon as the house was dark.

Sister Felicia was clever. He had to admire the way she blended into shadows and walls, shrubbery and trees. No matter how clever she was, though, she was still garbed in holy white. He, on the other hand, was dressed in dark jeans and shirt. If she was anywhere near the spring, he would find her before she found him. And if it was Sister Mary Grace he found instead, she would never know she had been watched.

There was almost no moon, and he picked his way cautiously, wasting precious time making certain he wasn't visible. When he was still a distance from the spring, he saw a flash of white. He ducked behind a tree and peered into the darkness. A robed figure sat on the rock where both Sister Mary Grace and Sister Felicia liked to perch.

Although she was turned toward the spring, he guessed the woman was Sister Mary Grace because she still wore her veil, and from his observations of Sister Felicia, she always stripped it away as soon as she was sure she was alone. There was no smoke wreathing this nun's head, either. She sat completely still, as if in deep contemplation. He wasn't sure that Sister Felicia could have sat that still if her life depended on it.

He realized he felt a keen jab of disappointment. What had he hoped for? Another striptease? Another night of playing Peeping Tom while he told himself lies about how he was peeping for strictly professional reasons?

He was afraid to move closer, because if that was Sister Mary Grace on the rock—and he felt almost certain it was—then Sister Felicia was somewhere nearby watching. He wanted to be sure it wasn't him that she watched. He couldn't stay there, though. He had to find a better position from which to survey the bushes at the spring's perimeter. Sister Felicia had never made any attempt to hurt Sister Mary Grace, but the best hired killers took their time. With unhurried precision they took the measure of their victims, watched and waited until they knew every idiosyncrasy, then struck with the deadly speed of a cobra.

He couldn't imagine Sister Felicia as a cobra, although that could certainly be wishful thinking. Assassins came in all shapes, sizes and disguises. They counted beautiful women in their ranks as well as beady-eyed men in business suits. There were people on Isla Tesoro who would go to any length to rid the world of one outspoken nun who cared too much. And the length they would go to could be Sister Felicia.

The pool into which the spring flowed was an oval, roughly equivalent in size to a suburban backyard. The edge where the nun sat was closest to the convent house, goat shed and garden. As the pool widened to the right, trees and shrubs grew denser, as if reaping the benefit of water just under the ground's surface. Far to the left, in the direction where Gallagher stood, was Ralph's house, and toward the opposite side of the pool from the nun but at least two hundred yards out of sight was the work shed and makeshift garage where the convent truck was kept.

Gallagher calculated where best to position himself. He had thoroughly scanned every corner of the area that he could see, but there was no glimpse of white, no suspicious movement. He couldn't shake the feeling that something was wrong, though. Once his instincts had been honed like sabers, lancing through the obvious to aim straight for the not-so-obvious truth. Now his instincts were rusty, but they creaked in protest as logic told him to move farther right.

He turned back to the left and stared into the darkness. His night vision was excellent, his hearing acute. Something crackled on the path he had just taken, a twig under a passing foot, perhaps, but just as possibly nothing more than branches brushing in the evening breeze.

He wondered if he had been wrong after all, if Sister Felicia had been watching him on the porch at Ralph's house and was now making her way toward the spring.

He took no chances, melting farther into the bushes surrounding him and crouching low. If she passed by, his job would be that much easier. He could follow her to her hiding place and watch both her and Sister Mary Grace. If someone else passed by? His hand slid to the .38 strapped in an ankle holster. If the noise had been footsteps, then he was ready.

* * *

Felice knew that Sister Mary Grace was probably back at the house and already sleeping, but she still couldn't make herself move off the rock. She faced the springs and stared toward distant Smoke Tree, where the lights were going off one by one.

She had failed, although she doubted anyone else would see it that way. She had gritted her teeth and made the best of a difficult situation for weeks. During that time she had kept a close eye on the nun she was being paid to protect. Sister Mary Grace was unharmed, although in no way could Felice take credit for that, since no one had tried to harm her. But Felice knew she had failed because she had let herself be discovered, and now she would have to leave.

Had she done it on purpose? She had been asking herself that question ever since Sister Mary Grace had taken the path to the house. She had chosen a difficult spot from which to watch, and she had moved closer tonight than ever before. Perhaps Sister Mary Grace had seen movement as well as a flash of white, and perhaps she herself had willed that to happen.

She didn't want to be here. Few people in the world relished this type of existence—witness the sparse number of nuns knocking on the Blessed Garden's iron-grilled door for admittance.

No, she didn't want to be here. She wanted to be back in Palm Springs in her own little condo looking out over a landscaped and manicured golf course. She wanted a facial and one of Rudolph's magical trims to make the best of the shearing she'd gotten from Mother Jeanne. She wanted to wear her favorite red silk blouse and dangling pearl earrings, and she wanted to go out for a leisurely gourmet feast with an adoring man and a bottle of Dom Perignon.

Two bottles.

Two men.

She could have all those things as early as tomorrow. But what was Sister Mary Grace going to have? Would she survive the rest of her stay here at the Blessed Garden? And after that, where would she go? What thoughts did she have each night as she sat in this very spot and looked toward the lights of Smoke

Tree? Was she planning to go back to Isla Tesoro to certain death?

Felice shivered, although the night was only pleasantly cool. She hadn't intended to get involved in this case. She had believed she was strong enough to do her job and forget it once it was done. But she had learned something about herself here. She wasn't as strong as she had thought.

Or perhaps she was stronger.

She cared about Sister Mary Grace. She cared about Luis and the agony he would now undergo knowing Sister Mary Grace was unprotected. She cared about the other nuns who might get caught in some bastard's line of fire. She cared that she had breached everyone's trust, that she had lived a lie even if her reasons had been good; that the church to which she had given no more than a passing thought in years might toss her out on her ear.

She was suddenly exhausted. She rested her face against her callused fingertips and tried to think about the pleasures awaiting her. She pictured herself at dinner with ... Josiah Gallagher? She wondered where that thought had come from. Gallagher was her biggest fear for Sister Mary Grace. If Kelley had been able to find out anything about him—and if anyone could, Kelley would be the one—she hadn't been able to get the information to Felice. He was still an unknown, a menace to the peace of the Blessed Garden. He was a self-proclaimed drifter with no references and eyes that saw everything.

She had to warn Sister Mary Grace about Gallagher.

The thought pumped just enough adrenaline into her system to give her the strength to lift her head. She opened her eyes and caught a movement out of the corner of her eye, not in the bushes but just beside her. She drew a sharp breath, but it was instantly clamped off by an arm against her throat. She twisted and struggled, but the harder she fought, the harder the arm pressed against her windpipe.

Her veil whipped across her face, blocking her view. She felt something securing the veil in place and realized she was being gagged, as well. She fought harder, but the lack of oxygen weakened her. Her head began to spin as her arms were savagely jerked behind her back and tied with something that bit into her wrists.

She thought someone spoke, although she couldn't discern what was said. The arm relaxed just enough to let her gasp for a small breath, then tightened again. She was on the verge of fainting. She could see nothing through her veil, but whirling patterns of light danced in front of her eyes anyway. She tried to duck her head, to struggle for more air, anything to keep herself from going under, but the arm pressed harder against her throat. She felt herself floating.

Then she felt nothing at all.

Chapter 6

The two men had come from the right. If Gallagher had followed his head and circled around to the right himself, he probably would have run straight into them.

They weren't the kind of men anyone wanted to run into.

Gun in hand, he watched as they tied up Sister Mary Grace, but there was nothing he could do, even though he had a clean shot at one of the men. If he fired, she was as good as dead.

As he watched, Sister Mary Grace stopped her struggles, and one of the men tossed her over his shoulder like a soldier's duffel bag. Then they started around the pool, silently but with little attempt to stay under cover. They had no reason to think they were being watched, which was Gallagher's only advantage.

He followed just as silently, blending with bushes and trees until the oasis was no more. The men were heading toward the back of the Blessed Garden's acreage and in the direction of the garage. He surveyed that area in his mind as he used the last of the shrubbery as cover. Most of the Blessed Garden was walled in thick adobe, keeping even a glimpse of the world from the sisters' serene gaze. But the acres behind the garage were barren desert and rarely visited by the nuns. They were fenced in wire to mark the Blessed Garden's boundaries. A gate broke the prison-like symmetry, leading to a dirt road that circled the property. He had used that gate on his trip to Smoke Tree in order not to alert Sister Felicia that he was leaving the convent property.

Now he guessed that the men and their unconscious captive would be leaving the same way.

He gave the men a good head start, gauging the distance they would be able to see in the dark before he trailed far behind them. He kept low and used what scrub there was to shelter himself as he followed. He could barely chart the two skulking shapes in the darkness. He just hoped that he would seem nothing more than a shadow if they turned.

They gave the garage a wide berth, heading, as he'd guessed for the path leading to the gate. Gallagher weighed his options. If he followed the men on foot and they reached a car on the opposite side of the gate, they would leave him in their dust. If he got the truck instead, they would surely hear his engine and Sister Mary Grace's life would be in even greater danger.

He compromised, flattening himself against the wall of the garage as he peered into the darkness. He could just make out the gate, and beyond it a shape that was probably their getaway car. When they were far enough away that he could no longer make them out, he headed inside to listen for the rumble of a distant motor.

Felice came to in the back of a moving vehicle. At least, she thought she was in the back. The moving vehicle part was a certainty, because she was being tossed against something hard, a seat perhaps, every time the driver hit a bump. And the driver hit a bump every other second.

She sucked in air through the smothering veil and gag, and little by little her head began to clear. She vaguely remembered the events before she'd passed out, but she had no sense of time. She could have lost consciousness minutes ago or as long as an hour. More important was what happened next.

Gallagher.

The thought penetrated the far reaches of her mental fog and shocked her fully awake. She had been thinking about Gallagher and the need to warn Sister Mary Grace when she'd been taken unaware. Now her personal alarm system clanged furiously. The man who had choked her and was even now speeding along some desert road must be Gallagher.

Had he somehow discovered her identity? Was he going to get rid of her so he could have a clear path to Sister Mary Grace?

Gallagher was not a man who would give a warning and let her go. Behind his "I'm just a little ol' drifter" facade lurked a ruthlessness that she'd recognized right from the beginning. Hadn't she imagined him with an Uzi on his knee? Why hadn't she made more of an attempt to find out about him? Why hadn't she used her lock-picking skills to get to the telephone in Mother Jeanne's office to call Kelley and find out what she'd learned?

The answer was unacceptable, but there it was anyway. Somewhere deep inside her, despite warning signals galore, she'd begun to trust him. It made no sense, unless it was purely the trickery of his considerable sex appeal, but it was true. She'd believed he was capable of ruthlessness, she'd believed he was something other than what he claimed, but she hadn't been able to make the logical leap and believe him to be a murderer.

Now she knew better.

And if he was a murderer, what better target upon which to practice his craft than one bound and gagged nun?

Felice bounced once more and desperately tried to pull together what she knew. She was on the floor of a car, not a truck. She could feel the bump of the rear axle beneath her stomach and the smooth backseat against her side every time she was jolted.

Either the car had no shocks or they weren't on paved highway. The latter and more probable was terrible news for her. On a highway she had a chance to be rescued if she was able to get away. If they were on some unpaved road, or worse, in the middle of the desert somewhere, her chances were zero. She could be shot and her bones picked clean by vultures before anyone noticed she wasn't in the chapel for matins.

She strained to remember those few moments when she'd struggled with her captor. He had spoken. To her? Or was there someone helping him? Ralph? The possibility existed, although she doubted Ralph could get along with anyone long enough to pull off a caper like this one. Maybe there was another man who had joined Gallagher, but her guess was that he had done this alone. He wasn't a man who would need or want help.

And if he was alone, speeding into the middle of the desert, who was watching her? She liked this answer better than any of the others. Gallagher would have to be concentrating on his driving. If the door wasn't locked, and who would bother locking it, with his captive bound and unconscious?—she could get up on all fours and use her head to butt the door handle. Then she could propel herself out of the car before Gallagher knew she was gone.

Of course, she could die. The question was whether she wanted to die trying to escape or by one well-placed bullet. The first way she had a chance, albeit one so small as to be microscopic. The second way she had no chance at all.

She had never hurled herself from a moving car, but she knew the odds were greatly improved if the car was moving slowly. Speed was hard to judge from her position, but she doubted they were burning up the sand. Neither unpaved road nor desert was speedway material. They were probably going no more than forty.

The odds were also greatly improved if the driver kept going after she made her escape. She was swift on her feet but blindfolded she would have no chance of eluding capture or ducking bullets. She could run, but the first cactus that got in her path would be her undoing.

There was no reason to think that Gallagher was going to let her flee unimpeded into the desert night. He would stop the car and catch her before she had stumbled more than a few feet—if she was still alive to stumble at all.

"Someone's following us."

The words came out of nowhere. At first Felice thought she'd imagined them; then she realized their import. The words hadn't been aimed at her. There *were* two people besides herself in the car, and a third somewhere in the desert behind them.

"She still out?"

A pause. "Looks like it."

Two men. Felice lay perfectly still and tried to figure out which one was Gallagher. Neither voice sounded familiar—in fact, one voice seemed faintly accented. Still, neither man had spoken enough words for a good test, and with her head on the floor, the engine noise masked subtleties.

"I don't see anyone behind us."

"I don't now, but I did."

"You're imagining it."

"No. There. See?"

Another pause. "Maybe," the second voice conceded.

"I'm speeding up and turning off my lights." There was a faint snap, as if he had made good his words. The car slowed considerably. "Help me watch where we're going."

"Shouldn't I keep my eye on the guy behind—"

"Do what I tell you!"

Hope surged through Felice, along with the need to do something to decide her fate. She had never sat idly by and let anyone else determine what was going to happen to her. If she had, she would have been married to a Santa Barbara millionaire right now, sipping cocktails at some charity event.

Which didn't sound half-bad at the moment.

She knew if she lay there and considered, she would lose her nerve; then, down the road a piece, she would probably lose her life. She had one chance to do something. If there was a car following them, the men weren't likely to stop and go after her. They weren't watching her now. Both of them had their eyes firmly on the desert in front of them.

It was now or never.

Felice lifted herself on all fours and found the door with the top of her head, praying the car was an older model without recessed handles. At the reassuring feel of metal, she snapped her head upwards. When the door swung open, she launched herself into empty space.

Gallagher didn't think twice. At the sight of a white blur flying clear of the four-wheel-drive wagon in front of him, he snapped on his lights and bore down on the accelerator. Grisly visions of new meaning for the title "flying nun" filled his head.

This particular flying nun landed in a wide gully to the right of the wagon and rolled to the bottom. He didn't have time to see more. The wagon pulled to a halt, and the front door opened. A man appeared, gun in hand, aiming straight for Gallagher's truck. He fired once, but the bullet went wild and low. The second bullet hit the truck. The third did the same.

Gallagher drew closer before he slammed on his brakes. The gunman was shooting low now, but there was no guarantee he'd continue. Gallagher grabbed his gun off the seat beside him, and, opening his door to use as a shield, he leapt to the ground, ducked and fired through the open window. He heard the sound of splintering glass and knew that he had hit what he'd intended.

Another round of shots was fired and absorbed by the truck. He returned fire and heard the whine of bullet against metal. Then he heard nothing. He hazarded a peek through the crack between door and truck body. No one stood beside the wagon any longer. He pictured the gunman making his way to the side of the gully and aiming at the figure in white at its bottom. With that picture fueling him, he began to circle the truck, gun ready.

The silence was broken by the sound of an engine. Wheels spun in sand, and he rounded the truck just in time to see the wagon take off across the desert.

He wanted nothing so badly as to give chase, but there was something more pressing awaiting him. When it was clear that the wagon was gone and not coming back, he slid down the gully to the heap of white at its bottom.

He didn't think that Sister Mary Grace had moved since she'd landed. The wagon had been traveling at a fair speed when she'd launched herself from it, and any number of broken bones could have resulted, including her neck or spine. Gallagher wasn't a squeamish man, but he didn't really want to be the one to discover whether the nun was alive or dead.

Unfortunately there was no one else to whom he could assign the task.

He approached her cautiously. She lay on her side, unmoving, her face still covered by her veil. Between the veil and the gag, he wasn't sure how she'd found the oxygen she needed to fly out the wagon door. One thing was certain, Sister Mary Grace had the kind of courage he wished for in the men who worked for him. If she was anything but a nun, he would have offered her a job.

His hands were oddly unsteady as he found the knot in her gag and untied it. He folded the fabric away from her face, taking no chances by moving her head. Then he brushed the veil back to give her more air.

Sister Mary Grace wasn't Sister Mary Grace.

Gallagher stared at Sister Felicia like a man who had just crossed over to the Twilight Zone. Not once since he'd seen her dragged away by the two men at the springs had he considered that the nun in captivity wasn't Sister Mary Grace. Yet here, beyond the shadow of a doubt, was the woman whom he had suspected of being behind the kidnapping.

And he *had* thought just that. As he'd made his long, frantic drive across the desert, he had put all the facts together and come out with Sister Felicia as bad guy. She had played the spy, determined Sister Mary Grace's pattern of movement and arranged to have her kidnapped. Yet here she was, the victim herself, and the neat little scheme he thought he'd figured out was collapsing around him.

She moaned, the first sign he'd had that she was definitely alive. Putting all doubts and questions behind him, he knelt beside her and touched her cheek. She moaned again, louder.

His hand brushed down her neck to her shoulder, then down her arm. It stopped at her wrist, where he quickly unknotted the rope that bound her. His cursory investigation hadn't revealed a thing, but he knew better than to be optimistic. If nothing else, she was sure to have a mild concussion and more bruises than an overripe peach.

He continued his search for broken bones, running two fingers along her spine. When that revealed nothing he moved to her rib cage, nudging the soft side of her breast.

He had a sudden, crazy flash of what that breast had looked like dappled by moonlight. At the same moment he realized that he cared whether she'd been hurt, not just as one human being cares about another, but as a man cares about a woman who has excited him. She had danced along the far reaches of his mind since the first day he'd seen her, hips swaying, green eyes sparkling, full, sassy lips promising things a nun could never even think.

His fingers dove to the narrow taper of her waist and down the ripe swell of her hip. He took a detour to her pelvis, trying not to think of how soft she felt as he satisfied himself that her bones were in one piece before he moved slowly down her leg.

He stopped not for broken bones or contorted limbs but for a suspicious lump against her thigh. His hands told him what his mind didn't want to believe. He hesitated a moment before proving what a fickle thing the mind could be; then he lifted the hem of her robe and smoothed it up her calf.

He stopped and stared at the place on her thigh where he'd felt the lump. The lump was a gun, a gun strapped low on her hips, just as his mind had insisted. He smoothed the robe farther up her leg and followed the narrow belt holding the holster to one irresistibly sexy pair of bikini pants.

A nun who wore X-rated underwear and topped it off with a .38.

A nun who obviously wasn't.

Gallagher forced his jaw back into place. He felt glad that question had been cleared up. He really did. He finally knew something for sure. There was just one thing he didn't know.

Who in the hell *was* she?

Felice awoke, but she didn't open her eyes. She had been far too young to die, and she wanted to put off the moment when she saw angels—or worse.

Dying was not what it was cracked up to be. At the very least there was supposed to be a cessation of pain, but here she was with the world's worst headache. Not to mention a million questions she had carried into eternity.

Of course, there was the teeniest possibility that she hadn't died at all and had that to look forward to in the near future instead.

She was amazed at how difficult that thought had been to form. Her head felt like someone had used it for sledgehammer practice, and the rest of her didn't feel much better. She couldn't remember what had brought her to this state exactly, only that it was some foolhardy thing she had done. She could almost hear her mother's voice.

"What sort of woman throws herself from a moving car?"

Her mother's voice had grown surprisingly deep. In fact, it wasn't her mother's at all.

Felice doubted the voice was St. Peter's, either. Her eyelids fluttered open before her brain gave them permission. Nothing changed; the world was still black.

Then a man's face came into focus.

"Jesus!"

"Not quite." Gallagher put his hands on her shoulders and held her to the ground as she struggled to sit up. "Don't move. You may be injured."

By her own muddy-headed assessment, she might be injured if she *didn't* move. She moistened lips gone surprisingly dry. "So it *was* you."

He wasn't sure what she'd said, but he was more interested in finding out how badly she was hurt. "Don't worry about anything right now. I'm just trying to find out if you've broken any bones."

"Why? So you can break them, if I didn't?"

He couldn't understand what she'd said. Her words sounded as if they were coming from under the ground somewhere. "Just lie still and relax."

"Relax?" She struggled to sit up again, but he held her firmly to the ground.

"Look, everything's going to be all right. The men who grabbed you are long gone. Unless you want to lie at the bottom of the gully for the rest of the night, let me finish my exam."

Everything was out of her grasp. All Felice could really understand was that Gallagher was here with her, and at least for the moment he didn't seem bent on killing her. She stopped struggling and let him continue his examination.

"I haven't found anything too interesting so far," he said conversationally as he felt along the side he hadn't yet examined for broken bones.

"Ouch!"

He stopped, then ran his fingers along her arm again. "This doesn't seem to be broken, but it may be badly sprained."

She muttered something that sounded like, "Big deal."

"Can you wiggle your fingers?"

"Since I was an infant," she croaked.

This time he understood her. Despite himself, he smiled. "Show me."

There was something degrading about wiggling her fingers at the man who had kidnapped her, but Felice forced herself to cooperate.

"Good." Gallagher ran his hand along her side, lingering extra seconds at her breast.

"Worried . . . that's broken, too?"

"Can't be too careful." He progressed reluctantly down her rib cage to her waist and hip. "Anyway, like I said, I really haven't found anything too interesting so far. Not unless I count your gun and underwear."

Her head was beginning to clear, although not to stop pounding. "Who are you?"

"I could ask you the same thing. Will, in fact. Who are *you*?"

"Sister Felicia—"

"Of the lace panties? Of the .38 revolver? Of the thousand lies?"

"The panties . . . were a gift from a friend. Even nuns have some fetishes."

"The gun's a fetish, too, I suppose."

She couldn't think of any story at all, much less a believable one.

"Try the truth," he said helpfully.

"I'm not obliged to tell you anything."

"Obliged? No. But would you be smart to tell me?" He let the question hang for a minute, as if he were actually considering. His hands trailed down her leg and finally to her foot. When he was finished, he sat back and folded his arms. "God must have been with you, *Sister*. Nothing seems to be broken."

"No thanks to you." Felice rolled over to her side and tried to push herself into a sitting position. Gallagher didn't move.

She finally lay back, exhausted and near tears from the pain in her head.

"A concussion. Mild, hopefully," he said.

"You're a doctor... as well as a drifter?"

"Actually, I'm with the FBI."

"And I'm a reincarnation of Saint Joan."

"Then you're used to roasting. Which is good, by the way, since that's what's going to happen tomorrow if we don't get out of here."

"Cute." Felice struggled to sit up again. Sheer grit made her succeed. Images swam in front of her eyes, and for a moment she thought she would pass out again. Then her vision cleared. She could see a blurry rendition of Gallagher sitting not more than three feet from her. He had a gun in his hand. "Thou shalt not steal," she said, waving ineffectually in his direction.

"*Thou* shalt not carry a gun without a license. And in case you hadn't noticed the subtle differences, this gun is mine. Yours is in here." He patted his pocket. "Who were you planning to use yours against? Sister Mary Grace?"

"Your line of work, not mine."

"What exactly is your line of work?"

"Goat herding."

"And you need a gun for that?"

"I was lying in wait... for Mary Poppins."

"What went wrong tonight? How come you were grabbed?"

"You did the grabbing. You should know." Her head was whirling again, and she wanted nothing more than to lie down, pull the sand over her and die peacefully. There were images that wouldn't let her, though. Men talking. Men. Not one man. Words. An accent of some sort. *Someone's following us.* She rested her head in her hands. It hurt to touch it.

She felt arms come around her. Gallagher had put away his gun and pulled her back against his chest to rest. There was something oddly comforting about his touch, even though she knew he was just trying to keep her from passing out. She struggled against the comfort as much as the captivity, but her struggle lacked strength.

"What do you remember about tonight?" The words were soft against her ear, and soothing. He was seducing her into letting down her guard.

She knew better than to let that happen. "I remember being manhandled."

"You were grabbed at the spring. By two men. I saw it happen, but there was nothing I could do, because I was afraid one of them would kill you if I shot the other."

"Nice of you to worry." She struggled again, but he held her tightly against him until she stopped.

"So I followed you in the convent truck. It's still parked on the road above us."

"Road?" she asked hopefully.

"An exaggeration."

"Are we far from the Blessed Garden?"

"Afraid so. I followed for miles before you threw yourself out of the wagon."

"They were going to kill me."

"You know that for a fact?"

She shrugged.

"Why would they want to kill you?"

She shrugged again.

He admired the sensation of her shoulders rubbing against his chest. She was slender but strong. Even with her head obviously pounding like a jackhammer, she had put up a worthy struggle when he'd set out to hold her. They were well matched.

Unaccountably, thoughts of friends flashed through Gallagher's head. He could almost see Tate and Simon, whose love affair he had admired from a distance. *They* were well matched, too, and Simon was fond of saying that he'd married Tate because she had always given as good as she'd gotten. Passive women weren't Simon's style.

Nuns and assassins had never been Gallagher's.

His arms tightened, but not from attraction. "I asked you why those men might want to kill you." His voice was no longer playful.

"I doubt it was me . . . they thought they were going to kill."

"Sister Mary Grace?" When she didn't answer, he went on. "I thought you were Sister Mary Grace until I untied your veil."

"Surprise."

"You know, I could leave you here."

"One of the nicer things you could do."

"I saved your life."

She wished she knew if that was true. Her brain was working in disjointed leaps. There had been two men, because she was sure she had heard two voices. And one of the men *had* said that someone was following them.

Had that someone been Gallagher?

"You thought I was Sister Mary Grace," she said slowly.

"That's right."

"And you wanted to save her life?"

"Right again."

Even as she formed her next question she wondered what the point was. She had no way to tell if Gallagher was lying. Even her instincts were bruised. She asked it anyway. "Why?"

"Because that's what the government is paying me to do."

"Government?"

"I told you. More than you told me, by the way."

"FBI?" she asked incredulously.

He reached in his pocket, pulled out his badge and flipped it open. In the darkness she could see nothing more than a glint, but it was enough. "A badge is easy to counterfeit," she said.

"I'm getting tired of this."

She tried desperately to make her brain work. "The FBI doesn't send in agents to act as bodyguards to nuns."

"They do if national security is an issue."

She closed her eyes and willed herself somewhere, anywhere, where she wouldn't have to think about one more thing.

"Sister Mary Grace," he said, "is a hot item in Isla Tesoro right now. Her death would be an even hotter item for the right people."

"I don't understand." She knew she sounded weak. Pathetic. She felt pathetic.

"Then listen closely, because I'm only going to tell you once. And when I'm done, you're going to talk to me. Got it?"

She didn't plan to agree, but there she was, nodding a head that felt as if it had grown two sizes. "If I like what you say," she added.

"Whether you like it or not."

She wanted to protest but found nothing inside her to do it with. "Talk."

"I was on vacation," he began. "Actually a leave of absence, when I got nailed for this assignment."

Chapter 7

"Why me?"

"Because you were a top-notch agent, and you've got the security clearance we need. Besides, you're available."

Gallagher swung down off the horse he'd been training and looped his reins over the fence.

"Not to mention," Barker added, "you look the part of a drifter these days."

"I'm on leave of absence. I came here to get away from the Justice Department."

"You know we wouldn't ask if there was anyone else who could do it." Gallagher's profane response made Barker wince. "Anyone else as good," he amended.

"There must be a hundred men with my security clearance, any one of whom's had more recent field experience than I have."

"But you're the one we're asking."

Gallagher knew exactly what all this meant. Someone more exalted in status than himself was trying to bring him back into the fold, using Barker to do the dirty work. Gallagher had done the unforgivable. He had taken a leave of absence, a perfectly legitimate act but one highly frowned upon, and one of his superiors had decided to rein him in.

The problem was that he didn't know about his future. He had come to work on a friend's dude ranch for a few months to clear his head. Two weeks of roping cows and breaking horses had cured him of his dream of quitting government service and buying his own small spread somewhere. Ranching wasn't the cure for the restlessness, the sense of futility that had pervaded every moment of the last year of his life.

He didn't know what the answer was, though. And it was possible that it still lay somewhere along the labyrinthine halls of the Justice Department. Which meant, quite simply, that he couldn't turn his back on a request like this one. Not if he ever hoped to go back to D.C. and pick up where he'd left off.

"You look ridiculous in that outfit," he snapped, waving his hand at Barker's stiff new jeans and brightly embroidered cowboy shirt.

Barker took no offense. "You look right at home in yours. Like you've been living in it for weeks now."

"A convent, for God's sake."

"Some would say that's exactly whose sake it *is* for." Barker shrugged at Gallagher's icy stare. He had worked for Gallagher long enough to know the man inside out and backward. Gallagher was always the best at whatever he did, and by the looks of him now, he already needed new challenges.

"How come they picked you to come and deliver the ultimatum?" Gallagher asked.

"They bribed me."

"With what?"

"Two weeks here. If you don't go to the convent and make like a handyman, you get to see my smiling baby face at every meal. And you have to be nice to me."

Gallagher swore like his fellow cowboys, but his heart wasn't in it. Barker was one of his favorite colleagues, an innocent-looking young man who could trick information from the craftiest con.

"You'll do it?" Barker asked.

"When?"

"Yesterday."

"It'll take me a day to wrap up here."

"It's about a four-hour drive. I'll take you there myself and introduce you to Father Melrose. He's not excited about one of us breaching the sanctity of the convent, but he's even less excited about any of the sisters being in danger."

"And the Mother Superior?"

"Doesn't know a thing. We plan to keep it that way."

"When are you going to brief me on the ins and outs."

"There's not a lot to tell. I told you about Sister Mary Grace and her stay on Isla Tesoro. Now we've got reason to believe that the right wing there wants to come here and finish her off. That'll stir up the peasants, which will prove that the folks in power now can't handle the country and create a rift that the right wing can slip into. When the smoke clears, they'll be in power."

"This country hasn't worried overmuch about supporting repressive right-wing regimes before."

"This one is real bad news."

"And the one in power now?"

"Weak but ideologically acceptable. If we can catch the bad guys in the act of going after Sister Mary Grace, then the Tesoro government will be grateful and we'll have some bargaining chips. Who knows, maybe it'll even be the push they need to start acting like men."

"Or like women."

Barker looked puzzled.

"From what you've said, the one person who's shown courage, real courage, on that island is a middle-aged nun."

Barker nodded. "Apparently she's something else. The peasants think she's a saint. The right wing thinks she's important enough to risk creating an international incident."

"And the department thinks she's important enough to protect with my life and my leave of absence."

"You got it."

Gallagher unlooped the reins of the young horse he'd been training and held them out to Barker. "Here."

"What for?"

"You're going to stay on a dude ranch, you've got to ride."

"You don't think I know how?"

Gallagher cocked one brow.

"I took lessons."

"When?"

"About twenty years ago."

"I'm sure you haven't forgotten a thing."

Barker took the reins, successfully pulled them over the horse's head and managed to mount, although the horse danced from side to side in anticipation.

"Just give him a kick when you're ready," Gallagher said helpfully.

Barker nudged the young stallion with his foot, and it took off like a shot around the ring.

"Barker," Gallagher called. "Just one thing. I forgot to tell you. He starts, but he's hard to stop. That's what I was teaching him when you arrived. Just click your tongue and kick him a little harder when you've finished with him. Maybe that'll work." He took off his battered cowboy hat and waved it at the horse as it came around the ring at a teeth-jarring trot. Then, satisfied as the horse began a rapid canter, he walked away.

Felice listened to Gallagher's story, aware that the four or five sentences he uttered hid more than they revealed. If he was the man he claimed he was, however, he would not reveal more, particularly not to someone he didn't trust. It was enough to know that the FBI was involved because they were afraid Sister Mary Grace's assassination would cause an unstable Isla Tesoro to erupt into worse violence. She had worked with the Feds often enough to know that they were always sticking their noses in places outside their own borders. This was just the kind of case they would kill for. Literally.

She was all too aware that Gallagher was still holding her tightly against him, though there was nothing affectionate about his grasp. Clearly he believed she was a woman who needed to be restrained.

He wasn't hurting her, though. She considered that piece of evidence as carefully as everything he had said. She had to make a decision, and she had to make it now. If Gallagher was the man he claimed to be, then she was safe in telling him her identity. If he wasn't, she was a goner. But then, she would be a goner if she didn't tell him, too. Her head still pounded, and her brain was still working in fits and starts, but that bit of adrenaline-carried logic seemed indisputable.

Her life was in Gallagher's hands.

As he had done, she told him an abbreviated version of her story, leaving out everything she could. "So this man convinced himself that someone had to go into the convent to protect Sister Mary Grace," she finished.

"And?"

"That someone was me. I'm a private investigator. I have an office with a partner in Palm Springs."

"That's good for a warm-up. Now let's hear the real story."

"That *is* the real story."

"You're saying you or anyone would sneak into a convent under false pretenses and bury yourself in the religious life just on the whim of some old man who's still in love with a nun?"

"Did I mention that he's paying me a fortune to do it?"

Gallagher was silent.

"We're not talking a hundred a day plus expenses," Felice said.

"What's your name?"

"Felice Cristy."

"I can break your story with one call."

"I know the Feds are everywhere, but I don't see a phone nearby." She felt the hands on her shoulders turning her to face him. She wished the night was lighter, so that she could read the expression in his eyes. But then, if the night had been lighter, she might be dead.

Gallagher lifted his hands to her head and tugged at her veil. Her hands rose of their own accord to stop him. "I'd rather you didn't do that."

"Why not?"

She swallowed, trying to be matter-of-fact. "Mother Jeanne did quite a number with the scissors when I arrived."

He smiled at her vanity. "I've seen your head uncovered. I've been watching you at the spring."

"You bastard." Felice thought back to the night she had given in completely to temptation and stripped off her robe for a swim. "Were you there the night I—"

"Certainly was. Some dreams I had that night."

She tried to shove him away, but he grasped her hands with one of his and tugged at her veil again. This time it came off. He unwrapped the wimple, clearly revealing her face.

He hadn't seen her this well up close before. He wasn't about to tell her, but the little-boy haircut—less skillfully done than she probably imagined—emphasized the perfect oval of her face, the delicate lift of her cheekbones, her long narrow nose and, God help him, her incredibly kissable mouth.

"Just what do you think you're going to see?" she asked indignantly.

"Truth or lies."

"I can say the same thing."

"I know." He dropped her hands. They went immediately to her head to smooth her hair.

He watched the very feminine response. A real nun wouldn't have worried about her hair or lack of it. An assassin? Well, his educated guess was that an assassin would have had other things on her mind, like doing whatever it took to get his gun. A private eye masquerading as a nun? There was no telling, since that particular combination was unique to him.

"Well, do you believe me?" she asked.

"Believing you would be a luxury." He pushed himself to his feet, towering over her. "How's your head?"

"It hurts like hell."

"Feel any lumps?"

"One in the back. One at the temple."

"You're lucky you weren't killed."

"Tell my head that."

He held out a hand. "By all rights you shouldn't move, but if we stay here, we're sitting ducks if our friends come back. Let's get you in the truck and back to the convent."

"Not there."

"No?"

"Sister Mary Grace caught me watching her tonight. I had to tell her who I was. She'll tell Mother Jeanne if I keep hanging around, and I'll be kicked out of the Blessed Garden and..."

"And?"

"The church."

She shrugged, but he saw the distress on her face. He moved one step closer to believing her story. "Then where shall I take you?"

"The closest town. I can call my partner."

"Don't you think the nuns will worry if you disappear?"

"Considering my reputation there, they probably won't be surprised—especially after Sister Mary Grace tells them about our little talk. But I'll call Mother Jeanne and tell her I'm all right."

"But not your real name."

"Minus that."

"And the other call?"

Felice managed to stand, using his hand for help. "What call?"

"The one to the Feds to find out if I'm telling the truth."

The night began to whirl in shades of black and blacker. She touched her forehead. "Would you expect any different?" Her own voice sounded far away.

"Are you all right?"

She nodded; at least, she thought she did. The whirling night sucked her into its vortex, and her body went limp. Just as she fell she thought she felt Gallagher's arms around her.

She awoke to the feel of fingertips against her cheek. Her eyes opened slowly to see Gallagher gazing down at her. "Keep your eyes open. I'm going to shine a light in them to check your pupils."

She was so exhausted that she couldn't form an answer. She flinched as the sudden beam of light struck, but Gallagher seemed satisfied after a moment's exam of both eyes. "Looks okay. And there's no sign of suspicious drainage, but the knot on the back of your head is swelling.

"Where'd you get the light?"

"From the truck."

"I thought we were headed that way."

"We were." He considered how best to give her the bad news. "We did. I carried you there."

"How come we're not in it?" She didn't want to move her head to find out where they were, but the stars above were a dead giveaway that it wasn't the truck.

"The truck's out of commission.'

She absorbed that bit of information. "How come?"

"Bullet holes."

"Bullets?"

"You slept through the little shooting match I had with the kidnappers. They didn't get me, but they made a real shooting gallery out of the truck."

She imagined the worst-case scenario, something she was especially good at. "The radiator?"

"Looks like swiss cheese."

"And the water's all drained away?"

"No trace of it, or the gas either."

"Tires?"

"Flat enough to pave a road with."

"How far would you say we are from civilization?"

"Farther than we should be."

"Shouldn't you be hoofing it for parts unknown?"

He didn't answer.

"Don't tell me you stayed around to take care of me."

"You'd be just the least bit vulnerable out here, injured and alone. When that sun comes up tomorrow, you're going to wish you *did* have some special alliance with God."

"Gallagher, get going. Leave my gun in case my bad-guy buddies come back looking for me. I'll get beside the truck for shade and wait for you. Or maybe somebody else will come along."

"We're way off the beaten path." He didn't add that he wasn't even sure where the beaten path was. The men who had grabbed her had zigzagged for miles along hill and gully, making hash out of the delicate desert ecology. Along the way they had zigzagged a few times too many to make Gallagher feel certain that he knew how to get anywhere now. His best hope was to follow his own tracks, and there was a wind rising, which threatened to mask even that bit of help.

"The world's chock-full of people. Someone's bound to find me."

"It may not be someone you want. Would you recognize the men who grabbed you?"

"No." She realized what he was getting at. If someone did rescue her, it might not be an accident. And it might not be a rescue.

"There's another matter of whether I could find you again if I came back looking for you."

"If you're really a Fed, you'd have access to helicopters and planes."

"And you might be as dried out as the desert floor by the time we completed a search. No, we've got a better chance of surviving this if we stay together."

"You mean *I've* got a better chance."

He didn't answer.

"I've been nothing but trouble for you."

"Something tells me there is a gaggle of people who can say that about you."

"I'm very good at what I do," she said indignantly. "I made detective after just a year and a half with the LAPD."

"And didn't stay there. To my profound regret."

She shut her eyes. "What are you planning?"

"With that concussion, I'm probably not supposed to let you get any sleep for a while, anyway. I suggest we try to get you on your feet again and get as far away from here as we can. It's not ideal, but being stranded in the desert's not ideal, either."

"Someone will notice you're gone tomorrow and send help."

"Probably not. I've made a convincing show of being a drifter. When Ralph finds I'm gone, he'll just assume I up and left. He wants me out, so the word probably won't get back to Father Melrose until one of the nuns asks Ralph where I went."

"Too bad neither of us was lovable enough for anybody to miss."

He didn't answer, but he was encouraged that her responses were so sharp. He was much more worried about possible brain injury than he was letting on to her. He'd had enough first-aid training to know that her second loss of consciousness could be a bad sign. And he'd had more than enough to know that she should spend the rest of the evening being carefully watched in a hospital bed, not roaming the desert.

There was nothing he could do, though, to change reality. He had to get her away from the truck in case the kidnappers returned, and he had to find civilization quickly, since no one up to any good was going to be searching for them until Father Melrose sounded the alarm. His contacts in the Bureau were used to hearing from him sporadically and wouldn't worry for a few more days.

"I don't know how far I can walk," Felice admitted. "But I'll do my best."

He felt an unwelcome surge of admiration for her. Her skull had to feel like a jet fighter was inside trying to escape, but she was struggling to ignore the pain and do what she had to. He didn't want to have good feelings about Felice Cristy. He was still suspicious, not because her story wasn't plausible but because his business was being suspicious. Period. But other feelings, like admiration and, worse, sexual attraction, were interfering with his suspicions and his logic.

They were going to be alone in the desert, trying to survive together, for at least a day and probably more. They had to cooperate, but he knew he was going to have to keep an emotional distance from her in order to watch her carefully. He just wasn't sure how he was going to do it.

"Do you know where to go?" she asked.

"Yeah," he lied.

"Then we'd better get going."

"Not so fast. I'm going to assemble a pack from the truck."

"Pack?"

"We'll need some survival gear." When he saw her brows draw together, he wished he hadn't used the word "survival." "We are in the desert," he pointed out, as casually as he could. "We'll need to take care of ourselves."

"You don't think we'll find civilization tonight?"

"We might."

"But you're not hopeful."

"I don't think we should count on it."

"This is California, for God's sake. There's not an inch somebody hasn't claimed."

"This is the desert, and there are still parts of it claimed mostly by scorpions and rattlesnakes."

"You don't know where to go, do you?"

"There's a star right up there telling me where."

"But if you're not sure where we are, what good does it do to know which way north is?"

"Look, you worry about your head and putting one foot in front of the other, I'll take care of getting us somewhere."

Felice knew she was capable of little more than he was suggesting. She managed a nod and gratefully realized it hadn't split her head in two.

"Good. I'll be gone a few minutes, twenty at most. You stay here and gather your strength. You're about five hundred yards from the truck, on the opposite side from the one where you took your tumble. If you hear an engine, stay down unless I tell you it's okay." He moved away, heading for the truck.

"Gallagher?"

"Yeah?"

"Rattlesnakes and scorpions?"

He wished the next day or two were going to be only that perilous. "Possibilities. But they're not going to come searching for you."

"Suppose this is their favorite meeting place?"

"Just rest and forget about them. They'll give you a wide berth."

"I'll do the same for them."

"Good idea." He hesitated a second, but when she didn't say anything else, he started off again.

He made a mental list as he approached the sadly tilting vehicle. The pickup would probably never run again. Now it was purely a scrap heap of items they might be able to use on their desert trek. He'd driven it so rarely that he hadn't paid much attention to what Ralph kept in it. He had been much more interested in getting the engine running smoothly. And it had, until it had been shot full of bullet holes.

He started in the truck bed. There were a variety of tools in a utility box that ran the width of the bed, just behind the cab. He couldn't see much use for screwdrivers or wrenches, but the camping-size hatchet looked promising. He threw it to the ground beside the truck and continued his search. When he'd finished he had a pack of flares, a small, ancient first-aid kit, a length of rope, what looked like half of a paint-splattered plastic drop cloth and a can of motor oil.

Wedged between the box and the wheel well was a five-gallon plastic jug of the type used to carry gasoline. With no need for fuel he almost bypassed it, but at the last moment he unscrewed the cap and sniffed for fumes. There were none. The jug held water, no doubt for radiator use.

He sent silent thanks to the old recluse, who certainly wouldn't have supplied this life-giving fluid if he had known whose life it was going to save. Gallagher lifted the jug and shook it. It wasn't full; probably not more than a gallon or two was inside, but that could make the difference between surviving and not.

In the truck cab he found matches and miscellaneous papers for starting fires, although the one document he wanted to find, a map, was absent. There were two pairs of sunglasses—one with a cracked lens, one with a broken earpiece—and a long-sleeved work shirt. There was a smashed granola bar and the remains of half an apple. Better yet was a can of Coke that had never been opened.

The seat was covered by an old Indian blanket. Gallagher stripped it off and made one more quick investigation with the flashlight to be sure he hadn't missed anything before he stepped outside.

The exterior of the truck yielded two more treasures: one utilitarian hubcap and—after a trip to the toolbox for the screwdriver he'd ignored—the side mirror. He wrapped everything but the water jug in the blanket and rolled and tied it with the length of rope. Then, blanket roll slung across his back and jug in hand, he went back to find Felice.

She was lying exactly where he'd left her, eyes closed, hands folded on her chest like a corpse. Her eyes opened when he reached her side.

"Put a pot on your head and you'd look just like Johnny Appleseed," she said.

"How are you feeling?" He squatted and shined the flashlight in her face.

"I was feeling better until you did that."

"Your pupils are still the same size."

"I told them to stay that way."

"You're pale."

"Who wouldn't be?"

"And sassy."

"An eternal condition."

"Then are you ready to make tracks?"

"Follow tracks, don't you mean?"

"That's right."

She pushed herself into a sitting position. Her head stayed on her neck, a reassuring sign.

Gallagher touched her shoulder. "All right?"

"So far."

"Put your hand on my shoulder, and we'll get up together."

"I don't need your help."

"No?" His voice grew softer and infinitely more dangerous. "Without my help, little desert flower, you'd dry up and blow away before you got out of here. Let's get one thing straight right now. I'm in charge, and you're not. If I tell you to do something, you do it. If I don't tell you to do something, you ask before you try it on your own. There can only be one boss on this expedition, and that boss is me."

"I still don't trust you."

"The feeling's mutual."

"How do I know you're who you say you are?"

"You don't. On the other hand, if I were anyone else, I'd have been long gone by now, wouldn't I?"

"And if I were anyone else, I wouldn't have been mistaken for Sister Mary Grace and kidnapped in her place."

"If that's what happened."

"Why else would I have been snatched?"

"No reason's occurred to me. Yet."

She considered her choices. She had only one. Reluctantly she laid her hand on his shoulder. He grunted his approval. Then, with his hand hovering at her back to catch her if she fell, they rose together.

The world wove crazily, then steadied. Felice felt Gallagher's arm come around her for support.

She was furious at him. She didn't like Neanderthal men, and she didn't like taking orders. On the other hand, she didn't like falling on her face, either. And she had done that tonight in more ways than one. Gallagher had been there to catch her every time. Where would she be without his help?

She could feel each individual finger dig reassuringly into her waist. He wasn't going to let her fall; he wasn't going to let her die. She turned toward him, and his arm clamped tighter.

She lifted her head and saw the question in his eyes. "I'm all right."

"Good." He didn't release her. He was all too aware that holding her was like grabbing a live wire, but he couldn't seem to let her go.

"Have I said thank you?"

"I don't know. It doesn't matter."

"Just doin' my job, ma'am?"

"Something like that."

"Thank you anyway."

"You forgot your veil."

Her hand went to her head. "My hair looks that bad, huh?"

"Desert flower, you've got to know that bald as a billiard ball you'd still be a movie star. The veil's to keep the sun off your head. You're going to need it."

She wanted to hang on to her anger. She wanted to hang on to something besides him. It was treacherous to trust him completely, even worse to get weak-kneed at the way he said "desert flower."

He thought she was beautiful. He'd as much as told her. Lots of men had thought so, but none of them had seen her this way, stripped bare of every feminine wile and crowning glory. And none of those men had been a man like this one.

She didn't let herself dwell on that, though she couldn't make herself move away.

"We'd better get going." Gallagher didn't take a step.

"I think I'll be able to walk."

"Good." He stared down at her, at the thickly lashed green eyes and the cheek that was already swelling with a bruise. He saw courage and vixen temper and reluctant gratitude mixed with something like the warmth growing in remote regions of his own body. "Damn," he said. Just before he kissed her.

She tasted like his most erotic dream; she felt like hopes he'd abandoned long ago. The desert night was hushed, as if it had waited for this merging of these unlikely humans. The only sound he heard was a low moan from the woman he kissed.

"Bad idea, Gallagher." Felice tried to push him away and ended up pulling him closer.

"The worst." He kissed her again, burying deep inside himself the sensation of her lips yielding beneath his. He made himself step away before he kissed her a third time. Her eyes were heavy-lidded and suspicious. They were also unmistakably blazing with life.

"No more of that." Now that he had already stepped away, Felice managed to shove him gently.

"No?"

"No!"

He smiled, flashing dimples—one shallow, one deep—that only made his face more rugged. "Then next time it'll be something different."

"Nothing." She rued the lack of conviction in her voice. Her legs were trembling, and she didn't know if it was her injuries or this man's surprisingly healing touch.

"I don't trust you, and you don't trust me. But there seems to be one thing we agree on." Gallagher bent and lifted her veil and wimple from the ground, folding them to stuff inside the blanket roll. "Ready?"

She wasn't sure what she was agreeing to, but she nodded.

"Then let's go."

An owl called from a thick grove of mesquite at the edge of a wide wash to their left. Another bird answered, and the night was no longer still. With Gallagher just in front of her, Felice began to walk.

Chapter 8

Sandals weren't made for desert hiking. Felice had to pause half a dozen times to brush debris off the soles of her feet, and she had to pick her way through the darkness with particular care, since cactus spines in the same place would have been excruciating.

She wouldn't have been moving at the speed of light, anyway. Her head wasn't pounding as hard, and the dizziness had almost disappeared, but she was sore from top to bottom. She knew that when the sun came up tomorrow, she would be looking at a multihued body.

Neither the aching head, the bruises, nor the arm which wasn't working quite right was much to have sustained after catapulting herself from a moving vehicle. Even if she was stranded in the desert with a suspicious man who didn't seem to know where he was going, she was a lucky woman. By all rights she should be dead about now.

She could tell herself that until the stars fell from the sky, but she didn't feel a damned bit lucky. She hurt; she was exhausted; she wanted a hot bath, a soft bed, and a man's arms around her.

And not just any man's.

Gallagher was a good five paces ahead of her. She knew he wanted to walk faster but had to stay close to guide her in the darkness. The night was cool. He hadn't talked about water and the need to cover ground before the sun came up, but she knew what he was thinking. There was some water in the jug he was carrying, but she knew it was very little compared to what they might need. As spartan as the life at the Blessed Garden had been, one thing no one had ever stinted on was water. All the sisters had been encouraged to drink more than they thought they needed. Felice knew how easy it was to become dehydrated in a climate that sucked water from the human body like a misinformed vampire.

"Are you doing all right?"

She watched Gallagher pull up short and wait for her. "I'm fine. Keep going."

"How's your head?"

"Still on my shoulders."

"You're a trooper."

She realized he was complimenting her. The words did something peculiar to her insides. Maybe it was just that she'd been living at the Blessed Garden so long that she wasn't used to hearing praise. Nuns didn't bother with it much, the theory being, she supposed, that God's opinion was the only one that really mattered.

So maybe she just hadn't heard a kind word about herself in too long. Or maybe it was the man who had uttered these particular kind words.

She didn't like that last thought. She'd been trying to shove Gallagher an emotional arm's length away since he'd kissed her. Or more accurately, she supposed, since they'd kissed—admittedly she had done her share.

And what had gotten into her to stand under the desert sky, head throbbing and knees knocking, and kiss a man whose identity was still suspect? Had she been without a man's touch so long?

It wasn't as if men were such a large part of her life that she couldn't live without them. She was a flirt, but men realized early on that she wasn't a tease or an easy mark. Perhaps all the years of convent school had made more of a difference in her than she had believed, or perhaps she had just been too wary of being tied down to get involved very often. Whatever the reason, despite her free-spirit demeanor, there had been dozens of men she had kissed, then pointed toward the door. And that was the way she had liked it.

Kissing Gallagher had been different. Maybe it was gratitude, or the near brush with death. Maybe it was weeks of deprivation of every type of sensuality.

And maybe it was the man.

She almost bumped into Gallagher, who had waited for her. "There's not much point in going farther," he said, reaching out to steady her. "We need to find a place to sleep."

"I can keep going."

"I know." He dropped his hands. "I'm not sure where we're going at this point, though. I'm going to need some light to get my bearings and see if I can find any tracks. Besides, the wind's picking up. Even though it's cool enough now, the wind will dehydrate us. We need to lie low and conserve water."

"How much is in the jug?"

"Enough to get us where we're going."

"You don't know where we're going, do you, Josiah?" His first name came naturally to her tongue. She liked the sound of it and the way it humanized him somehow. She suspected everyone in the world called him Gallagher, except maybe his mother...and his wife, if he had one.

"I'll get you somewhere."

"Undoubtedly." She watched him turn and start off again. "Josiah?"

"Very few people have lived long enough to call me that twice."

"What few?" She started after him.

He thought about Simon and Tate, who rarely called him anything but. And once there had been a woman with laughing brown eyes and a smile that made his heart soar like the Concorde.

When he didn't answer, Felice rephrased her question. "Are you married? Or isn't that any of my business?"

"No."

She wasn't sure which question he'd answered. But she was sure she'd better not ask again. That "no" had been fraught with finality.

There was a rise just ahead. Gallagher stopped and pointed. "Can you climb?"

"I can do anything."

"I am a strong, invincible woman?"

"You got it."

"Come on." Gallagher started toward the rise, one of a series of low foothills leading eventually to a small mountain range. "I'll lead the way, and we'll go slow. Even if you are invincible, you're hurt and you're wearing sandals."

"I wish I had boots."

"Wouldn't that look cute with your habit?"

"Cute's never been high on my agenda."

"I'll bet you thought you were something in a cop's uniform."

"I was something. But not cute."

Gallagher knew that climbing straight up would tire her too much. He zigzagged up the hill, carefully choosing his path and staying right in front of her. He pulled out the flashlight, using its light sparingly to help guide them. He was afraid the battery was going to run low, and he wanted to save some power to use it for signaling if that became necessary.

Halfway up they came to a plateau, just the right width for two bodies under a blanket. He wondered how Felice was going to like the idea of sleeping with him. "We'll camp here."

Felice was too sore and exhausted to climb another foot, although she would have walked to hell and back before admitting that to Gallagher. "I hope you don't toss and turn in your sleep."

"I'll be taking you down the hill with me if I do."

"Which means?"

"One blanket, which we're going to share."

"It doesn't look easy to tear."

"Share. Together."

"There were two firm rules in my division. Never tell the Feds anything they didn't know enough to ask about, and never, never sleep with them."

"You work on your own now, you can do what you want. And you want to sleep with me, because if you don't you're going to get cold, not to mention scared as hell when the first coyote howls."

"Cold, maybe. I've been cold before."

"Your choice."

She wasn't scared of coyotes, but the thought of a rattlesnake cuddling up for company didn't thrill her. And she was already shivering, from shock or the dropping temperature. Whichever it was, she didn't look forward to a night of it. "Are we going to sleep right on the ground?"

"Unless you have a better idea."

"Leaves?"

"We're not exactly in a forest." Gallagher stooped and began to brush the ground with his hands, scooping up the largest rocks and tossing them to one side. Felice knelt beside him to help.

"This means I get the pleasure of your company?" he asked.

"Whatever pleasure it gives you to sleep with a fully robed nun."

"Whatever made you think you could pull off being a nun, Sister Felicia?"

She'd been asked that once before tonight, but this time her answer wasn't the same. Not for Gallagher. "I did pull it off. For a long time, anyway."

"And you hated every minute of it."

She almost agreed, until she realized it wasn't true. She hadn't had time to put her weeks at the Blessed Garden in any kind of perspective, but when she did, she had the curious feeling that she might actually look back at them fondly.

"No, I didn't hate every minute," she said. "And if I had a choice between the Blessed Garden and this, I wouldn't have to think long or hard."

"Between the relative safety there and the danger here? Or between celibacy and sleeping with a man?"

"Sleeping with a man can mean one of two things. In this case I'll remain celibate, so there's no choice, is there?"

Gallagher was satisfied they'd cleared the spot as much as they would be able to. He could sleep anywhere, but he felt a real pang of sympathy for the bruised and aching woman beside him. The ground was going to be no treat for her.

"I wish I could do better for you. This isn't going to be comfortable."

Felice had been waiting for another wisecrack. It took her a second to adjust. "Umm...I guess I'm lucky to be able to sleep anywhere at all, considering what might have happened to me. Besides, the mattresses at the Blessed Garden were stuffed with rocks. At least, that's how they felt."

"One thing about you. You don't whine."

"Only one thing?" She watched him turn toward her. She could barely read the expression in his eyes, and she couldn't interpret it at all.

"You want me to tell you what else?"

"Maybe not."

"You gave me nightmares when I thought you were a nun."

"I gave myself nightmares," she said lightly.

"You have a walk that asks a man to reconsider his life plans."

"That's two things, Josiah. Enough."

"Three's my lucky number, so I'll tell you something else. But this one's about me. I'm in California because I don't seem to know what I want anymore. But I know what I don't want, and that's getting tangled up right now. So whatever you're worried about, don't worry about me."

"I've never wanted to get tangled up." She watched him unroll the blanket and wondered why he'd said one thing and sounded like he'd meant another. She didn't know him; she still wasn't sure she even could believe he was the man he said he was. But she knew people, and she knew when they were lying to themselves. She also knew when to leave well enough alone.

"Quite a pack rat, aren't you?" she said, purposely changing the subject.

"I hope we won't need all of this."

"A hubcap?"

"In lieu of a shovel."

"A mirror?"

"For signaling."

"Lord, now I'll be able to see what I look like tomorrow."

"You might want to leave that for another time."

"Like next year." She watched him pull the plastic out.

"Can we sleep on that?"

"Tonight we can. We might need it to catch water later."

"Sure. In case we get a thunderstorm."

"It has been known to rain this time of year."

"If it does, there'll be camera crews out here to film it, and we can hitch a ride back home."

"I suggest you say a few prayers."

"If I do, it won't be rain I'll pray for."

"What will it be?" Gallagher spread the plastic. It was paint-spattered and dusty, but it was some protection from the ground.

"I'll pray for a town around the first bend. One with a luxury motel."

"I'll settle for a telephone."

"If I'm going to pray, I'm not going to waste my effort on the mundane." Felice watched Gallagher gesture toward the plastic. She realized he was planning to wedge her against the hillside. "What? Me first?" she asked.

"If one of us rolls downhill, it ought to be me. You probably wouldn't survive another tumble tonight."

She looked with gratitude toward the far side of the drop cloth, which snuggled up against the hillside. "Thanks."

"I'll be back in a minute."

"Where are you going?" She figured it out without his help. "Oh. Well, don't step on any scorpions."

"You don't need to make a pilgrimage?"

"No." She forced her aching body to bend and kneel, then crawled across the plastic, which did nothing to soften the hard ground beneath. The Blessed Garden's mattresses had been feather beds in comparison. She could tell herself until sunrise how lucky she was to be alive, but the ground was still going to feel like solid granite.

Flat on her back, she realized just how uncomfortable sleeping in her robe was going to be. Even when she loosened the cord at her waist and the loops at her wrists, she felt swaddled in fabric. The cotton was coarsely woven, and she itched where it pressed against her. With little time to weigh the pros and cons, she stripped it off to sleep in her undershirt and pants. The air was cool against her skin, but not unpleasant as she pulled the blanket over her.

Other than brief minutes at the spring, it had been weeks since she'd worn so few clothes, and even without Gallagher there to complicate matters, she felt curiously disoriented, as if her body belonged to a stranger. In some ways, perhaps, it did. She had played the part of Sister Felicia for so long that the good sister still dwelled somewhere inside her. She would never be exactly the person she'd been before walking through the Blessed Garden's gates.

With the robe rolled into a makeshift pillow, she settled on her left side, facing away from the hillside. Her right arm throbbed, guaranteeing that she would get no sleep on that side. Since the ground sloped gently, there was no choice where to put her head, not unless she wanted all her blood to drain into her brain during the night. She was going to be forced to sleep facing Gallagher. She told herself she'd be able to keep an eye on him that way and waited for him to return.

He crept back to camp so silently that he was almost on top of her before she knew it. As she watched, he kicked off his shoes. His pants slid down his long legs, and her breath caught as she fully expected him to continue. He didn't, however. He sat on the plastic and rolled his pants into a pillow. Much as she had rolled her robe. Then he slid under the blanket.

The blanket was more suited to one than to two. Felice wanted to protest how closely he lay beside her, but she knew she had no right. There was a benefit, too. She could feel the heat radiating from his body. At least she wasn't going to be cold.

"I saw two jackrabbits," he said.

She couldn't believe he sounded so delighted. "This isn't 'The Wild Kingdom.' We're not having an adventure."

"When I was a kid, my father and I went desert camping for the fun of it."

"Right from the beginning I knew there was something strange about you."

"I'm trying to tell you that we can make it out here if we have to. I know what to do."

"Based on skills you learned as a kid? How come I'm not reassured?"

"I've used them a time or two since," he said cryptically.

"Broke some of your biggest cases in Death Valley, did you?"

"We're not in Death Valley."

"A mere figure of speech, Josiah."

"Just so you'll know, we're in the Upper Colorado portion of the Sonoran Desert, edging along the Mojave. Overall, the Sonoran's the hottest desert in North America, and it gets the least precipitation."

"Well, at least when we do something, we do it big."

"I make it my business to know where I am."

"I knew we weren't in Death Valley," she insisted.

"It's a good thing we aren't. A man without water in Death Valley can't survive two summer days."

"I'm feeling better already."

"What does it take to turn off your sass?"

"Sleep."

"Then by all means indulge."

She waited for him to close his eyes; obviously he was waiting for her. Even this close, it was too dark to get more than an impression of what he was probably thinking, but she thought she knew. "I'm not going anywhere."

"I know."

"Then shut your eyes," she said irritably.

"Can you think of any reason why someone would kidnap you, other than mistaking you for Sister Mary Grace?"

"No!" His eyes closed, but Felice wasn't fooled. "I've told you the truth! I am who I say I am."

"For your sake, I hope so."

"You know, you don't exactly look like the Feds I knew in L.A. You look more like something that crawled off a carnival midway."

"We'll see who looks worse when this is over."

"Well, at least neither of us will be tempted to..." Her voice trailed off.

His eyes opened. "To what?"

"To use your highly literate phrase, get tangled up."

"Go to sleep, desert flower, before I show you just exactly what that phrase means."

She did go to sleep eventually, but not before erotic visions of exactly what he'd meant convinced her that the convent hadn't changed her too much after all.

Gallagher woke first. The sun wasn't up yet, but the sky was growing light. A warm, satisfying weight rested against his chest and abdomen. A head rested against his shoulder.

His arms tightened around Felice in automatic response. His hand splayed across the bare skin of her back. He caressed it lightly, moving up her spine until he felt the rumpled cloth of her undershirt.

She felt as perfect as she had looked the night he'd seen her naked in the moonlight. Not surprisingly, his body was behaving exactly the same way, too.

He knew better. Even if the woman lying in his arms was the private investigator she claimed to be, that didn't change anything important. He was reacting this way because it had been too long since he'd held a woman against him or dreamed of one as he had dreamed of Felice last night. His work had become his life, so all consuming and ever present that even an attempt to leave it behind for a while hadn't succeeded.

But restlessness and abstinence weren't reasons enough for starting something. Felice was not his kind of woman. On the rare occasions when he envisioned a woman sharing his life now, he envisioned one like Rebecca. Not that there were too many of those in the world. Rebecca had been one of a kind, a will-o'-the-wisp who had merged her life so fully with his that for weeks after she left him he had still felt her presence everywhere.

Of course, there was no one he could tell that to. Few people even knew that he had been married for a short time, or that after Rebecca left, his progression through the FBI, then the Justice Department ranks, had been the only thing that had made getting up in the morning worthwhile.

Felice stirred in his arms and moaned softly. Gallagher was alarmed. She had been through so much, and she had more to go through today. He felt nothing special for her, except a good dose of sexual attraction, but she was a human being and she was suffering. Certainly that was why he wanted to protect her—although that was a little like wanting to protect a side-winder.

She moaned again, and his arms tightened around her, despite the best of intentions. "Felice," he whispered softly. "Are you all right?"

She awoke slowly, then wished she hadn't. Every cell of her body felt as if it had been reshaped, and not just because she had jumped from a moving car. Gallagher was holding her much too close, and it felt entirely too good.

She lifted her head and discovered that his face was only a few blurry inches from hers.

His hair curled over his forehead in a tangle that did nothing to reduce the unrepentant masculinity of his face. His eyes were heavy-lidded from sleep but smoldering, like a banked fire about to blaze once more. She felt each of his fingers press against the bare skin of her back, seducing her with the simple pressure as surely as if he were kissing her.

He was a dangerous man, and not just because she had no proof he was who he claimed. He was a man she could easily fall prey to, a man who could change a life she didn't want changed. For the first time she understood what it meant to have met one's match, and the thought sent frissons of fear through her.

"Felice?" His brows drew together. "Are you all right?"

She fed his concern. "Who are you?" she asked plaintively.

He looked as if he'd been slapped. "What do you remember?"

She moaned. Pitifully.

Gallagher slid his hand to the small of her back, clutching the fabric of her undershirt as he went so that she was covered as best he could manage. Gently he lifted her head back to her ersatz pillow and moved away from her. "Do you know who you are?"

She pushed herself to a sitting position and stared down at him, eyes narrowed. "I'm exactly who I told you I was yesterday! And who do you think you are, clutching me like your personal teddy bear?"

His eyes narrowed, too. "I'm a man about to get upset."

"I don't like being handled."

"I'll bet."

"What's that supposed to mean?"

"Figure it out." Gallagher rolled over and pushed himself to his feet. The morning air and her verbal assault brought him back to reality. "We need to get out of here and do some walking before the sun gets very high in the sky."

She wanted to work up more anger, although more wasn't coming through very reliably. What was coming through was the unaccountably pleasurable sight of his long, muscular legs. "Look, we're stuck with each other for a little while, but when this is over I want to be able to forget any of it happened."

"Just for the record, who snuggled up to whom is entirely unclear."

"Well, who broke it up isn't!"

"You can drop the nun act this morning. Waking up with a man isn't strange to you."

"Waking up with one I didn't choose certainly is."

Against his better judgment he admired the flash of her green eyes. The blanket had worked its way down to her waist, and the firm curves of her breasts were clearly outlined under her shirt. His fingertips still tingled with the feel of her bare skin against them.

He grinned at her. He couldn't help himself. She was spitting fire, and he was feeling it in places that still reveled in the early morning warmth of her. "Mad enough?"

"What are you talking about?"

"Mad enough to forget how good it felt to wake up in my arms?"

Of course he was right, but she wasn't going to give him the satisfaction of admitting it. "What did you do, Josiah? Lie awake all night pumping up your ego?" She reached for her robe and unrolled it, shaking it out carefully before she slipped it over her head.

He had lain awake longer than he wanted to admit, though his ego hadn't had anything to do with it. "We've got a long way to go this morning. Now that your adrenaline's flowing nicely, we'd better get started."

She stood, and the robe slid to her ankles. She belted it loosely for better circulation. When she looked up, he was dressed and busy slipping on his shoes.

"Truce?" she asked.

He glanced up and nodded, but his eyes confirmed what she already knew. They could wave white flags and call a truce every other minute, but underneath the words and the flags was something that wasn't going to stop heating up until it boiled over. And when it did, the desert was going to seem cool in comparison.

Chapter 9

"I've got a comb." Gallagher pulled a small one from his pocket and handed it to Felice.

She didn't bother to protest that it wasn't going to make any difference and ran it across her head before she gave it back to him.

"You'll want to wear your veil."

"Why? Do you think it's going to make a difference to the rattlesnakes if they think I'm a real nun?"

"When the sun comes up it'll make a difference to you."

"Do you have a hat?"

"I'm going to make one."

She watched in fascination as he wrapped her wimple into something that looked like a cross between a pirate's bandanna and a maharaja's turban. "Fetching." She stepped forward and adjusted it so it shaded both his ears. "Could be the start of something big for the fashion industry."

He couldn't help himself. He smiled.

She couldn't help herself. Her insides twanged in response. She stepped away. "Can we go?"

He stooped beside his small stash of treasures and rose with two pairs of sunglasses, holding them out to her. "Take your pick."

She examined them both. "Either I go blind in one eye or I walk with a finger on my nose." She chose the pair with the broken earpiece and slipped it over one ear. Immediately it dangled halfway down her face. She slid it back in place and held it on. "We can trade off."

"See if you can anchor it with your veil."

She didn't want to wear the veil, but she knew he was right. The sun would bake her brain without it. She picked it up and slipped it on her head. It was no help with the glasses, and she resigned herself to a day of adjusting them repeatedly once the sun came up.

"Ready for some breakfast?" Gallagher asked.

Her mouth watered at the words. "Really?"

"Half an old granola bar, two bites of withered apple and a cup of water."

"Shouldn't we save the water until later, when we're really thirsty?"

"Men have died in the desert with water in their canteens. Water can't help if you don't drink it. Besides, it's easier to carry inside you than out."

She stretched out her hand for her portion of the granola bar. It was little more than a handful of oats and nuts once bound together by honey, but it tasted heavenly. The apple wasn't bad, either.

"We don't have anything else to eat," Gallagher informed her. "But we can go a long time without food."

"And water?"

"We'll find civilization before we run out. And there's always the chance we'll find some along the way."

"Make mine Perrier."

Gallagher stooped and rolled his booty in the blanket, tying it again with the length of rope, but not before he donned Ralph's old work shirt. Torn and dirty, it smelled like Ralph, but it would keep his arms from blistering and his sweat from evaporating before it could cool his body.

"I guess we're ready." He held out the water jug to Felice.

"What? No Waterford crystal?"

"You know, when the sun comes up, you're going to have to stop talking and keep your mouth shut. It conserves water."

"Who'll keep your spirits up?"

As she drank, he thought about all the women who would be dissolving into tears about now. Not all women dissolved, certainly, and not all men were immune to tears or fright. But Felice was unusual in her courage—for either sex. The word special almost came to mind.

"Your turn." She held the water jug out to him. "I'll be counting swallows."

He finished his share and capped the jug. "All set?"

She nodded.

"Your biggest enemy besides the sun is going to be cactus. You're way too vulnerable in those sandals. If you get stuck, don't touch the spines. I'll get them out."

"Okay."

"Watch out for snakes, but as soon as the sun gets high enough in the sky, they won't be too much of a problem. Most scorpions aren't lethal, and even the ones that can be don't always kill their victims."

"Gosh, I feel better."

"If you don't reach under deadwood or rocks, you probably won't run into any, so don't worry about being one of the few who drop dead."

"Better and better."

"We'll probably see a variety of lizards. None of the California types are poisonous."

"And if the ones that are just didn't happen to read the sign at the state border, we'll send 'em back." She looked up from the knot she'd been retying at her waist. "What are you grinning at?"

"I'm getting it over with before the sun comes up." He couldn't help himself. He reached over and touched her bruised cheek. For just the shadow of a second she looked vulnerable and very much in need of comfort. Then the moment passed. "We're going to be all right," he promised.

"Not if we stand here talking."

"Let's go." Gallagher turned and started zigzagging his way down the hill where they'd camped.

It was nearly noon before Gallagher had to admit he wasn't sure where he was going. A compass would have helped. A map would have helped more. Even a watch with hands that could have served as a makeshift compass would have been something. But he was stuck with a digital watch, a landscape that looked as if no human had ever set foot there and car tracks that had vanished.

There were a myriad of other tracks, though. The characteristic X of the roadrunner, the roughly parallel tracks of a sidewinder, and various other reptile and mammal prints that he couldn't identify with certainty.

He guided Felice along a flat sandy plain, or *bajada,* dotted with creosote and burro bush interspersed with ocotillos and barrel cactus. He noted with satisfaction that Felice had heeded his warning and walked with great care around the cactus. He was relieved that so far they'd had no accidents.

Since early morning they had stopped to drink and rest twice, but he could feel the sun's effect anyway, and he knew it was time to rest until it dipped halfway to the horizon. The miles they could cover now wouldn't be productive when balanced against the water they would need. Surviving the desert was a constant balancing act, and anything that tipped the scales the wrong way could be fatal.

There were trees in the near distance, and he stopped and pointed in their direction. He guessed they grew along a dry wash, an arroyo, but there was always the chance that there could be water there. Whether there was or not, the shade the trees provided would be enough reason to detour in that direction.

It took most of an hour to reach the sparse grove. Felice looked as if she were ready to drop, although she'd never once asked him to walk slower or to pass the water jug. She dropped down in the dubious shade of a clump of skinny mesquites and stripped off her veil.

Gallagher sprawled beside her and unscrewed the cap of the water jug, offering it to her first.

She drank with gusto, careful not to spill a drop, and handed it back to him.

"We'll stay here until the sun goes down a bit," he said when he'd finished. The water jug was growing alarmingly light.

"Do you have any idea where we are?"

He was perfectly capable of lying if any good could come from it. This wasn't one of those occasions. "I think we're heading in the right direction."

"But you don't know."

"Any direction could be the right one. That's just the way it is."

His words came as no surprise. "At least tell me we're not walking in circles."

"We aren't."

"Then we have to be heading somewhere."

"That's my theory."

"Of course, that somewhere could be a hundred miles away."

"Like you said, this is California. There'll be someone on skates or a surfboard around the next corner."

"There are trees growing here. Doesn't that mean water?"

"Way, way down. So far down that even if we reached it, we'd use up every drop of water in our bodies and the jug getting there. And probably for less water."

"How do you know? It could be just below the surface."

"Wrong kind of trees. If there was a real water source here we'd have cottonwoods and sycamores, maybe even fan-tail palms. We've got mesquite and smoke trees and palos verdes."

"The smoke trees are lovely, aren't they?"

He was surprised she had the strength to notice or care. Ten yards away there were blooms of purple glory amidst the ashy gray foliage that gave the smoke tree its name. "I could do with a spreading oak beside a river myself."

"The smoke tree reminds me . . ." Her voice trailed off.

He expected some sentimental memory. "Of what?"

"Cigarettes. I'd sell the water left in our jug for a cigarette about now."

"Smoking can kill you."

"This can kill you, too. I'll take my chances with tobacco, thanks."

"If you managed at the convent with one cigarette a night, you'll manage out here without any. And if the water starts to get low, the last thing you'll want is something that dries out your throat."

"How are we going to get water when this runs out?"

"There are ways."

"That's what I'm asking."

"Chew cactus pulp."

She made a face.

"Look for natural water tanks. Water collects in low-lying rock pools, even in the desert. Watch for places where animal tracks converge and lead to a watering hole. Dig at the bottom of a dry riverbed."

"So there are things we can do."

"Always."

"How hot do you think it is?"

He didn't want to guess. Certainly not as hot as it would be in six weeks, but a hell of a lot hotter than it had been six weeks before. "Hot enough," he answered.

"Are we still under your rule of silence, or are we allowed to talk some more?"

"Talk away." Gallagher adjusted his body so that he was completely in shade, not an easy feat to manage, because the mesquite was hardly more than scrub. "Just try not to open your mouth when you do."

Despite herself, she chuckled. "How do you know so much about the desert? It can't just be from a camping trip or two."

He didn't really want to talk about his life, but he knew the value of passing the time and keeping calm. "I grew up outside Bakersfield. My father had a small ranch in the middle of nowhere. More desert than pasture."

"How did you get hooked up with the Feds, then?"

"Looking for excitement. My father died when I was in law school. I sold the ranch to get enough money to finish school without killing myself working two jobs."

Felice heard regret in his voice. "Sorry you did?"

He was angry at himself for telling her so much. "I don't know."

Which meant, she assumed, that he didn't want to say. "You said you were on a leave of absence when you got called to go to the Blessed Garden," she continued.

"Yeah." Gallagher opened his eyes. "Are you curious or probing?"

"Both."

"I needed a break."

"Trying to assess your life?"

He realized he'd said something like that the night before. "More like I was just tired."

"Tired of what?"

"What I was doing."

"Which was?"

"Classified."

"I love talking to a Fed." Felice closed her eyes. "When I was a cop, there was this case I worked on. A little boy disappeared, and nobody else would pay any attention when his mother insisted he'd been kidnapped. The kid's parents were divorced, and the father had been furious at the mother over the settlement. Nobody could find him for questioning, so everybody thought he'd just grabbed the kid and run."

"A logical assumption."

She ignored him. "Only the mother didn't think her ex was smart enough or committed enough to grab his own kid. She thought he'd just gone off somewhere on a binge, like he'd done when they were married. She was sure he didn't have the boy."

"Did he?"

"No." She thought about all the off-duty hours she'd put in on that case, all the dead ends and false hopes, all the razzing she'd taken from her fellow cops. Everybody but Kelley had thought she was crazy to be wasting her time.

"What happened?"

"I found the father. Finally. He was in Tijuana, boozing it up and living with a woman with eight kids. He sure didn't need another one. He hadn't seen the boy since he left the States."

"Did you ever find the kid?"

She snorted. "I got that far, then the Feds took over. I wasn't allowed near the evidence after that. The Feds wouldn't even tell me what they knew. I was the one who had proved he'd been kidnapped by a stranger, and they wouldn't even share their damned information with me. The kid's mother stopped speaking to me, claimed I didn't care anymore. I was told to tell the Feds everything I knew and forget I'd ever been part of the case. Eventually they found the kid with some psycho woman who thought he was hers. Apparently he was as all right as a kid who'd lived through that could be. The agent who found him got all kinds of attention. I didn't even get a nod.''

"How long ago was all this?"

"Just before I came to Palm Springs."

"You quit over that?"

"That and a lot of things."

"You're not a team player."

"That about sums it up." She opened her eyes. "I don't play on teams. The rules are stupid."

"No. Now you follow your own stupid rules, like pretending you're a nun and getting kidnapped yourself."

"I'd do it again. Sister Mary Grace needed protection."

"You're saying you did it to help her and not for the money?"

Her eyes snapped shut. "I'm going to take a nap."

"That *is* what you're saying."

"Don't put words in my mouth."

"What else do you do because it's right and good? Take photos of married men going in and out of motel rooms? Spy on some bozo's ancient aunt to see when she's going to kick off so the bozo can start spending his inheritance?"

"Enough!" She sat up and glared at him. "What I don't do is play stupid political games. Maybe the main reason I went to the the Blessed Garden was because I was being paid a whopping fee to do it, but I also wanted to watch out for Sister Mary Grace. Can you say the same thing? Or wasn't your stay there just one of those 'my country right or wrong' things that you Feds are so fond of screwing up?"

She saw his eyes narrow, but she didn't care. "Don't tell me what a great record you folks have. You're a bunch of lousy spies, and half the time you're spying on the wrong people!"

"Finished?"

"Finished!" She lay back and realized that she'd probably sweated off an ounce of water.

"I am not a lousy spy."

"So you're a good spy with lousy reasons for what you do. Big deal."

"You really got hurt, didn't you?"

She'd expected anything except compassion. "It doesn't matter."

"How effective can you be if you get so involved?"

"I don't. And I'm damned effective. Ask anybody who's hired me."

"Then what are you doing hanging out in the desert with a lousy spy when you're supposed to be watching Sister Mary Grace?"

She opened her mouth to retort, but his smile stopped her. "I wish you wouldn't do that."

"What?"

"Grin like that. Show that nice deep dimple in your right cheek."

"Why not?"

"Because it makes it hard for me to remember who you are."

"Who I am is a not-so-lousy 'spy,' as you put it, who believes he's made a difference in the world."

"And that's why you're a Fed? Or is it because of the excitement? The money?"

"I don't know anymore."

She was surprised he was so honest—or seemed to be. She wanted to give him some word of encouragement, but something more pressing drew her attention. "Remember when you mentioned the lizard thing?"

"What?"

"The lizard thing. You know, about no lizards being poisonous in California?"

"Yeah."

"Well, there's a big guy standing on the rock behind you who looks like he might not have heard."

Gallagher turned slowly and saw a chuckwalla about five yards away. It was close to a foot long, head to tail tip, and camouflaged nicely by the rock it was sunning on.

"Lunch," Gallagher said.

"Who? Us or him?"

"Him."

"Over my dead body."

"No. His."

"You'd better be kidding."

"I am. For now. Digestion takes water, and we can't spare any." Gallagher got slowly to his feet. "Want to see one of nature's miracles?"

"If it doesn't involve lizard stew."

Gallagher gestured for her to join him. She left the shade reluctantly, and they advanced on the lizard together. Several feet away Gallagher clapped his hands. The startled lizard took off like a shot for the crack between his rock and the one close beside it.

"Quick on his feet, isn't he?" Gallagher moved closer.

"Boy, that was a regular circus act," she said, starting back toward the shade.

He grasped her arm. "You're about to see the fat lady."

"You mean it gets better?"

He pulled her to his side and draped an arm over her shoulders. "Watch."

"I'm all a-twitter." She found herself leaning on him, and she didn't have the strength to straighten up.

"Notice anything?"

She peered at the lizard. Strangely enough, he seemed to be growing before her eyes. "What's he doing?"

"Swallowing air."

"What for?"

"What do you think?"

She considered. "Because predators don't like fat, ugly lizards?"

"Guess again."

The chuckwalla continued to balloon until it had nearly filled the narrow space between the rocks. Despite herself, Felice was fascinated. "He's wedging himself in, isn't he?"

"Exactly."

"So, no lizard stew," she said triumphantly.

"If we wanted to eat him, there would still be ways."

"I'd just as soon not hear about them."

"A cop with tender sensibilities?"

"Better than a cop with a tender lizard lunch."

"Survival sometimes depends on doing things that don't appeal to you under normal circumstances."

"Don't worry. I can do anything I have to. It's just that I don't have to eat lizard."

"Not yet."

She nodded. "Not yet."

Gallagher knew they should get back in the shade, but he turned her to him first. "You kind of remind me of the chuckwalla."

"Every woman's dream."

"You fill yourself full of hot air to protect yourself. I just haven't figured out from what enemy."

"If you're thinking of a career change, don't consider psychiatry. Or poetry. Your metaphors need a lot of work."

"Does anyone ever really get close to you?"

"I could ask the same."

"You're saying we're two of a kind?"

"Has a nasty ring to it, doesn't it?"

He didn't want a woman in his life. And if he did, Felice was nothing like the one he would want. She was bruised and bedraggled. Her face was streaked with dust, and what hair she had was plastered to her head from wearing the veil all morning. She was feisty and irreverent and materialistic; she had no idea how to stroke a man's ego.

And he was becoming hopelessly "tangled up." Despite every gut instinct that told him to run the other way.

"If we're two of a kind," he said slowly, "then you're feeling it, too."

"It? What?"

"This damned pull between us."

She didn't, couldn't, answer.

He dropped his hands. "We'd better get back in the shade."

"Heatstroke," she said. "That's what it is."

He wasn't about to admit that "it" had begun for him at a cool, palm-studded oasis when he'd seen the loveliest vision of his life outlined in moonlight. He watched her flop down in the shade and close her eyes. He told himself that once they were back in civilization, he probably wouldn't even remember her name.

But he couldn't make himself believe it.

They camped for the night on the edge of another arroyo and shared all but a cup or two of the remaining water. The night was clear, and the sliver of a moon christened them with spidery moonbeams. Gallagher gathered fallen branches of mesquite and built a fire.

"You're not worried about being spotted? You don't think we're in danger of being found by the wrong people?" Felice asked, moving closer to the flames for warmth in the rapidly dropping temperature.

"We're in more danger of not being found by the right people."

Somewhere in the distance, a coyote howled. Another answered, and for seconds they sang a duet.

"If you're who you say you are, don't you check in with somebody?" Felice asked. "Wouldn't someone get worried if you didn't call?"

"Not for a while."

"If this was important enough to pull you away from your vacation, then how come no one is paying closer attention to what happens?"

"They couldn't very well send a dozen men to the Blessed Garden and make them Ralph's helpers without raising suspicions. There are other people working on other fronts."

Felice gave a humorless laugh. "They could have sent in some women to pose as nuns."

"I imagine they thought that was too stupid to consider."

"You folks have more brains than I've given you credit for." Gallagher stretched out, his shoulder nearly touching hers. "I'm going to make a shallow well to catch tomorrow's dew."

"Great. I need a bath and a shampoo."

"I'll have to use the plastic."

"Oh." She thought about how quickly she'd gotten attached to the relative luxury of something separating her from the ground. "Can I help?"

FREE BOOKS!

FREE GIFTS!

PLAY THE "LUCKY 7" SLOT MACHINE GAME !

AND YOU COULD GET FREE BOOKS, A FREE VICTORIAN PICTURE FRAME AND A SURPRISE GIFT!

NO COST! NO OBLIGATION TO BUY!
NO PURCHASE NECESSARY!

PLAY "LUCKY 7"
AND GET AS MANY AS SIX FREE GIFTS...

HOW TO PLAY:

1. With a coin, carefully scratch off the silver box at the right. This makes you eligible to receive one or more free books, and possibly other gifts, depending on what is revealed beneath the scratch-off area.

2. You'll receive brand-new Silhouette Intimate Moments® novels. When you return this card, we'll send you the books and gifts you qualify for *absolutely free!*

3. If we don't hear from you, every month we'll send you 4 additional novels to read and enjoy. You can return them and owe nothing but if you decide to keep them, you'll pay only $2.92* per book, a saving of 33¢ each off the cover price. There is *no* extra charge for postage and handling. There are **no** hidden extras.

4. When you join the Silhouette Reader Service™, you'll get our subscribers'-only newsletter, as well as additional free gifts from time to time, just for being a subscriber.

5. You must be completely satisfied. You may cancel at any time simply by sending us a note or a shipping statement marked ''cancel'' or by returning any shipment to us at our cost.

*Terms and prices subject to change without notice.
Sales tax applicable in N.Y.
© 1990 HARLEQUIN ENTERPRISES LIMITED

This lovely Victorian pewter-finish miniature is perfect for displaying a treasured photograph— and it's yours absolutely free—when you accept our no-risk offer.

DETACH AND MAIL CARD TODAY

PLAY "LUCKY 7"

Just scratch off the silver box with a coin.
Then check below to see which gifts you get.

YES! I have scratched off the silver box. Please send me all the gifts for which I qualify. I understand I am under no obligation to purchase any books, as explained on the opposite page.

240 CIS ADET
(U-SIL-IM-10/91)

NAME

ADDRESS   APT.

CITY   STATE   ZIP

7	7	7	WORTH FOUR FREE BOOKS, FREE VICTORIAN PICTURE FRAME AND MYSTERY BONUS
🍒	🍒	🍒	WORTH FOUR FREE BOOKS AND MYSTERY BONUS
⬤	⬤	⬤	WORTH FOUR FREE BOOKS
🔔	🔔	🍒	WORTH TWO FREE BOOKS

Offer limited to one per household and not valid to current
Silhouette Intimate Moments® subscribers. All orders subject to approval.
© 1990 HARLEQUIN ENTERPRISES LIMITED.   PRINTED IN U.S.A.

SILHOUETTE ''NO RISK'' GUARANTEE
- You're not required to buy a single book—ever!
- You must be completely satisfied or you may cancel at any time simply by sending us a note or a shipping statement marked ''cancel'' or by returning any shipment to us at our cost. Either way, you will receive no more books; you'll have no obligation to buy.
- The free books and gifts you receive from this ''Lucky 7'' offer remain yours to keep no matter what you decide.

If offer card is missing, write to:
Silhouette Reader Service, 3010 Walden Ave., P.O. Box 1867, Buffalo, N.Y. 14269-1867

DETACH AND MAIL CARD TODAY

BUSINESS REPLY MAIL

FIRST CLASS MAIL   PERMIT NO. 717   BUFFALO, NY

POSTAGE WILL BE PAID BY ADDRESSEE

SILHOUETTE READER SERVICE
3010 WALDEN AVE
PO BOX 1867
BUFFALO NY 14240-9952

NO POSTAGE
NECESSARY
IF MAILED
IN THE
UNITED STATES

"If you want."

"The spirit's willing."

"And the flesh?"

She turned a little so she could see him. "Is wiped out."

He touched her hair, brushing the short strands against her ear. "When you were a kid, did you ever cry?"

"As little as possible."

"Why?"

"Why did I cry?"

"Why didn't you?"

She lay back and thought about his question for a moment. "Did you have a happy childhood, Josiah?"

He had never really asked himself. "I suppose."

"I had everything that's supposed to make a childhood happy. Money. Lots of money. Every toy and opportunity that money could buy. Parents who wanted me and loved me to death . . ." Her voice trailed off.

"To death?"

"They wanted a kid they didn't get. So they loved me to death, hoping the kid they'd gotten would pass on and a new, better kid would take her place."

"What did they want?"

"Someone who was just like them. I figured out early that if I cried, they thought they had clay in their hands that they could mold the way they wanted. So I stopped crying. And I stopped complaining. And I stopped arguing. I just waited until I could leave, and I did."

"And now?"

"Now I'm a grown-up. I visit them, and I smile a lot. I do anything I can to make them happy. And when I start to feel like clay again, I kiss them goodbye and leave."

"If your parents have so much money, why are you taking crazy jobs? Did they cut you off when they figured they couldn't mold you into the person they wanted?"

"Nope. They'd give me anything I wanted. Any time I wanted it. But you see, I don't want it. Not from them. Anything I get, I want to earn myself."

"Trying to prove something?"

"That I'm a person in my own right, I suppose."

"So why do you need a lot of money?" He moved closer and propped himself on his side, so he could make out her face in the firelight. His fingers trailed as if magnetically drawn to her cheekbone and traced the perimeter of the bruise marring it.

"I want to buy a house."

"Why?"

She frowned. "I've got to live somewhere."

"You don't live anywhere now?"

"It's a great house, in one of the nicer country-club estates. Roomy. Well designed."

"And fancy enough to impress Mommy and Daddy?"

She stared at him.

His finger stopped at the corner of her lips. "Well?"

"Maybe psychiatry wouldn't be such a bad bet for you after all," she said finally.

"So I'm right?"

"I wish you weren't."

He liked her flippant, and he liked her this way, too—vulnerable, honest and softer-edged. Fact was, he liked her every way. And he didn't like that. Not at all.

"Will they be impressed?" he asked, drawing his hand back to his side.

"I don't know. I wish I could say I don't care."

"I guess we all have somebody whose good opinion is crucial to us."

"Who's your somebody?"

He lay back and put his hands behind his head, so that he wouldn't be tempted to touch her again. The question hit much closer to home than he wanted to admit. But somehow the desert night and her own honesty made it hard for him to push the question aside.

"My wife," he said at last. "Ex-wife," he amended. "Ex-somebody."

"I knew you were too good a catch to have stayed off the hook forever."

"Just yesterday you said I'd crawled out of a carnival midway."

She ignored that. "If she's your ex, why do you care what she thinks?"

He didn't want to talk about Rebecca. He never did, not even to the people closest to him. But he found himself talking anyway. "Maybe I still love her."

"Baloney." She moved closer and leaned over so that she could see his face. "Josiah, if you still loved this Rebecca, you'd be with her tonight instead of in the middle of some godforsaken desert with me."

"What a thought."

"You don't love her."

He lay back, too. "Well, that takes care of that," he said cynically.

"What was she like?"

"What are you like?"

"We both know the answer to that."

"Well, she was everything you aren't."

"A woman to treasure." This time she propped herself up and touched the dimple that creased his cheek. She'd been wanting to do it all day.

He covered her hand, but he didn't push it away. "She was a born homemaker, soft and feminine and maternal." The word "clinging" came to mind, although it had rarely occurred to him before. "She said I was her life."

"I can't imagine you with a woman like that."

He grunted. "Apparently neither could she."

"She left you?"

"Lock, stock and divorce decree. She said I'd never be a real husband, that what I did was more important to me than who I went home to."

"Was she right?"

"I wasn't willing to quit my job with the department to practice law in her father's firm in Alabama. In her eyes, that was proof enough."

"That only seems to prove that you weren't willing to submit to blackmail. Actually, your Rebecca sounds like she'd get along great with my parents."

"Maybe you and I need a superhuman dose of patience to be tolerated."

"Actually, I find you pretty tolerable." Felice was touched both that he'd listened to her and that he'd shared his own story. "Within limits, of course."

His hands lifted to her shoulders, and he pulled her toward him. "What limits?"

"The ones you're about to step over."

"Or expand." He drew her closer.

"I'm nothing like your Rebecca," she reminded him. "The opposite, remember?"

"She would never have launched herself from a moving car."

"Smart woman."

"She would have fit right in at the Blessed Garden."

"A real saint." Her lips were only inches from his.

"And she would have cried several times by now." He tried the words out and realized they were true. He realized it was also the first negative thing he'd ever admitted about Rebecca. And it was opening a floodgate of others. Rebecca would have complained. And . . . whined.

"Maybe not a saint?"

"Maybe not." He tugged her the inches he needed to meet her lips. Felice melted against him, but she was not Rebecca. She didn't twine herself around his soul, trying to make one person where two existed. She was a separate, distinct personality who would never want to change anyone to meet her own needs.

She was Felice, and he was glad.

Her cheek tasted faintly of salt, but her lips tasted like the sweetest, purest water from a desert oasis. He could feel each soft curve of her body accommodate the firmer planes of his chest and hips, and he could feel himself growing harder in response.

For just a moment he let himself think of making love to her, of stripping off the preposterous robe and tasting each inch of her skin, of finding what gave her pleasure and taking his own pleasure in hers. He had few thoughts that they might not survive this ordeal. He had been in worse situations and come out unscathed. But there was little joy in what they had already undergone, or in what they still had waiting for them. They could give each other joy now.

And forever be haunted by one night in the desert, when two guarded people had made themselves vulnerable.

She was the first one who pulled away. Reluctantly. "We keep doing that."

He forced himself to let her go. "Can't figure out why."

"You said something about a well."

"Yeah."

"We're going to need water."

He could think of other things he needed, just as life-giving and thirst quenching, but he knew this wasn't the time. That time should never come. "Yeah." He sat up.

"Josiah?"

"Yeah."

"I'm glad you didn't change for her. If you had, where would I be now?"

He pushed himself to his feet and held out his hand to help her up. "Get the hubcap. We're going to dig."

"Right."

Lying beside Felice that night, listening to the soft rhythm of her breathing, he thought about her words. He was glad to be there with her, despite what he had left behind and in spite of what might happen in the next few days. He shouldn't be, but he was. It was enough of a mystery to keep him awake until the dew they were counting on for sustenance began to settle.

Chapter 10

They shared the Coke before sunrise, lingering over each sip as if there might never be another one.

"Think of all the times when someone's offered you a drink and you've turned them down," Felice said, handing the can to Gallagher for his last drink.

"Think of all the water we waste when we shower or brush our teeth."

"A shower. Do you think we'll ever take a shower again?"

"Tonight, hopefully."

"Do you really think so?"

"Yeah."

"If anyone who knows me could see me now..." Without the plastic to protect her from the ground, Felice had chosen to sleep in her robe. It would never even approach white again, nor, she was sure, would her face, which between bruises, dirt and sunburn had to be a grotesque rainbow. She hadn't been able to make herself look in the mirror to find out.

"You'll bloom again, desert flower, just as soon as you mix with a little water."

She managed a smile. "Did you check the well?"

The "well" was really nothing more than a hole they'd dug at the bottom of the wash, then lined with plastic weighted by cool stones excavated from a distance beneath the ground's surface. Gallagher didn't have a lot of hope for it, but it had given them something concrete to do without expending too much energy.

"Let's check it now," he said. "We'll need a piece of cloth to sop up what moisture we've trapped."

"I'd hoped we'd get enough to scoop it up with the hub-cap."

"We'll be lucky if there's enough to soak a handkerchief."

"Do you have a handkerchief?"

He shook his head, and his eyes fell to the hem of her robe. Felice knew what he was thinking. "Unh-uh. We can use Ralph's work shirt."

"And then the water will taste like Ralph smells."

"Bad idea," she admitted.

"You're well covered. A patch from the bottom of your robe won't hurt anything."

"Sister Marietta weaves this fabric herself. And I did some of the work on this robe."

"Sister Marietta wouldn't expect you to die of thirst to protect her creation."

She grimaced, but she knew he was right. "Fine, but I'll do it."

"Better let me. The middle of the back hem will be best. That way the tops of your feet won't be exposed."

"Oh, go ahead." She felt petulant this morning, but she wasn't sure exactly why. Maybe it was because they had another day of desert trekking in front of them. That would be enough to make anyone petulant, especially since they weren't sure that they were trekking anywhere in particular.

Or maybe it was something else. Maybe it was because she had awakened in Gallagher's arms again and found herself wishing she was there for another reason.

She was going to have to be careful not to let a little thing like being thrown together with him in a life-and-death situation affect her libido. She had gone from the life of the convent to that of a desert rat. Certainly she needed comfort and human warmth. Who wouldn't? But she had never been a person who let her needs dictate her actions.

She felt Gallagher tugging at her robe. She tried not to picture this further assault to her vanity. Who cared what she looked like? Who was there to see her except a taciturn FBI agent who was probably going to turn her over for interrogation just as soon as he could find a telephone?

She heard the fabric tear and winced at the sound, trying not to picture sweet-faced Sister Marietta, who wove the fabric on a loom that belonged in the Smithsonian. Sister Marietta had fussed over the hem on this robe, making sure it was the perfect length. "We don't want you tripping, Sister," she had said. "God wouldn't look kindly on our carelessness if you broke a leg."

Unexpectedly her eyes stung, as if she was about to cry. Tears, for heaven's sake, when she hadn't cried for years. Tears, when she needed every drop of bodily fluid to survive.

"This ought to do it." Gallagher stood and held out a ragged square of fabric.

Felice blinked back her tears angrily. "It's so dusty it'll pollute the water!"

Gallagher whipped the rag against his leg to dislodge what dust he could. "You know what they say about beggars and choosers."

"Let's just get going, okay?"

He frowned. "Are you all right?"

"Dandy."

"Do you want to see what we get from the well?"

"It had better be at least a gallon."

"Come on." Gallagher led the way down the arroyo. She followed behind, scanning the ground for cactus.

As Gallagher had predicted, the well yielded just enough to wet the handkerchief-sized scrap of fabric. He sopped up every drop he could, then, over Felice's protests, squeezed it carefully into their water bottle. "Water is water," he said bluntly.

"If that's the best we can do, then we're going to dry up and blow away."

"We're going to look for water as we walk." Gallagher threw the stones to one side and carefully folded the plastic before placing it in his blanket roll.

She wanted to pick a fight with him. The idea was pleasure itself, but she was hopelessly mature. She couldn't take out her fears, her incomprehensible desires, on Gallagher. He was trying to get them both to safety. At least he deserved her cooperation. "If I see a river or a lake, I'll let you know."

"Look for animal tracks converging."

They walked until the sun was a fact and the desert was washed in early morning gold. Felice scanned the ground for tracks and knew that Gallagher was doing the same.

At ten o'clock they stopped and rested in the shade of a low rise. Gallagher uncapped the water jug and handed it to her. "Drink just what you think you need," he cautioned.

She took a swallow and handed it back to him. The water was faintly gritty but palatable.

He took a swallow, too, and capped it quickly.

"Sunglasses time." Felice pulled hers from her pocket and perched them on her nose, guiding the remaining earpiece inside her veil. It came off in her hand. "Terrific." She wrinkled her nose and scrunched her face, trying to balance the glasses without either earpiece.

Gallagher lifted the glasses from her nose. "That's never going to work."

"It's got to, unless you've got some chewing gum I can stick them back together with."

"I've got another idea." He unrolled the blanket and took out the can of motor oil, using the tip of the screwdriver to make a tiny hole in the lid. He let drops of the thick black oil ooze onto his finger, then stood, still clutching the can. "Come here."

"Why?"

"You'll see."

"I don't think I'm going to like this." She backed away a step.

"You're probably right." He advanced toward her. "Come here. It might save your eyesight."

"Seeing well's never been that important to me."

"Fe . . . li . . . ice."

She had never heard her name wheedled quite that way. She sighed and stood still as Gallagher drew half-moons under her eyes. She'd watched enough war movies and football games to know the smudges would cut the glare, but all those movies also helped her visualize exactly what she looked like.

Gallagher seemed to know what she was thinking. "It's very becoming. Matches your hair."

"You might as well put a dab on the end of my nose to keep it from blistering in the sun."

He obliged her, then handed her the can. "Do my eyes, would you? My sunglasses are worse than nothing."

She took a certain pleasure in obliging him. The generous half-moons she drew did little to detract from his image, however. He looked rakish and dangerous, a desert pirate who would just as gladly slit a throat as kiss one.

"Is that what you brought the oil for?" she asked, when she'd finished.

"No. When we stop at noon we're going to light a signal fire. The oil on mesquite will make thick black smoke. Anyone who happens to be nearby will see it."

"*If* anyone happens to be nearby."

"A detail."

"Gallagher, what if we're not going anywhere?"

"Anywhere we go is somewhere."

"But what if the somewhere we're going is nowhere?"

"Nowhere is somewhere."

"What if somewhere doesn't have a water supply?" she demanded.

"There's no point in using energy to worry. You worry, you need more water." He reached over and straightened her veil. It fluttered like a giant albino moth around her shoulders. Rarely had he seen such a pitiful figure. She was "The Sound of Music" and "The Nun's Story" gone berserk. "In the meantime, keep looking for animal tracks."

"Sure. Maybe we can find a grizzly to finish us off quicker."

He plugged up the oil can with a piece of the rag he'd ripped from her hem, then set the can back in the roll so that it would be upright when the bundle was across his back. "There used to be grizzlies in the San Jacintos. Until man came along and hunted them into extinction."

"This is no time to rail against the horrors of civilization. A man, with or without a gun, would look pretty good about now."

"Unless the gun was pointed at you." Gallagher hefted the blanket roll to his back. "Or me."

"You're armed. Remember? I'm the one who isn't."

"You want your gun back?"

"Second to a glass of iced tea and a shower."

"The gun I can do." He lifted the gun from inside his belt and handed it to her, butt first.

"Do I get bullets, too?"

"Have you been a good girl?"

"Never."

He nodded, fished in the bottom of his pocket for bullets and handed them to her.

"Does this mean you trust me?"

"Any man would be a fool to trust you completely."

"So you'll be sleeping with your eyes open." She slid the gun into the deep front pocket of her robe.

"And here I thought I'd get the pleasure of watching you put it in your holster."

"When I was at the Blessed Garden I snipped the threads of my side pocket so I could reach down and grab my gun if I needed it. It wouldn't have done to keep it where anyone could see it. I don't have any reason to hide it now." She looked at him. "And I don't have any reason to show you my legs."

"Except to make a man blissfully happy."

"That's rarely been my mission."

"And never since we met." Gallagher pointed toward a ridge along the side of a steep hill. "We're going to climb. See that clump of trees over on the left? We'll reach it just about noon."

"It's closer than that."

"Distances are deceptive out here. A rule of thumb is to guess how far something is and multiply by three. If we think it'll take half an hour to get somewhere, it'll probably take an hour and a half."

"Why do we even want to climb? Shouldn't we stay on level ground and not tire ourselves?"

"It may be high enough to get our bearings, but if not, it'll still be good for a signal fire."

"We might ignite by the time we climb that close to the sun."

"We'll be fine." Gallagher started in the direction he'd indicated, not looking behind to see if she was following. "Of course, if you've got a better idea, you're always welcome to go off on your own. You can drink your share of the water now."

She trudged along behind him, but not without asking herself why.

Felice was asleep in the heart of the cluster of ironwoods by the time Gallagher climbed partway down the hillside to join her. He had found enough deadwood and used his ax to chop enough green that his motor-oil-drenched fire on the top of the hill would last a good long time. He could leave it unattended without fear of anything else catching on fire. There was nothing likely to burn between here and Smoke Tree. Wherever that was.

She stirred as he flopped beside her. "See anything?" she asked sleepily.

"Yeah."

"What?"

"I'm not sure, but I may have spotted a road."

She perked up immediately. "A road? Really?"

"It's pretty far in the distance, but it's a place to head for."

"A road," She said the words wonderingly. Just a few days ago a road had been nothing more than a strip of asphalt, a man-made, litter-lined necessity to carry her from one place to another. Now it was a prayer answered. "How long would it take us to get there?"

"A night's walk. Maybe two." Gallagher turned to his side so he could see her better. "I haven't wanted to walk in the dark. It's too dangerous. Rattlesnakes come out because it's cooler, and cactus looks like just another rock until you're right on top of it. But we don't have much of a choice if we're going to make the road. We can't walk in the sun anymore. We're using up our body water too fast, and the temperature's too high.''

Felice was exhausted from a climb that normally wouldn't have made her breathe heavily. She knew she was beginning to suffer the effects of dehydration. The thought of staying put until sundown was welcome. ''What do you think the temperature is?''

''Eighty-five in the shade.''

''How long could we last without water?''

''If we walked at night until we got too tired to walk any farther? A week maybe.''

''That long?''

''Maybe.''

''The wind's not helping, is it?'' A light wind had picked up as noon had approached. Even now, against the shelter of the hillside, Felice could feel it dance along her skin.

''It's helping fan the flames of my fire.''

''If there's a road, maybe someone will see the fire.''

''I'm not counting on it. The wind's also dispersing the smoke.''

''The human body's made up of something like two-thirds water.'' Felice smiled wanly. ''I remember that from biology class in college. Mine's more like two-fifths about now.''

''What did you need with college if you became a cop?''

She recognized the change of subject and respected it. This was no time to give in to self-pity. ''I was in my sophomore year when I was recruited to do a little campus espionage. The local police knew somebody was dealing drugs to the fraternity and sorority houses. They weren't overly concerned about the small stuff, but the drugs were getting big-time. A girl in my house overdosed and died. The cops asked me to work for them. At her funeral.''

''And hooked you in the process.''

''Boy, did they. I'd already gotten bored with the college scene. I switched my major to criminology, helped catch a few drug dealers and finished school in three years instead of four. Then I joined the LAPD.''

''And you find being a detective as exciting?''

"I know what you think about my work." She yawned. "It is exciting, though. And rewarding. I can pick and choose who I help. I've had cases where I've made a real difference. I've reunited people with the mothers and fathers who had to give them away at birth. I've helped women, powerless women, get child support or alimony when the government couldn't do a thing."

"I'm sure you help."

Her eyes were in the process of closing until he spoke. "That's not what you said before."

"I like to bait you."

She rolled to her back and put her hands under her head. "You'd be surprised at the people who come to me. Palm Springs is still a playground for the rich and famous."

"They come to you?"

"They can get themselves in real messes."

"Which you clean up?"

"If I can. I helped the wife of a major TV idol last year. He's everybody's father figure on the screen, but in real life he's the worst kind of philanderer. She wanted a divorce. He didn't want the publicity. By the time I was finished tailing him, the publicity he could have gotten would have ruined his career. He gave her the divorce and everything she was entitled to. She re-married—a high-school teacher, I think—and she's as happy as a clam. I went to the wedding."

Her words had slowed until he wasn't sure she was going to finish her last sentence. Her eyes drifted shut, and he watched her drop back into sleep. He shut his own eyes and made himself comfortable. He wouldn't sleep, in case someone did see the fire and came shouting for them, but he planned to rest. They would need every spare bit of energy they possessed tonight.

So far Felice had kept up with him, despite her injuries and smaller, more vulnerable size. But she wasn't superhuman. She was beginning to feel the effects of too little water and too much sun. She wouldn't last more than a few days at most. Unfortunately, finding water might be harder than he'd indicated. The flat strip he'd glimpsed in the distance could be nothing more than a mirage.

He wasn't going to tell her that, though. He had said clearly that he thought he'd seen a road. She hadn't questioned him about the possibility it was something else. She wanted to believe in miracles, and so did he. The strip was a road. Period. And it could be reached with steady night walking.

One night. Maybe two. He had to believe it, because his bag of tricks was getting lighter and lighter. Sooner or later he was going to reach inside and his hand was going to come up empty.

"Cactus and snakes." Gallagher pulled his blanket roll over his shoulders. "Just remember to be careful."

"Which way are we heading?"

"Down, around and over thataway." He pointed to his right.

"Can we really find our way to the road in the dark?"

He handed her the water jug. "Finish this off and stop asking questions I can't answer."

She took two swallows and handed it back. "Drink your share or I'll pour it on your boots."

He took a swallow and passed it back to her. "Finish it."

"That's not—"

"You'll be a real hazard if you start stumbling around out there from thirst. You're smaller than I am, and you don't store as much water. Drink."

Felice knew he was growing dehydrated, too. Neither of them had taken any private side trips in the last twenty-four hours. What water they drank they sweated away immediately, but the desert heat was so intense that they never even felt the moisture on their skin. It dried instantly. She swallowed the last of the water and wished she could waste a few tears. She tucked the empty jug under her arm. "Let's go."

"We're going to walk as fast as we can, but not so fast that we get worn out right off the bat. I've got the flashlight, but we'll want to use it in emergencies only. There's enough moonlight to make this possible, but only just. Stay alert and stay close. Let me know if I move too fast for you."

"You're really used to being in command." Felice started after him. "You're no junior G-man, are you?"

A short laugh was all the answer she got.

She'd dealt with enough men like him to know just how far that line of questioning would get her. She wanted to talk about something, though. Maybe talking used up water and energy, prime requisites for getting to Gallagher's road—if it was a road, and she had her doubts, unspoken though they were—but talking also gave her heart. And she was beginning to need that as much as water.

She chose a subject that had been on her mind since the moment she'd been kidnapped. "Josiah, I keep worrying about Sister Mary Grace. What if those men go back for her while we're out here playing desert survival?"

"Under the circumstances, I wouldn't waste my energy worrying about anyone else right now."

"I can't help it. I was hired to protect her. You were, too, if you're telling the truth." His head spun, and he favored her with a particularly dirty look. "Sorry," she said, "but you said it best. I can't trust you completely, either. Maybe you were hired to lead me into the heart of the desert. Maybe this 'road' we're going toward is really Death Valley."

"Maybe you should stop talking and save your energy." They walked five hundred yards before he spoke again. "Don't worry about Sister Mary Grace. If you're telling the truth and the men had no reason to kidnap you, then they think they've already gotten Sister Mary Grace. If that's the case, why would they go back and kidnap her again? They left her in the middle of a desert, injured from her dive out of the car. And they left the truck that had come after her disabled. That should be good enough for them."

"If they're professionals, they'll keep an eye open, just to see if she makes it back to the Blessed Garden. They won't leave anything to chance. What a surprise they'll get when they discover she's not gone at all."

"I doubt they're that professional. More likely they're just political zealots from Tesoro, ex-altar boys who wish someone else had been sent to murder the troublemaker nun. That's why they didn't shoot you in the car and dump your body out the door." He heard a pathetic wheeze behind him, but kept on walking. "They're long gone by now, back in Tesoro sucking on the worm from some good Mexican tequila and waiting to sneak into confession when nobody's looking.''

''Nice try, Josiah.''

He shrugged and kept walking.

Two hours later they were still walking. It was close to midnight, and clouds had drifted across the sliver of moon that had helped light their way. The flashlight battery was getting weaker, and Felice was walking slower, even after rest periods.

Her head no longer ached, but it did feel suspiciously light. She tried to ignore her thirst, but it was becoming ever present. Soon she knew she would be able to think of nothing else.

''Let's take a rest.'' Gallagher eased the blanket roll off his shoulders and dropped it in the path.

''If we're going to rest, let's do it right.'' Felice pointed toward a pile of rocks.

''Too dangerous,'' Gallagher reminded her. ''Snakes and scorpions. Remember?''

She stared longingly at what looked as good as a chair to lean against, but she knew he was right. She lowered herself to the hard ground beside him and lay down flat to look up at the stars. A coyote howled, an echo of her own feelings. ''I'm holding you back,'' she said. ''You'd be halfway there by now if it weren't for me.''

''You're doing fine. And I'd have to walk slower at night, anyway. It's dangerous country to race through in the dark.''

''Look, we've got to talk about you leaving me behind. We both know it's coming.''

''We don't both know that.'' Gallagher obeyed a very human instinct. He reached out and pulled her close, propping her head on his arm. The night had grown cool, and the warmth of her body against his was welcome.

She was welcome. Even though he was filthy, thirsty, exhausted and doubtful he was heading anywhere in particular, he was still a man and she was a woman. True, even the beauty that she was, few men would find her desirable now, but it wasn't her model's face and figure that were most attractive about her. It was her unquenchable spirit, and though she was filthy, thirsty, exhausted and doubtful he was heading anywhere in particular, too, that spirit hadn't wavered.

"I can't think of anybody I'd rather have with me out here," he said, resting his cheek against hers.

She felt his whiskers scratch her skin, but the experience was somehow energizing. "How about somebody who knows where a water hole is located?"

"Don't push it."

She snuggled a little closer. "We should have made love last night."

Every muscle in his body contracted. "What?"

"While we still could." She rested her hand on his chest. She liked the breadth of it, the fine play of his muscles. She wished it was bare. "Before our faces were streaked with motor oil and our bodies started drying up."

His hand covered hers. "You're one night late mentioning it."

She sighed. "Did you want to make love to me, Josiah?"

His hand tightened convulsively at the thought. He might be two quarts low, but all his parts were still working. "What brings this on, desert flower?"

A coyote howled. Closer this time. An owl hooted in answer. "We could die out here, and only that coyote and that owl would know it. And the buzzards."

"Shh . . ." Gallagher kissed her cheek. "That's not going to help. We're heading for a road. We'll get there, maybe even tonight."

"I already feel like I ran a marathon."

"I know."

"I don't think I'm going to make it to a road. Not unless it's just over the next rise."

"It's not like you to give up."

"I'm not. I just think our chances are going to be better if you go on without me. You can send help when you get wherever you're going."

"And help might not find you until your bones are bleaching at the bottom of some arroyo."

"Do you have to be so graphic?"

He kissed her cheek again. "We'll stay together."

"Are you as tired as I am?"

"I doubt it."

"Male superiority?"

"I didn't launch myself from a moving vehicle. I don't know how you've made it this far."

She basked in what passed for a compliment, while she plotted what to do next. "Does your watch have an alarm?"

"If I could see to set it."

"Use the flashlight and set it for half an hour. We can sleep. I'll feel more rested afterward and able to walk."

He considered. "We can make it an hour. We'll still have hours to walk before sunrise."

"Okay. An hour." She thought that would be even better. She watched him rise and unroll the blanket.

"Do you want to sleep on it or under it?"

"On it. It's not that cold yet."

He shook the blanket and spread it on the ground. She moved over to her half and waited for him to join her. He lay down on his half, but he didn't touch her again.

"You never really answered my question," she said softly.

"Which one?"

"Did you want to make love to me?"

He put his arms under his head and stared at the stars. "Yeah."

"Because we're stranded in the middle of nowhere?"

He was silent for so long that she thought he had fallen asleep; then he answered. Softly. "If we were stranded in the middle of New York City, I'd still want to make love to you."

She felt his words like a warm, loving caress. "Maybe New York's over the next hill."

"Better chance it's L.A."

"I wanted to make love to you last night." She turned on her side. "I'm not even sure you're who you say you are, and I wanted to make love to you." She stretched out her hand to touch his cheek.

Reluctantly he turned toward her. "We're going to make it out of here, and the next time we have this conversation it won't be about what might have been."

He didn't touch her, but his eyes burned right through her in the darkness. "The next time we talk about making love, we'll be doing it. In a bed somewhere. You'll be full of water and food and sass, and I'll have to kiss you hard to make you shut up. But you will.''

Her eyes felt funny, like tears were supposed to be there, but her dehydrated body wouldn't cooperate. ''I can't wait.''

''You might have to wait a little while. But not long, desert flower. We're going to make it out of here.''

''I know.''

She didn't, and he knew it, but there was nothing more that he could say. He brought her hand to his face and kissed the palm. ''Go to sleep.''

She fingered the whiskery warmth of his cheek, then reluctantly pulled her hand away. ''Okay.''

''And have good dreams.''

She shut her eyes and composed her features. She was glad it was too dark for him to read every nuance of her expression. She was a good actress, but he was a better critic.

She took deep breaths and let the rhythm grow slower, as it would naturally if she was falling asleep. She listened as Gallagher fidgeted; then his breathing slowed, too. Finally sure that he was asleep, she cracked her eyelids.

He wasn't moving, and his eyes were closed. She could read exhaustion across his features. One chestnut curl spilled over his forehead boyishly, softening the lines burned there by sun and worry. Something twisted inside her at the sight. He was an unusual man, and probably who he said he was. He had come after her at the risk of his own life, and he had stuck by her when no one else would have.

Now she was about to save him.

She sat up slowly, her gaze plastered on him as she did. He slept on. Every muscle in her body screamed a protest, but she abused them anyway, hauling herself to her blistered feet without making a sound or even a ripple in the blanket.

Gallagher slept on.

Earlier she had determined where she would go, if she got the chance. There were hills not too far away, a distant sawtooth ridge that blocked that corner of the sky. She was going to go there and hide. When Gallagher awoke he would know what she had done. If he was smart—and of that she had no doubt—he would continue the way they had been heading. He would know that she would come back to this place as soon as he was gone and that she would wait there—or in the nearest shade— for him to come back with help.

She also knew he would be furious, but if he returned for her and she was still alive, she could live with his fury. What she couldn't live with was the certainty that she was slowing him down so much that they might never make the road that he swore was only just in the distance. By himself he might get out alive. With her, the chances were narrowed considerably.

The beauty of darkness was that ten or twenty yards from camp she would no longer be visible. When he awoke she would be gone as surely as if she'd ascended into heaven. He could call to her, but if she didn't want to be found she wouldn't be.

She told herself she wasn't being noble. The Blessed Garden hadn't rubbed off on her that much. She was giving both of them the best chance they had. Gallagher was just too stubborn to realize it.

A hundred yards from the blanket she relaxed a little. She wasn't looking forward to being in the desert alone. In fact, until that moment, she hadn't realized just how empty, how eerie, it would be. But she was still sure she had done the right thing.

She had left the flashlight for Gallagher. In fact, she had left everything. Desert survival tools were his bailiwick, not hers. She had learned a thing or two about how to walk an urban sidewalk and live to tell about it. She had also survived her share of Sissy Forrester's stultifying Rancho Mirage pool parties, so she could rub shoulders with Hollywood's vacationing galaxy of stars who might someday need her services. But she knew nothing about survival in the desert, and a can of motor oil or a seen-better-days hubcap weren't going to magically produce water or point the direction to Smoke Tree.

The only thing she had wanted was the blanket, and there had been little she could do about that. She couldn't have ripped it out from under Gallagher like a third-rate magician with a tablecloth, hoping he wouldn't wake up. She just hoped that when he packed to leave he'd realize the blanket would be of more use to her than to him and leave it behind for her to find.

A coyote howled again, and the sound seemed much closer than it had before. She put her hands in her pocket and fingered her revolver for reassurance. Coyotes didn't attack humans—or at least that was what she thought she'd heard. Of course, she didn't look human anymore. Anyone coming upon her now would think she was haunting the desert, the Ghost of the Sonoran who wanders the desert searching and pleading for water in a place where there is none. Doomed eternally.

She had gone so far that she was no longer sure if she could have found her way back to Gallagher if she'd tried. The moon was still partly under cloud, but light trickled at her feet in pale golden drops, and she walked slowly, careful that each step was safe.

Each step would have been, if it hadn't been for the rattlesnake. She was still telling herself not to worry about the coyote when she sensed movement at her right, near what looked like a pile of decaying wood. Startled, she jumped away from the pile, veering sharply to her left. She hadn't even steadied herself for another jump before she heard the telltale rattle assuring her that she was in danger. She couldn't see anything, but she wasn't about to stay around and verify her fears. She jumped left again.

Into empty space.

Chapter 11

Gallagher awoke to a scream. It wasn't as pleasant as an alarm clock, but it did the trick nicely. He was on his feet before he remembered where he was.

The sound died almost as soon as it had been born.

"Felice?" He spoke softly, scanning the immediate area as far as his sleep-fogged eyes could penetrate. "Felice?"

His .38 was in his hand and ready to fire. Clearly Felice was nowhere in his limited field of vision. And he knew better than to believe she had gone off for a few moments of privacy.

He considered, then dismissed, the possibility that the kidnappers had struck again. Not here, and not without him knowing. No, Felice had taken off on her own, probably so that he could move faster without her.

And somewhere along her heroic trek, she had gotten herself into trouble.

"Felice!" He shouted this time, and his voice seemed to go on forever in the clear desert air. "Felice!"

His shout was met with silence.

"I know you're out there, and I know what you're doing. I'm not going anywhere until you get back here."

There was no answer. He knelt and felt for the flashlight, shining it on his watch to gauge how long she had been gone and how much distance she might have covered. He was about to give up calling and start combing the area to find her when he heard a weak cry.

"Josiah?"

"Where the hell are you?"

"How the hell am I supposed to tell you that?"

He grinned despite himself. Whatever had caused her to scream hadn't scared the spunk out of her. "Just keep talking. I'll find you!"

"Be careful. I heard a rattler."

"Get your gun out!"

"I don't think he followed me. I sort of . . . I'm sort of in the bottom of a ravine."

He cursed and set off in the direction he thought her voice was coming from.

"I was heading for the hills."

Gallagher adjusted his steps accordingly. "Keep talking."

"There's a pile of wood near where I . . . went over the side of this . . ." He could almost hear her struggle for a word less flashy than "ravine." "This gully," she said.

"How far did you fall?"

"Far enough to brush up against a cactus or two."

He cursed again. She sounded in pain. Now he knew the reason why. "Was the snake near the woodpile?"

"Yes. I remembered what you'd said and jumped left. The second time I jumped I landed here."

"He's probably not interested in vengeance, but get ready to shoot, just in case."

"You should just leave me here."

"The thought's crossed my mind." Gallagher knew he was getting closer. Her voice was clearer, off to his left somewhere. He shone his wavering light in a circle, looking for what she had called a woodpile near a drop-off. He saw a likely candidate just at the edge of his light. This pile of wood was at the bottom of a hill, flush against its side. His heart slowed mid-beat. "Keep talking," he ordered.

"I wanted to give you a chance to go off on your own."

"I figured that out."

"It was a good idea!"

"Oh, better than good. Excellent."

"You don't have to be sarcastic!"

"And you don't have to be heroic. You were a nun too long."

"I'm not the idiot who keeps saying we'll get out of this together. I was trying to give us both a real chance."

Gallagher approached the woodpile carefully. He heard the same rattle that Felice had. The sound jump started his heartbeat again. "Felice?"

"Down here. Be careful."

"Just worry about you right now. Okay?"

"Sure. I'll just lie here and wallow in my misery while the sidewinder who ate Cincinnati digests you!"

"I'm as safe as I can be." Gallagher stood at the side of the ravine and peered down. Gully had been a better word. Ditch would have done nicely. It wasn't nearly as deep as the one in which he had found her after her kidnappers' exit. He shone his light and spotted her, five yards back the way he had just come. "Hi, there."

She blinked and shaded her eyes. "You're not very far away."

"I bet you thought you'd hit the bottom of the Grand Canyon."

"Distances are deceptive out here, remember?"

He admired her sass. From the look on her face it was a supreme effort. The side of the wash was dotted with cactus, and he winced just thinking about where some of that cactus had ended up.

"I'm coming down to get you." Gallagher realized he was still holding his gun. He flicked on the safety and stuck it in his belt.

"I can make it up. Just shine the light."

He ignored her and started down, picking his way carefully. He was beside her in a few moments.

She was the portrait of human misery. He knelt beside her, but he didn't pull her close, the way he wanted to. He didn't know where the cactus spines were embedded, and he didn't want to make them worse. "Did you break anything?"

"My bones must be made of rubber."

"And your brain."

"Please. I feel bad enough. Okay?"

He relented. "Okay, desert flower. Where do you hurt?"

Her hand hovered high over her left thigh.

"Can you lie down on your other side and let me see?"

"What are you planning to do?"

"Get the spines out."

"I don't think—"

"We don't have all night."

She knew that voice, had heard it from cops and troopers and Feds since the first day she'd realized her life's calling wasn't to be a debutante. She'd used it herself. Now, as usual, it worked. She turned over on her right side and eased her robe up her leg. "Don't go pretending you're a surgeon. It hurts like hell."

"Be a brave soldier." Gallagher shone the light on her leg and felt an instant tug of sympathy. But sympathy wasn't going to get the cactus spines out of her flesh. Not one, and not the twenty or so that he could see protruding from her skin. They were in the fleshiest portion of her thigh. Had they been four inches higher, they would be studding the lace of her bikini panties.

He took his comb from his pocket, explaining so she wouldn't jump when he touched her. "There are two ways to deal with these. If they're big enough I can use my comb to pull them out."

"Great, I've got more to comb on my leg than my head."

He rubbed her back soothingly and wondered how someone who felt so delicate could survive so much. "If they're not big enough, I'll have to break them off so they don't rub against your robe and drive you crazy."

"Every sadist's dream job."

"Hopefully it won't come to that. But you'll have to lie completely still and let me work at them with the comb. I've got to flip them away so they don't touch either of us. Otherwise they'll embed themselves somewhere else."

"As still as a . . ." She was still trying to think of a good comparison when he pulled out the first spine. She winced, but didn't jerk.

"I'm going to have to get you up on my lap to get the rest of them."

"I'll bet."

"You don't have to worry. I've never been attracted to porcupines." Gallagher nudged her legs apart, then slid his own between hers and positioned her top leg across his lap. Despite his words, he schooled himself not to think about the other, more intimate way their legs could be entwined. "Good girl."

"Forget the encouragement. Get back to work."

He propped the flashlight in the crook of his neck and inched his fingers along her flesh, wielding the comb with finesse. She lay perfectly still, although he knew she was in pain. Five minutes later he was finished. "I think that's it. You must have hit a cholla. The pain's worse, but the spines are easier to remove."

"Thanks."

"I know it hurts."

Felice tried to extricate herself, but they were hopelessly entangled. "Just tell me you've had this happen to you, and I won't feel so stupid."

"More times than I can count. Twice a day at my desk in Washington." Gallagher ran his hand along her thigh, slowly, like a man searching for something he'd lost. "Just checking to be sure I got them all."

She covered his hand, stopping its sensuous glide. "It's going to look pretty damned silly if we die here knotted together like a pretzel."

He slid his legs from between hers, and, with as much dignity as she could manage, she pulled her robe down. Her leg still felt like it was on fire. She didn't want to look at him, but he turned her face to his. "Listen," he said "you've been through an ordeal, and I'm not going to rub your nose it it. But try something like this again, and you're buzzard bait."

All the starch had gone out of her spine. "Josiah, we could die out here. One of us has to be honest about that."

He smoothed her veil back from her shoulders and wondered why he hadn't noticed before that she hadn't taken it off when they'd stopped to sleep. It had been a dead giveaway that she was planning something like this. His water-starved brain was working at half speed.

"We're not going to die," he promised her. A more wretched-looking woman didn't exist, but he didn't care. He leaned forward and brushed his parched lips across hers, once, then again. She sighed and leaned against him, and her hands circled his neck.

"I just wanted to give you a chance," she said softly. "You're not such a bad guy. You deserve better than you've gotten since you met me."

"Let's get out of this hole."

"The snake—"

"Isn't."

"I heard a rattle."

"Lots of things rattle." He tried to sound nonchalant. "Branches rattle in the wind. Tin rattles when water strikes it."

"Water?"

"Just an example."

"What are you trying to say?"

"That I want to get out of here. Are you coming?"

She got to her feet, feet that felt twice as large as they ever had before. She took his hand and let him guide her up the slope in silence; she estimated that the trip took ten times as long as her spectacular cactus-studded slide. At the top Gallagher started toward the woodpile, and she followed cautiously, still holding his hand. Only when the weak beam of the flashlight struck a gleam of silver did she understand.

"It's some kind of well, isn't it?" She couldn't believe it. A well in the middle of the desert, covered with a rusted slab of tin.

"Maybe not a well, but something close. At least, I hope so."

"Why? Who?" She was babbling and she knew it, but she didn't care.

"Probably something as simple as someone who spends time in this area protecting a known water source. Indians, maybe, or off-road campers." He pointed to the hillside. "The water probably comes from a trickling spring up there somewhere. It follows a path down the rocks, then pools here. There's probably a natural rock basin under this scrap heap."

"Why the roof?"

"To hold evaporation to a minimum and keep animals out."

"And the rattle was drops hitting the tin?"

"I'd guess the tin's blown too close to the edge, and the water's striking it before it runs off into the basin."

He was moving closer as he spoke, cautiously, in case his theory wasn't correct, but not too cautiously. At the edge he dropped her hand and lifted the slab of tin to peer beneath it, shining his light. The shallow gleam of water shone back at him. "Bingo!"

"Do you think it's safe to drink?" She didn't know whether to shout or cry from joy.

"Do you think it's safe not to drink it?"

"We need something to scoop it out with."

"You stay here. I'll go back for our stuff."

"I found this!" Felice grabbed his arm and shook him. "If I hadn't taken off—"

"We'd be halfway to the road by now."

"And thirsty as hell."

He grinned at her. "Go ahead and crow. And get ready for a big drink." He grabbed her and hauled her against him, kissing her hard, then disappeared into the night.

The desert, which had seemed so endless and eerie, now seemed like a trusted friend.

They forced themselves to drink even more than they wanted and rested just long enough to let the water rejuvenate them. Then, renewed and invigorated, they started toward the road with a water jug that was filled to the top.

Sunrise lit the sky with a spectacular display of color. Even better was the visible strip of pavement half a day's hike in the distance.

Felice ignored the blisters that throbbed each time she took a step. She ignored the sand rubbing new blisters against the soles of her feet and the pain radiating from her thigh. She ignored the aches in body parts she'd never given much thought to and the hunger gnawing a hole inside her. An hour after drinking as much water as she could hold, she had realized she was going to make it.

They were going to make it.

Gallagher no longer led the way. They paused twice to dampen their faces with the rag soaked in their new water wealth, but other than that they trudged side by side without talking, husbanding every calorie of energy left to them for the next step, then the next.

Under the blazing sun of high noon they reached the road.

"I haven't seen a car," Felice said, putting into words what neither of them had yet admitted.

The road—a charitable term—was paved, but only just. The California Highway Department hadn't sunk big bucks into a route that would clearly never be a superhighway.

"One will come." Gallagher gestured to a rock by the road-side. Something approximating shade crept away from one side. "We'll rest over there and wait to see what happens."

"If nothing comes, I think we should follow the road a ways. What do you think?"

"We'll wait until late afternoon and do it if we have the energy."

"I feel like I could walk a hundred miles."

"Adrenaline and water are lifesaving." Gallagher leaned back against the rock after a thorough check.

Felice joined him. "Where do you suppose the road goes?"

"Somewhere."

She shut her eyes. "What are you going to do when we get back to civilization?"

"Besides take a shower and eat?"

"About Sister Mary Grace."

"I'm going to call my contacts and report what's happened, exactly the same thing you'll do... if you are who you say you are."

"You know I am, don't you?"

"Yeah."

"And I know you're a Fed."

"Compensation for living through hell."

"We're not out yet."

"No?" Gallagher waited a moment. "Listen."

Felice was quiet, but the only sound she heard was the cry of a hawk. "I don't hear—"

"Shh..."

She listened harder. Just as she was about to give up, she heard the faintest rumble. Then something that sounded almost like bleating. "I must not have recovered as much as I'd thought. I could swear I hear..."

"Goats?"

"It couldn't be."

Gallagher stood and unknotted the wimple that had been his makeshift hat since they had set out.

"What are you doing?" Felice asked, puzzled.

"Getting ready to flag down a truck." He pointed.

She stood, too. There was a truck behind the shimmers of heat waves at the edge of the horizon. And it was heading right for them. She squinted and shaded her eyes. "Two trucks." She was too moved to say more.

The trucks drew nearer. The rumbling grew louder. The bleating grew louder.

"Goats," Gallagher said decisively.

"I've died, and this isn't heaven." She watched the truck rumble closer.

"When do the sisters send the goats up to the mountains?"

"About now," she said. The words were a croak.

Gallagher took his eyes off the trucks just long enough to shoot her a grin. "I'll put Bulldozer on my lap, if you'll take Mary Poppins."

She told him what she thought of him until the trucks screeched to a halt in front of them and the men driving ushered them to prime seating in the back with the convent goats.

"You were very lucky, Miss Cristy. Nothing's broken, and your arm's not sprained too badly."

"I'm feeling tre*men*dously lucky," Felice told the doctor.

The old man looked up from her chart. "Apparently your concussion wasn't too serious, either, if you've still got the wit to be sarcastic with me, young lady."

"Look, let's test your hearing. I've got to get to a telephone. Did you hear that? Your nurse doesn't seem to hear too well, either. I told her an hour ago. I'd go looking for one myself, but I might scare your other patients dressed this way." She pulled the backless hospital gown away from her chest.

"A shower first."

"You're going to let me take a shower?" Felice slapped her hand over her heart.

The faintest glimmer of a smile cracked through a face that was desert-dry and withered. "We're going to demand you take one."

"All I've wanted since the moment they brought me in here was a phone and a shower. That's all I wanted. I never asked for an examination or an X ray or a tetanus shot or your damned antibiotics."

"But aren't you glad you got them?" Dr. Collins consulted her chart again. "A shower, and then another quart of water. Or I'll hook you up to an IV," he promised, when she tried to argue. "After you get enough to drink, my nurse will treat and bandage your feet and your leg." He shook his head. "You're not leaving my clinic until you do what I say."

"And how are you going to keep me here?" she asked.

"Any way I have to." There was no longer a smile glimmering in the deep furrows around his mouth. "People have died out in that desert. You suffered some effects, even if you don't want to admit it. You let us take care of you, then we'll let you go." He paused. "After you talk to the sheriff."

"Sheriff?"

"Did you think I wouldn't report this?"

She glared at him. "When do I get to use the phone? Christmas? Easter?"

"As soon as you've done what you're supposed to."

"What about Gallagher?"

"What about him?"

"How is he? Where is he?"

"He is in the shower," Dr. Collins said.

"Not quite," said a voice from the doorway.

The doctor turned his head and nodded to his nurse. She could have been his female twin, although Felice had found her twice as unbending. "What do you mean, Lily?" he asked.

"I went into Mr. Gallagher's room to check his pulse after he got out of the shower. He's taken off."

Felice shut her eyes.

"Gone?" the doctor asked.

"Gone. Wearing those filthy clothes." Nurse Lily made it clear that, in her opinion, the clothes were his greatest crime. "And I didn't even get his insurance number!"

Dr. Collins sighed. "Keep your eye on Saint Teresa, here. I'll see if I can find him."

Felice opened her eyes. "Don't bother looking. If he's gone, he's gone." She slid off the examining table and watched the disapproval on Nurse Lily's face when she saw how dirty it was. It was almost as much disapproval as she had shown when she'd discovered Felice was carrying a gun.

Felice took a step toward her. "I'm going to take that shower and drink that water. Then I'm making my phone call. Got it? I'll answer your sheriff's questions after I've called someone to come get me."

Nurse Lily harrumphed. "Don't tell us—"

"Don't mess with me!" Felice narrowed her eyes and slapped her hands on her hips. She knew what she must look like, even after swabbing a wet washcloth over her face, the most Nurse Lily had allowed her to this point. "I don't feel like being messed with anymore. You let Gallagher get away, and for all I know he's as dangerous as the men who put me here. Now get that shower running, or get out of my way so I can do it!"

Nurse Lily sniffed, but she started toward the adjoining bathroom.

Felice followed, but the doctor's hand on her arm stopped her. "Just one more thing, Miss Cristy."

"What?"

"There's a mirror in there. I wouldn't advise a look in it just yet."

She pulled her arm from his grasp. "I've been kidnapped and shot at, starved and dehydrated. I've been covered with cactus and bruises, and God knows what kind of germs were in that water we found. You think I can't take a peek in the mirror?"

He shook his head.

He was right. One peek was all she took. One self-indulgent sob of outraged vanity was proof that she was no longer dehydrated.

*   *   *

"You look like you were run over by a truck!"

Felice sat back in the passenger seat of Kelley's car. "Boy, Kell, what are friends for?"

"Do I get to trade on this for a while? Do I get to be the glamour girl in the office until you're back in shape?"

"You've always been a glamour girl." Felice examined her friend with eyes that could barely stay open. Kelley was dressed in a sundress of a vivid pink she shouldn't be able to wear but somehow pulled off anyway. Her hair curled away from her face like a living thing and sprang down to her shoulders as if it were practicing a gymnastics routine. She wasn't wearing makeup, and her peach-tinted skin was getting a new crop of summertime freckles. "You know you're gorgeous."

"I keep forgetting." Kelley pulled out to the road. "Goodbye, Smoke Tree."

"I could have died out in that desert."

Kelley patted Felice on the knee. "Well, you were in good hands. Shall I tell you what I found out about Josiah Gallagher?"

Kelley had already told Felice that Gallagher really did work for the Justice Department, but with Nurse Lily ticking off the seconds of the long-distance call, there hadn't been time for Felice to ask more. "I might as well hear it all."

"It's almost not correct to say he works 'for' the Justice Department. He practically *is* the Justice Department. He's way up at the top, and his position is so hush-hush that nobody would give me any good details."

"This can't be the same Josiah Gallagher."

"Why not?"

With distaste Felice tugged the T-shirt Kelley had brought her away from her chest. Kelley was four inches shorter and ten pounds lighter, and without making a stop by Felice's condo, the only clothes that she'd had that would fit Felice were a faded oversized orange T-shirt that said Jed's Bar and Grill in fluorescent green, and a pair of plum-colored jogging pants. Felice had almost preferred her robe.

"It can't be the same man," she answered, "because this one was posing as a bum. Does the Justice Department waste its top resources that way?"

"It's the same guy. I was told he was on a leave of absence." She paused. "After I called in about a dozen favors."

Felice sat back and closed her eyes. She always closed her eyes when Kelley drove. Her station wagon might be ten years old and crotchety, but Kelley drove it like an Alfa-Romeo. "Well, I'm off the case now, anyway. Sister Mary Grace knows who I am, and she doesn't want me watching her anymore."

Kelley said nothing.

Felice was drained of energy. She had refused to eat more than a piece of toast at the clinic, and she was starving. Kelley had raided a fast-food restaurant on the way to pick her up, but the paper bag still sat at Felice's feet. She was too tired to lift it to her lap.

She was too tired to think. The days in the desert with Gallagher, her escape from a moving car, her weeks at the Blessed Garden, even the morning's trip back to Smoke Tree with the goats, seemed a million years in the past. Reality was this moment, bouncing over the pockmarked road leading away from Smoke Tree, and the thought of twenty-four hours of sleep in her very own bed.

Almost the only reality. Her eyes opened, and she turned her head toward Kelley. "What about Sister Mary Grace?"

Kelley looked pained. "You don't need to worry about anyone except yourself right now. You've just crawled out of the desert. There'll be plenty of time to think about work later."

"Kelley!"

Kelley sighed. "She's gone."

"Gone?"

"She disappeared the same night you did. She left the Mother Superior a note and told her that she had to be alone to think."

"It's my fault." Felice almost strangled on the words. "I did that to her. I made her leave the Blessed Garden. She knew Luis had traced her there, and she knew that we'd probably find some way to keep watching her, so she took off."

"She said something about you in the note."

Felice shook her head. "Mother Jeanne's probably already called the pope. My picture will be hung in every church between here and Australia. I'll be barred at every door."

"Nothing like that. The note said that Sister Mary Grace had talked to you, and that you would be leaving, too, although she didn't say why. She asked Mother Jeanne not to be too hard on you."

"How do you know all this?"

"Mother Jeanne called the Mother Superior of your order in L.A."

Since the order in L.A. was nothing more than a recently installed telephone in a friend's apartment in Studio City, Felice understood. "And she told Sue the whole story?"

"Sue as Mother John the Baptist. Yes. That number was good insurance."

"That number was a lie. One of a million."

"All for good reasons, Felice. You were trying to save someone's life. Don't forget that."

"And now that someone is wandering somewhere trying to find some peace."

"You need food and sleep. Then you can try to put this in perspective."

"Does Luis know?"

"I felt I had to call him."

"What did you say?"

"I told him what I knew, but of course I didn't know much, just that you and Sister Mary Grace had both disappeared. I assumed you were still tailing her. By yesterday, though, I was getting worried, since I hadn't heard from you."

"Did you know Gallagher was gone, too?"

"No. I couldn't very well call the convent and ask if the new handyman had disappeared with the two missing nuns." With her eyes still on the road, Kelley leaned down and picked up the bag at Felice's feet. "Eat!"

Obediently Felice took the bag and gnawed at a cold french fry. "I'll have to call Luis when I get home."

"Why don't you practice your story on me? I'd love to know every detail. I've been remarkably patient."

Felice worked her way slowly to the end of the fry. "I don't think I can accurately describe it," she said when she'd finished. She felt a huge empty place inside her that had nothing to do with hunger—at least, not the digestive kind.

She thought of Gallagher, gone from her life now. His job had ended; his reason to stay with her had ended, too. If he was the powerful man Kelley had described, then he was on his way back to the East Coast right now.

So? What had she expected? He was neither an ignorant drifter nor a skillful assassin. He was a highly placed administrator in the Justice Department. His life and job were in Washington, and his heart was entrenched in bureaucracy. She must have looked pretty silly to a man like Josiah Gallagher.

"If you won't eat, maybe you'd like one of these?" Kelley held out a pack of cigarettes.

"I thought you quit?" Felice didn't take the pack.

"I bought these for you."

Felice thought about how thoroughly her life had changed. "I don't want them."

"No?"

"No."

Kelley tossed the pack in the back seat. "I don't know what to make of you, Felice."

"Me either." Felice stared out the window at the passing desert scenery. "Me either."

Chapter 12

Her condo was a palace. Felice wandered through the five rooms in wonder. No king, no maharaja, had ever lived more sumptuously. She stroked her calloused fingers over the raw oyster silk that covered the sofa, let the smooth taupe walls cool a sunburned cheek. She hugged a velvet pillow to her chest as she stood at the door to her balcony looking over the eighteenth hole of the condominium's pristine fairway.

Why did one person need all this room?

In the background she could hear the twelfth message on her answering machine. Her mother had called from Madrid. Did Felice want to join her parents there for a few days? Sissy Forrester was call number thirteen. Why had Felice missed her party? Frank Sinatra had planned to come. Hadn't Felice wanted to meet Frank Sinatra?

"I already have, thanks," Felice answered automatically. She doubted Frank liked Sissy's parties, either.

Number fourteen was her mother calling from Lisbon. Didn't Felice want to meet her parents in Lisbon for a few days?

Felice found her way to the answering machine, perched on a table from an exclusive Palm Springs gallery. The table was painted to look like a desert at sunrise; the legs were carved like barrel cactus and painted a sickly green. She made a mental note to get rid of it tomorrow.

She rewound the answering-machine tape and flicked it off, along with the ringer. The apartment seemed unbearably still, and she wandered across the room to turn on her stereo. Fusion jazz snaked its way through the room, perfect for the room, inappropriate for her mood. She flicked the music off, too.

Where was Gallagher now? Over Colorado, most likely. Maybe even as far away as Kansas. Why hadn't he said goodbye? Certainly he'd needed to check her out first, but one phone call would have bought him the assurance that she was the person she'd said she was. Why hadn't he told her he was leaving? What had been the awful hurry?

Maybe nothing that had happened in the desert had held any meaning for him. At heart he was a good guy. He'd felt compassion for her and tried to keep her spirits up. At the clinic she'd seen what she looked like. What man would think fondly of a sunburned and cactus-spangled, black and blue, nearly bald woman streaked with motor oil and dirt? And what man would think fondly of a woman who had pulled any of the stunts she had?

She had hoped that maybe Gallagher would.

Fatigue and depression settled over her like a smothering blanket. Curiously, she knew her bed was going to seem too soft.

And too empty.

She headed for her bedroom anyway. She was too exhausted to put her life in perspective, and too exhausted to do anything about the way she looked. She was going to sleep, for as long as she needed. And then she would allow herself the luxury of thought.

But she wasn't going to think about Gallagher anymore. He was gone, without even saying goodbye. And she was not a woman who let a man reject her twice.

Gallagher took in the condominium complex with an experienced eye. A team of gardeners passed, going home for the evening, and he lifted his hand in polite farewell. He wondered what the men found to do. Every blade of grass was a uniform height. If a noxious native plant had ever grown in any of the impeccably boring flower beds, it had been tried and convicted years ago.

He consulted the scrap of paper in his hand. Felice's apartment was number twelve, on the second floor overlooking the golf course. He wondered why she had chosen to entertain herself by watching men in funny pants ride from hole to hole in canopied carts. He wondered if she ever looked out her windows.

He entered the complex through the air-conditioned garage. He supposed it was air-conditioned so that no condo owner would ever have to face the trial of rolling down his windows to cool his car.

He found Felice's apartment with no trouble. His knock brought no response, so he knocked louder. He had resorted to banging when he heard the dead bolt click. A bleary-eyed vision appeared through a crack in the door.

She was dressed in a huge orange T-shirt that made the ones he'd worn at the Blessed Garden look civilized. Her chopped off hair was spiked, as if the wind had been her hairdresser of choice, and without motor oil covering her face, he could clearly see the fading gold of her bruised cheek.

He had never seen a more beautiful woman.

She narrowed her eyes. "You're supposed to be in Washington."

"Why?"

"Because you practically run the Justice Department, and they can't do justice without you." She cracked the door wider. "Look at you." Her eyes were beginning to focus and send messages to her brain.

Gallagher looked like a million dollars, the pot of gold at the end of a desert rainbow. He was dressed in charcoal slacks and a pin-striped shirt. His jacket was a lighter gray and made of a fabric that was a textile manufacturer's dream. His hair had been cut by someone in Palm Springs—certainly not Smoke Tree—and he was clean shaven, which only spotlighted more effectively the deep, cynical dimple in his right cheek.

She tried to shut the door. "Come back tomorrow," she croaked.

His shoe filled the crack. "Not a chance."

"I was sleeping."

"I guessed that much."

"I'm a wreck."

"Half a wreck." He wedged what he could of himself in the doorway and began to inch the door wider.

"This isn't fair!"

"Hardly anything is."

She knew when to give up and stepped away from the door, but she didn't know what to say when he was inside facing her. She pulled the hem of Kelley's T-shirt away from her hips. "This isn't mine."

"Felice." He said her name like a caress.

Her eyes flashed to his face. "You didn't say goodbye."

"I didn't have to." He didn't touch her, but not because he didn't want to. He sensed just how slow he had to take this and schooled himself to patience.

"You didn't even leave your insurance number."

"Blue Cross concerns you?" She turned away from him, and he watched her smooth her hair—he wasn't going to tell her it was a lost cause. Her hands didn't look quite steady. "Or were you concerned about something else?"

"What makes you think I'm concerned?" she asked.

Gallagher rested his hands lightly on her shoulders. "Did you check me out?"

"You passed with flying colors. Fed *extraordinaire.*"

"You passed, too. Three commendations for bravery while you were on the force in L.A. You upset a lot of people when you left."

"Doing a little recruiting for the Bureau while you're here?"

He turned her. Gently. Obviously she wanted to come. "Sorry, but you're not exactly what we look for."

"Thank God."

"I am recruiting, though." His thumbs brushed her cheeks. She couldn't miss his meaning. "There are likelier candidates."

"No."

"Josiah, maybe it was just those desert nights. Did you think about that? We were thrown together. Life and death. That can do things to a person."

"Amazing things," he agreed.

She stared into his whiskey brown eyes and saw something she hadn't expected. He wasn't sure of himself. He had been supremely confident in the desert, but here, in Palm Springs, he wasn't sure of either of them.

She tried to buy time. "Would you like a drink? Do you remember talking about all those times you'd turned down a..." She realized he was drawing her closer. "Josiah..."

"Do you want to know what I remember? I remember thinking that if I had to get lost in the desert, I'd chosen the right woman to do it with. Then, at night, I'd lie awake and listen to your breathing, and I'd think that when we were safe, I was going to have to get out of your life fast, or I'd end up in the midst of something I couldn't handle."

"But you're here."

"I'm not going to pretend anything, desert flower. I still don't want to get tangled up with you or anyone. But I don't want to leave, either. Not yet."

"The ground between those alternatives isn't very firm."

"I'll take my chances." His thumbs stroked the soft hollow at the base of her throat. "Will you take yours?"

Blindfolded and bound, she had launched herself from a moving car. She had taken off alone into a dark desert night, and she had walked endless miles in the hot desert sun with a man she wasn't sure of. She was a champion at taking chances, a foolhardy gambler who walked life's razor edge just for the thrill of it.

But now she didn't know what to say.

"Shall I take the chance for both of us, then?" he asked.

"Josiah." It was as good as saying yes.

He pulled her the final inches so that their lips could meet. She sighed and curved against him, and her body was familiar to his. He felt her breasts push against his chest, and the feeling inside him was familiar, too.

The man holding her was strangely unfamiliar to Felice. He was not the drifter nor the desert trailblazer. He was Josiah

Gallagher, a man who kept secrets for a living, and what he wanted, what he felt, was as much a mystery as the weakness in her knees, the warmth flooding through her.

Somehow that didn't matter. Nothing mattered except that he hadn't left without saying goodbye, that he had come to Palm Springs to find her, and that he was here with her now. It didn't even matter that she was beginning to suspect she might never want to say goodbye to him. That was later; this was now. Now he was here, his body setting hers ablaze. She would be crazy to worry about more.

"If the shirt's not yours, whose is it?"

For a moment Felice was thrown off balance. She didn't understand. Then she thought she might. "Kelley's."

"Kelley?"

She pulled away just far enough to see his eyes. "Your research should have turned that up."

"Your partner?"

"Right."

His research had been done quickly, and there were gaps. "Kelley can be male or female."

She suppressed a smile. "That's true."

"And?"

"Female." She touched his chin, tracing a line to the corner of his mouth. "I suppose this is a roundabout way of asking about the men in my life."

"It's none of my business. There must have been life before the Blessed Garden."

"I work too hard. Just like you."

"Meaning?"

"There's no one waiting in the wings. No one important. There hasn't been for a long time."

He nodded as his hands settled at her hips, but he didn't draw her close again. "Not that I'm trying to own you."

"Of course you're not." This time she allowed a smile. "You don't want to get tangled up. You'd probably be happy if you were just part of a long string of men I kept dangling. Even happier if you had to make an appointment weeks ahead of time to sleep with me."

He silenced her in the most effective way he knew. Her lips gave under his; her flesh was resilient under the pressure of his fingers. She was slender but not fragile, as if the work at the convent and the days in the desert had melted her down to the essence of the woman who had once lived in this apartment. He knew that if he could fly through time to the days before the Blessed Garden, it would be a very different Felice Cristy he would be holding in his arms

Something had melted inside him, too. He didn't know what, or why, and he certainly didn't understand how. But he wanted this woman in a way that was unfamiliar to him. And yes, she was right, damn it. In her penetrating, infuriating way she had seen right through him. He didn't want to be one of a string of men in her life. He didn't know what he wanted, but he didn't want that. In some unfathomable way, she was his already. He didn't want to share her.

And he didn't want to think about the reasons why. Not now. Maybe not ever.

"Is there a bedroom in this place?" He sounded like he felt: impatient, more than a little angry at himself for needing to come here, more than a little angry at her for making him need her.

"More than one."

His fingers trailed to her legs, then under the hem of the shirt. "One will do."

"I could show you both, and you could choose."

"I don't want a tour." He said the words against her ear. His breath was warm, and she shuddered when he blew a lock of her hair behind it. His teeth tugged at her earlobe, and she felt the sensation in scattered places that seemed miles away.

Her knees grew weaker. They had been strong enough to get her through the desert, but she wondered if they would move her the required number of yards to her bedroom. "You haven't said exactly what you do want."

"You."

"Succinct, aren't you?"

"In a bed or somewhere closer." The preposterous T-shirt pooled over the back of his hands. He lifted his hands to her waist, disappointed to find she wore pants beneath the shirt. "The rug looks soft," he whispered.

More sparks showered through her body. "I'll show you my bedroom." She dropped her hands over his and pushed. Reluctantly he let the T-shirt fall back over her hips. "You've got to promise not to laugh."

"Can't say I feel like laughing." He smiled a little, but it did nothing to lessen the intensity of his gaze.

She shivered and wondered what she was letting herself in for. She was trying to stay in control, to defuse the passion that was building so quickly between them. She was frightened by it, and frightened by the intimacy that was building, too. Wanting Gallagher was one thing. Having him would be something else.

She turned before he could touch her again. Her bedroom was at the end of the hallway. She almost stopped at the spare bedroom, instead. It was furnished like most of the rest of the apartment, modern and chic, with neutral tones and occasional touches of whimsy. She passed it, though, and led him farther, opening the door to a part of her he probably hadn't expected.

Gallagher didn't laugh. He felt the romanticism, the lyric sentimentality, like a punch to the gut. There was nothing of the wisecracking, irreverent private eye in this room. The room was unrepentantly feminine, with walls lined in pale yellow silk and flowered curtains that drifted in clouds of chiffon from floor to ceiling. Her bed was a carved monument to the nineteenth century, and instead of a canopy, more fabric of the palest pastels twisted over the canopy frame and spiraled to the floor.

And yet, this woman was no stranger. He had seen glimpses of her in Sister Felicia, glimpses of her in the desert. He had felt this woman when he'd kissed the other, and the hint of this woman intrigued him.

"My mother would love this room."

He heard the apology in her words. "It looks like the daughter she wanted was there all along."

"A part of me," she acknowledged. "But I could never be this person around her, because then she wouldn't have understood the parts of me that were different." She turned a little,

and he saw the woman who had created this room in her eyes.
"Does that make sense?"

The only thing that made sense was that he should get out of
there. He could handle Felice Cristy. He could make love to her,
take untold pleasure from her body and, later, get on with his
life as she got on with hers. But this woman complicated things.
Extraordinarily.

"You probably think this is silly." Felice leaned against the
door frame, the T-shirt tightening over her breasts. She waved
her hand at the room. "It doesn't really mean that much. I was
tired of earth tones and good taste. I—"

His lips silenced hers. If he'd ever had any sense, he'd lost it
the first night a worldly young nun had stripped off her veil and
bared her head to the moonlight. He pinned her to the door
frame with his hands and kissed her until her lips parted under
his. Then, because it was that kind of room and in it she was
that kind of woman, he lifted her in his arms and strode toward the bed.

Her bedspread was watered silk. She felt it against the backs
of her legs before she could protest. Still dressed, Gallagher lay
on his side facing her. His hand splayed across her cheek and
his fingers twined in her hair.

She sighed as he kissed her again, a shuddering, imploring
sigh that did nothing to make him withdraw. She felt him shift
her to her side, felt his hand trail down her neck, down her
spine to her hip. His hands were large, large enough to make her
feel small and at his mercy. She felt the slow slide of cotton up
her side and the warmth of his hand following it.

She murmured dissent and pushed his sports coat off his
shoulders. "You first." She ignored the low rumble of his
laughter. "I mean it, Josiah."

"Do you now?" He inched the T-shirt to her waist.

"I do." The sports coat slid down his arms, and she started
on the buttons of his shirt.

"I've seen you naked. You've slept with me." His hand
trailed beneath the T-shirt to the side of her breast, lingering but
not stroking.

She moaned a little, and her hands faltered on his buttons.

"I've made love to you a thousand times in my mind." He felt her shudder, and his body responded accordingly. "I know what your breasts feel like against my palm."

She knew what his chest felt like against hers, but she didn't tell him that. The power of speech was abandoning her.

"I know how soft you are, how perfectly we fit together." He felt the tremor in her hands as the last button of his shirt was freed. "I know what it feels like to explode inside—"

"Stop it." She covered his lips with hers as he pulled the shirt higher. She clasped him against her, and the sensation was nothing either of them could have fantasized.

They rocked together, locked in each other's arms, until Gallagher finally broke away. He gathered the T-shirt in his hands to pull it over her head, but she stopped him. "Not yet."

"I want to see all of you."

She wanted that, too. She wanted him naked beside her, and she wanted more. She just wasn't ready.

"Desert flower?" He tipped her head and read the expression in her eyes. "Sister Felicia?"

"That's crazy!"

"Maybe not."

He smiled, and her heart flip-flopped. "I'm not a nun."

"Thank God for that."

"I'm just feeling... We're rushing..." She stopped.

He pushed her gently back on the bed. He made no move to finish undressing her, even though the T-shirt hung tantalizingly askew and gave him just enough of a view to drive him crazy. He stretched out beside her and brushed her hair back from her face, following the caress of his fingers with his lips.

She rested her hands on his shoulders, kneading them slowly as he kissed her. She shut her eyes, and they were in the desert again, lying together under the stars. She opened them and saw gossamer yards of pink and blue above his head. On his face she saw strained patience and something else she was afraid to name.

"Josiah." Her voice was a sigh.

He was moved beyond words. No matter what he'd told himself, this wasn't just about sex. It wasn't just about two people who found each other attractive and sought pleasure in that attraction. He touched her cheek, her neck, her shoulder. His hand smoothed a path to her waist. Her skin was warm and taut. He knew how it would taste, how it would feel against his lips. He knew how she would move beneath his hand as he stroked her, and he knew he shouldn't stroke her. Not yet. Not until she understood, too, that more would come of this than a physical release. He didn't know exactly what would come of their coupling, but whatever did, neither of them would soon forget it.

"Felice." He said her name again, this time against her lips. Then he lifted his head so that he could see her eyes. "This is new for me, too."

She didn't know what that meant for him, didn't even know if she wanted to understand. But she did know that what was happening between them was new for her. She wanted this to last forever, and she wanted it finished. She wanted him to make love to her eternally, and at the same time she wanted to lie in his arms when it was over and tell herself that nothing had happened.

His hand slid slowly to her breast. What she wanted and what she needed were no longer subjects for thought. Thought scattered and all she could do was feel, not only the glorious sensation of his hand just exactly where it belonged but emotions she hadn't even known existed.

She moved against his palm, felt his long fingers begin a slow, torturous rotation. Whatever sensibility had stopped her from letting him remove the T-shirt vanished. She squirmed and adjusted enough to pull it over her head. She saw the light in his eyes kindle into flame just before his lips followed the path of his fingers.

She swam in sensation and knew that she never had before. Strangely her heart, a part of her he couldn't touch, was most affected by the brush of his fingers and lips, the feel of his bare skin against hers, the clean scent of his hair, the magic of moving toward the moment when they would become one.

She had known pleasure; she had never known ecstasy. But ecstasy was the heat infusing the deepest parts of her. Thought was smothered by it; instinct prevailed. She arched against him, offering herself. He took more.

She twisted beneath him, trying to get closer, and somehow he was closer than anyone had ever been. Her heart beat faster, her hands moved over him, frustrated by what clothing remained. He moved away just long enough to rid himself of it and just long enough to make her mourn his loss. Then he was beside her again, his legs stretched against hers, his body hard and uncompromising.

She was uncompromising, too. She demanded and gave with equal fervor. He took, like a man long denied, but he made his own demands. His hands caressed and altered her flesh until she was no longer the same woman. His lips taunted hers, his body sought and found the answer to every question a man could ask.

He spoke, and for a moment, she wasn't sure what she had heard. Then she understood.

"New," he whispered.

"Oh, yes," she answered, and knew that it was true.

She felt him move above her, felt the welcome, invasive heat of his arousal. She opened herself to him in a way she had never opened herself to anyone before. She gave him her body and she gave him her heart. And in the storm that resulted, she was buoyed by the knowledge that he took what she offered.

She awoke at dawn and realized she hadn't told Gallagher that Sister Mary Grace had left the convent. But then, she hadn't exactly been thinking straight since he'd arrived.

The room was cool with a soft desert breeze. Sometime during the night he had gotten up to open a window, and in the rosy glow of sunrise her curtains waltzed together.

She turned her head to watch Gallagher instead, and that was all it took to wake him. His eyes opened, and for a moment she read questions, regrets, apologies in them, then she read only the defenses of a man who was used to none of those things.

"It's all right," she said, bringing his hand to her cheek. "You didn't marry me."

"What does that mean?"

"That you're free to get up and leave if you want." She smiled and suspected it was a good one. She kissed his palm and folded his fingers over the kiss. Then she sat up. "And I'm going to get up and take a shower."

His hand at the back of her neck stopped her. "What's your hurry?"

She wasn't sure, exactly. But something told her that she shouldn't lie there with him anymore. She hadn't wanted many things in her life that she hadn't been able to get. She wasn't sure how to cope with wanting this man.

"I've got work to do." She faced him again. "I've got a nun to find."

"So you know Sister Mary Grace left the convent."

"Apparently you know it, too."

"What else do you know?"

She shrugged. "Probably not as much as you."

"We don't know where she is, but there are a dozen highly trained operatives out there looking for her."

"So I can relax?"

He nodded warily.

"Forget it." Felice stood. The only thing in reach was Kelley's T-shirt. She slipped it over her head. It wasn't exactly armor, but she felt better protected.

Arms circled her waist; hands crept to her breasts. The T-shirt was no protection at all. "Forget leaving."

Memories of last night's lovemaking came flooding back as he caressed her. Her knees felt like water, a sensation growing all too familiar since Gallagher had entered her life. She let him pull her to his lap, and she felt how ready he was to make love to her again.

"Josiah," she moaned. "You know this isn't smart."

"Do I?"

"Last night was one thing. This is something else. Don't form any habits you'll have to break."

"I'm not thinking about breaking anything. Except the ice." He turned her and saw the same questions in her eyes that had been in his when he'd seen her lying beside him in dawn's rosy glow. He wanted to make love to her until all her questions were answered. But he didn't have a lifetime. He had this morning, and not even all of that.

He drew her head down to his. She resisted, but not enough to stop him. Her lips softened under his, her body flowed against him. This time he had the pleasure of stripping away the T-shirt. He tossed it over his shoulder and hoped she'd never find it.

She found it later, when she awoke again, but there was no need to wear it. Gallagher was gone, and her apartment was too large and too empty once more.

Chapter 13

Rudolph was anything but pleased that Felice had let anyone, anyone, cut her hair but him. She had placated him with the promise that someday she might possibly, just possibly, be able to tell him the whole horrible story. He had been enchanted enough at the prospect to set to work on her, though his gasps and grumbles had been enough to convince her that even his magical bony fingers didn't possess enough skill to rectify Mother Jeanne's handiwork.

She couldn't watch more of her hair disappear. Instead, she had Rudolph turn the chair so that she could watch some of Palm Springs's leading beauties get pummeled and creamed, bleached and shorn. Thinking about the contrast to the Blessed Garden was enough to keep her mind off Rudolph's groans.

There was nothing to groan about when he turned her around to see what he had done. There was a flirtatious fringe decorating her forehead and the nape of her neck. Her ears were bare, and the top of her hair was still long enough to swirl when she moved. The rest was in graduated layers, one hundred percent feminine and flattering.

Rudolph blushed when she kissed him, then sent her along to the next magic maker, who gasped and grumbled as she mixed up a potion to start Felice's sunburned, roughened complexion on the road to recovery, then another to help hide her bruise while it healed. The third magic maker generously shared everything she'd ever heard about the Gabor sisters, as she soaked, filed and buffed what was left of Felice's nails.

Felice left Rudolph's looking like a new woman. Silver earrings dangled from her ears; a black-and-white print sundress brushed the tops of her knees. She was a long way from the bedraggled desert rat who had gulped down a sob when she'd taken her first glance in the clinic mirror.

But that forlorn woman was gone forever, anyway, courtesy of one Josiah Gallagher, who, for a brief while, had made her feel beautiful. Even before her trip to Rudolph's.

Kelley was already at her desk by the time Felice got to the office. She made a face when Felice walked through the door.

"I thought I got to be the glamour girl for a while."

"In jeans and a T-shirt?" Felice narrowed her eyes to read the familiar slogan on Kelley's chest. She'd been wearing that slogan herself yesterday. "You had two of those shirts?"

"Great shirt. Can't have too many." Kelley pushed herself away from the desk. "I'm going to hang out on a bar stool in Cathedral City this afternoon."

"Waiting for somebody?"

"A guy who owes some child support." She stood. "You should be taking it easy today, kiddo. Don't try to do anything. Just see what's been going down since you took your vows, then go home and take a nap."

"I've got to see Luis. Then I'm off to find Sister Mary Grace."

"Think so?" The voice in Kelley's doorway was unmistakably Gallagher's.

Felice turned casually, as if she had been expecting him. But she hadn't been, not after his silent morning exit. He had made it clear, right from the beginning, that he wanted no ties. She had known his feelings when she'd taken him to her bed, and his disappearance had only been one more reminder.

Now she tried not to let the glow she felt at his reappearance show. He had come back. Suddenly anything seemed possible. "Come in and meet Kelley."

"We met this morning. Early," Kelley added. "He's a persistent cuss."

"Early?" Felice watched Gallagher examine her. His wasn't a face that showed his thoughts. For a moment she felt silly and hopelessly feminine for giving in to vanity and spending time at Rudolph's. She had told herself it was necessary—that looking the way she had, no one would take her seriously on her quest to find Sister Mary Grace. But now she wished she had just worn a scarf and washed her face, come into the office in jeans and a T-shirt, like Kelley....

Until she saw Gallagher smile. And heard his soft, spontaneous whistle. "Well, desert flower, I knew the makings were there."

She could feel her cheeks heat, and not from sunburn. "Early?" she repeated.

"I went out to get some groceries for breakfast," he said. "Your refrigerator was empty. When I got back, the door was locked and you were gone."

"Someone's going to have to teach you how to write a note."

"Why don't you apply for the job. Over lunch."

Felice glanced at Kelley. There was definitely a smirk on her face. She looked back at Gallagher. "I've got to speak to Luis."

"I already have."

"What do you mean you already—"

"This morning. While you were getting beautiful. He knows the situation, and he knows the government's looking."

"And in a few minutes he'll know I'm looking, too."

"He already knows, and he knows I'll be looking with you."

"You two don't need me," Kelley said. "Feel free to take up space in here. I'm going to see if anybody made more coffee."

Felice watched Kelley try to discipline a smile as she threaded her way between them and disappeared out the door. Felice lifted a paperweight off Kelley's desk. It was a Palm Springs Christmas scene with a garish yellow sun and a sandstorm when it was turned upside down. She tossed it from hand to hand and considered tossing it at the man in front of her.

"You know," she said, "I was in business before I met you, and I'll be in business when you go back to running whatever department it is you run. I've been shot at and beaten up, and once somebody tried to hit me with a car. I'm still here to tell the story."

"So?"

"So I don't want and I don't need your protection. This isn't the desert. I can take care of myself just fine."

He had moved closer as she'd talked, and now he was almost on top of her. She didn't give ground. "This isn't about protection," he said. "It's about two people who know Sister Mary Grace on sight getting together to find her."

She set down the paperweight with a bang. "You're a Fed. I know what you think of anyone who isn't. You won't share anything with me, because I'm not a Fed, too. You'll—" She stopped as his words finally sank in. "You're not trying to keep me out of trouble?"

"I don't attempt the impossible."

She perched on the edge of Kelley's desk. "We'd work together? As equals? You'll tell me what your people have found out?"

"Everything I can."

She nodded. "Strictly business?"

"What's that supposed to mean?" He touched her hair. It clung to his fingers.

She didn't let her reaction, a subtle contraction of all her muscles, an unheard of urge to rub her head against his fingers, show. "I don't want to be humored. I'm good at what I do."

"I know."

"I don't want to be lied to."

"Do you want to be kissed?"

She sighed. "I don't know what to do about you."

He tilted her head and brought his lips to hers. He smelled faintly like sunshine and more like warm, healthy male. His lips moved over hers as if he were staking a claim. She didn't dispute his boundaries. "Lunch?" he asked, when he finally pulled away.

"Lunch."

"You've got groceries in your refrigerator now."

"How did you get insi—" She stopped at his self-satisfied smile. "Never mind."

"I could cook you an omelet for lunch. We could make our plans for the rest of the day."

"We could do that at Nate's Deli."

"There are other things we couldn't do there."

She didn't ask what; his eyes and the very same smile told her everything she had to know. She picked up her purse and followed him out the door.

Gallagher struggled to get used to the fourth and latest Felice Cristy standing in front of him, chattering away in Spanish. Sister Felicia, with the Madonna face and the stealth of an assassin had been his introduction to this multifaceted woman. Felice number two, pathetic but courageous desert survivor, had been someone completely different. Felice number three, sensuous, feminine and altogether addictive, was someone he couldn't yet think clearly about. Now this fourth Felice, talented, competent professional, was another side of his changeling lover.

All four Felices were much too appealing.

"So you dropped the nun off a few miles outside of Palm Springs?" Felice forced herself to ignore the rooster pecking at the buckle on the largest shoes she owned. She had wrung a few feathered necks in her weeks at the Blessed Garden, and she soothed herself with that vision.

The old man answered. *"Sí."* He described the place. "She said she wanted to walk, that God had given her legs to use them. I think she would have walked all the way from Smoke Tree if I hadn't stopped and asked if she wanted a ride in my truck."

"How was she dressed?"

He shrugged. "Like a nun."

"In a robe like a monk? Sandals?"

"No. In a black skirt, white blouse. Short black veil. A modern nun."

That was new information for Felice. Gallagher's contacts had led them to the old man with the homestead several miles from the Blessed Garden. He had been reluctant to tell Gallagher's men much, only that he had given a middle-aged nun a lift in his truck the night Sister Mary Grace had left the Blessed Garden.

The homestead was nothing more than a shack and a wind-driven pump that dredged up enough water to satisfy a scrawny cow and a flock of chickens. The rusted machinery scattered over the landscape was as old as the man himself, and he could have been anywhere between fifty and a hundred. He lived alone and obviously liked it that way.

Although Felice suspected the man spoke English, she continued in Spanish. If nothing else, it impressed Gallagher and kept him in the dark. "Did you ask her where she might be going?"

"You ask a nun to pray for you. That's all."

Felice smiled. "Well, did she just happen to say?"

He smiled, a toothless beatific smile that told her he was enjoying this. "She did."

"Mind telling me where?"

"To a friend's."

"Anything else?'

"This man…" He inclined his head to Gallagher. "He's your boyfriend?"

She examined Gallagher, then turned back to the old man. "I guess you could say that."

"Too bad."

"Why? Are you interested?" she teased.

He cackled and slapped his knee with his hat. "Do you work with those other men who were here?"

"Men in suits and ties with faces like this?" She wrinkled her brow and tightened the corners of her mouth.

He cackled again. "Those men, yes. And the others, too."

"Others?"

"California sleaze," he said. "Two of them. Chains around their necks that would buy my cow hay for both her stomachs. Shirts open to here." He pointed to his navel.

Her internal alarm system clanged. "Josiah," she said in English. "Do you have agents who parade around dressed like Hollywood talent scouts? Gold chains? Hairy chests?"

"No."

She turned back to the old man. "Would you mind telling me more about these men?"

He shrugged again, as if his shoulders needed the exercise.

She turned up the voltage on her smile. *"¿Por favor?"*

"They asked me if I'd seen a nun on the road nearby, too. I told them I'd given one a ride. Nothing more."

"When did they come?"

"Yesterday? The day before?"

She imagined that one day was pretty much like the other to him. "But after the others came?"

"After."

"Anything else you can remember?"

"One was bald. One wasn't."

She stepped a little closer and lowered her voice. "They could be trying to hurt the sister. You don't want that, and neither do I."

"I knew they were no good." He leaned a little closer. "Do you think I'm stupid?"

She stepped a little closer. "Would I be here talking to you if I thought that?"

He cackled again, obviously enjoying her answer. He leaned a little closer still. "I like you. I'll tell you what I told them. I told them I took her to Los Angeles so she could catch a bus to San Diego." This time his smile was wily. "They won't find her before you do."

She laughed with him. Only after she had already said goodbye—and only after the rooster had pecked her twice more and ruined her panty hose—did she think to check out one last thing. "I forgot to ask. Those two men. Were they Latinos? Did they speak Spanish?"

He answered in English. "No. One spoke like he was from Alabamah." "Alabama" was said with a perfect Southern twang.

Felice put her hands on her hips. "Well, thanks for letting me practice my Spanish."

"You need work on your accent, you come back anytime." He winked at her, set his hat back on his head and shut his eyes for a nap.

In the car, Gallagher was silent until Felice had pulled onto the road. "So I'm your boyfriend," he said.

"You were listening!"

"I was standing right there, desert flower."

"You were listening in Spanish."

"You just assumed I didn't understand." He put his hand on the back of her neck and rubbed. "For that matter, you assumed he didn't speak English."

"You know I did no such thing. We started in English. He refused to answer."

"And you liked showing off. Come on, admit it."

Defeated, she stretched her neck against his fingers and wallowed in the pleasure threading through her. "Well, how'd I do?"

"You got some good information." He wondered how anyone's skin could feel so silky. Wisps of hair tickled the back of his fingers, and he realized, not entirely with pleasure, that he wanted her again, although they'd made love only hours ago. Someday that had to be different. Someday soon sanity would have to return, sanity and self-control and the capacity to say goodbye. His hand fell back to the top of her seat.

"Some good information? That's the best you can do? What about the fact that she was wearing her regular habit, not her Sisters of the Garden robe?" she asked.

He stared out the window. "We don't have her in hand yet."

"We will. I know the intersection he described in Palm Springs. We'll go there next."

"Have any theories on the men with the chains?"

She knew that asking her opinion was his way of letting her know she had done all right. "What do you think about that?"

"I don't. Not yet."

"They could be hired killers."

"I doubt the right wing on Tesoro flew over to Hollywood or down to 'Alabamah' to hire someone to knock off Sister Mary Grace."

"Anything's possible."

"Yeah. Look at you and me sitting here together."

She turned her head long enough to shoot him a smile, but he was staring at the horizon.

By eight o'clock, after hours of knocking on doors, they knew they were going to have to give up for the day. They had interviewed everyone who had been at home within a block's radius from the spot where the old man had dropped off Sister Mary Grace, and no one remembered anything. There was nothing more they could do until the next morning.

"I owe you a meal out, since lunch was in," Gallagher said, as they walked back to Felice's car.

He had hardly said a personal word to her since leaving the old man's homestead. She wondered exactly what he was thinking. "I don't care if we go out. We could fix dinner at my place."

"I'll take you out. You choose where."

She weighed what he'd said and thought she understood. Every time they had made love, she had felt him move closer in a way that was unfamiliar to her. She imagined it was the same for him. He wanted time; he needed perspective.

He was remembering that they had to say goodbye.

With regret she realized Gallagher was already putting on the brakes and slowing down the breakneck progress of a relationship that had been doomed from the beginning. Neither of them had the time or the inclination for a permanent, live-in lover. They were independent, work-addicted risk takers. Two of them under one roof was impossible, and even if it wasn't, she was settled in Palm Springs and he was settled in the nation's capitol. They had days to look forward to, maybe even weeks, but they should slow down, apply a good dose of caution. He was right.

And she didn't care if he was.

"I know a place you'll like," she said, plans forming as she spoke. She didn't look at him. "You won't need to get too dressed up."

"Drop me off at your place to get my car, and I'll go back to my hotel to change."

"You'll have to show the desk some ID. They haven't seen much of you."

They didn't speak again until she pulled into her garage, where his car was parked. "I'll make the reservation," she said. "Pick me up in an hour?"

Gallagher had to fight off the temptation to follow her inside and order a meal sent in. But he knew this was better. A quiet, public meal. A late, quiet, public meal with no fireworks, then a night alone for both of them. Perspective was the only way to deal with wanting to drag her into bed every time she smiled at him, every time he touched her or smelled the entwined scents that reminded him of a desert oasis. Every time he remembered what she felt like in his arms.

"An hour," he said. He didn't even kiss her goodbye.

She was too busy making plans to pay much attention.

An hour later Gallagher stood at her door and knocked. He hadn't thought much about what to expect, not from Felice, anyway. He had thought a lot about what to expect from himself, and he had convinced himself that his self-control extended far enough that he could use some of it to master his desire for her.

He reminded himself that he cared too much about her to use her or to make promises by his actions that he wasn't prepared to keep.

Until he saw her in the doorway.

"Ready?" Her smile was the picture of innocence; the rest of her was the picture of anything but.

Her tank top was a soft, black knit that clung to every curve of her breasts with the tenacity of a man's imagination. It exposed her shoulders, but the neckline was demure, as if doing penance for the perfection of the fit. With it she wore harem pants that clasped her slender waist and hips, then flared in yards of filmy, swirling colors to her ankles, where they were cinched above flirty silver sandals. Her jewelry was silver, too, large and bold. A slave bracelet decorated one arm. Earrings dangled to her chin.

"I thought we'd try a Moroccan place I know." She searched inside a small leather purse for her keys. "I don't know your tastes, but there'll be something there you'll like. The food's outstanding."

"You look lovely."

She looked up. "Oh. Do you think so?"

"You know I do."

"Well, I hoped." She stepped out in the hallway beside him and locked the door behind her. He smelled citrus and gardenias and felt the self-control he'd talked himself into vanishing.

She chatted as he drove, pointing out landmarks and telling funny stories. He said little, but she wasn't worried. She had seen the look in his eyes when she'd appeared in the doorway.

The restaurant was behind a shopping center on Bob Hope Drive. "Don't let the outside fool you," Felice warned as Gallagher parked his Sterling. They walked past a fountain and entered through ornate brass doors. Instantly they were in another time and place.

She took his arm, the way she would have taken the arm of a friend. "I thought you might be in the mood for some fantasy tonight."

"I've been in the middle of a fantasy since I met you, desert flower."

She patted his hand. "Good."

Their host led them through the reception area to their seats. Gallagher watched Felice's smile warm the room as they were seated on low pillow-laden sofas covered in the earth tones of Berber carpeting. Felice snuggled back against one and patted the seat beside her.

Their table and the surrounding ones were enclosed in the folds of a beige-and-brown tent. Outside their window was an elaborate cactus garden.

"I've always loved Morocco," she said. "I've been to Casablanca half a dozen times to visit family friends. This is a little like being in their home."

"So you just wanted a little nostalgia?"

"Something like that."

"You didn't have any ulterior motives for choosing a place that drips romance, did you?"

She was wide-eyed. "I can't imagine what you mean."

Their elaborately garbed waiter—or servant, as he told them he was to be referred to for the rest of the evening—arrived to begin their meal with a hand-washing ceremony. He set a large urn on the table and poured water over their cupped hands from a silver spouted pot.

Felice splashed Gallagher's face with a fine spray of water. Her laughter was deep and throaty, and when it was finished, he could still hear its echoes.

She leaned over and kissed away the drops on his cheek. "You look too serious."

"I'm a serious kind of guy."

"No, you're not. Not really. Only when you think you have to be."

He watched their servant and urn disappear. "So what was that all about? They don't have soap and water in the rest rooms?"

Felice sat back, but not before she had untied and removed his tie and unbuttoned the top buttons of his shirt. "We'll be eating with our fingers." She looked as pleased as if she had begun the custom herself.

"Why?" he asked, although he already knew.

"Why? The food feels as good as it tastes and looks. Eating should be a sensuous experience. One sensory delight layered on top of another." Her smile was mysterious and seductive. "Like making love."

"That comparison just came to you?"

"Out of nowhere. Just now."

He rested his fingertips on the back of her neck and felt her stretch toward them like a cat. "Do you always get what you want, desert flower?"

"There haven't been that many things I've wanted."

"No?"

"No. Just the chance to live my life the way I want to."

"And now?"

"Now?"

"What do you want now?"

She pretended to consider. "Well, I'd like to find Sister Mary Grace and keep her safe."

"What about right now?"

"Immediate goals, you mean?" She considered again. "Well, I suppose I'd like to just let the evening unfold and see what happens."

"See what you can make happen."

"That sounds like work, and I have no intention of working tonight."

They sat in silence until their food began to arrive. Reluctantly Gallagher withdrew his hand. Felice reached over and took it, unbuttoning his cuff and folding it back over his wrist. She did the other next, and her fingers lingered on the skin she'd exposed, just at his pulse point. "Do you have goals for the evening?" she asked, smiling provocatively up at him.

He didn't answer, but she was satisfied enough at the detectable leap in his heartbeat. She sat back as wine was poured for them. She held up her glass when Gallagher's was full, too. "To goals," she said. "And to both of us getting what we really want."

He raised his glass in silence.

The meal began with eggplant cooked in an exotic mixture of spices, and a concoction of cooked cucumbers and carrots, which they scooped up with triangles of bread cut from a round loaf. Felice chatted as they ate, telling him about her visits to Morocco as a child and the summers she had spent in Spain. One moment she was the small mischievous child who had escaped her nanny and run through a bazaar, freeing wooden crates of doves meant for someone's dinner table, the next she was the endlessly seductive woman offering him a bite of bread, the last taste of eggplant.

They progressed to *b'stilla,* a mixture of chicken and almonds baked in a sugar-and-cinnamon-sprinkled pastry shell, and then on to the main course.

"You were all set to eat giant lizard, but you balk at pigeon?" Felice teased, as they worked on lamb in a sauce of prunes and almonds instead.

"I've been to Central Park." He toyed with the lamb. "I've been to Casablanca, too."

"Have you?" She smiled and offered him more of the Moroccan wine they'd ordered. "Then you should be telling stories, too."

He had been almost everywhere, and never, during any of his explorations, had he met a woman like the one snuggled next to him on the sofa. He turned to see her better, although he knew how dangerous that could be. "I would have thought that after our vacation in the desert, you would have chosen something with a different theme for tonight."

"Interesting." She pondered that as she offered him a particularly succulent piece of lamb.

He hesitated, then took it from her fingertips. She smiled slowly and brought them back to her own lips to languorously lick off the sauce.

"I suppose," she said, as he watched, his eyes banked coals, "that our time in the desert's taken on new meaning to me, now that it's over. If we hadn't been thrown together that way, we might never have . . ." She paused and smiled a little. " . . . gotten to know each other?"

He waited until their table had been cleared and the next course, couscous with vegetables served over it, had been set before them before he answered. "Then you would have had to look for . . . adventure . . . someplace else, wouldn't you?"

"I'm not sure that's how I think of you." She offered him couscous. "An adventure?" She thought about it. "No. Too mundane."

"What, then?" He opened his mouth for the couscous.

"A challenge. A possibility." She shrugged. "Kismet?"

"Our meeting was prearranged, then? By whom? The gods? One God in particular?"

She shrugged again. "Do you believe that's possible?"

"No."

"You'll have to confess our meeting was odd."

"Odd's hardly the word."

Her smile would have struck sparks off an iceberg. "Odd but . . . advantageous, wouldn't you say?"

He was fast reaching the point where he would say almost anything she wanted. He was not without experience with beautiful women, but he had never been at either end of such a perfectly planned seduction. The wine, the atmosphere, the food and, most especially, the woman had reduced his logical self to a screaming tangle of impulses, not the least of which was to drag her out of the restaurant by her beautifully cut hair and make love to her in the parking lot.

"What are you trying to do to us?" he asked, fully aware of the answer.

She looked puzzled. "Didn't you ask something like that before?"

He pushed the couscous away. "Shall we tell our servant to bring the check?"

Puzzled became more puzzled. "Not yet, Josiah. There's more coming."

"I can't eat another bite, and neither can you."

"Trust me, you don't want to miss this." Her cheek brushed his as she leaned over and kissed him lightly. "Trust me," she said, promise in her words.

The table was cleared again before he could protest. Then the music started.

He could hear the excitement building in the room beside theirs. The music was performed on instruments whose names he didn't know and promised pleasures whose names he did. He could almost feel the dust of the desert, smell the fragrance of cinnamon and rosemary, the pungent odors of leather saddles and camels.

The man in red who had served them so well appeared and poured a long stream of steaming mint tea into glasses he'd placed in front of them. A bowl of fresh figs, oranges and walnuts was set on the table alongside a platter of freshly fried pastries dipped in honey.

The music grew louder.

"And the excitement builds," Felice said. She held a fig to Gallagher's lips. He took it, but he held her fingers there, kissing each one.

Her smile was not quite so assured when he had finished.

"In this world we reap what we sow," he said softly. "Did you ever meditate on that at the Blessed Garden?"

"All the time."

"Good."

Excitement curled along her spine and settled in the pit of her stomach. "I've never sat back and waited for anything to happen to me."

"You do make things happen."

"Life is very, very short."

"Another subject for meditation?"

"Yours? Or mine?"

Neither of them was smiling now. He searched her face for proof that she could handle whatever happened between them, and then for proof that when he left, it wouldn't change her. There was no proof there, nor, he was sure, was there any on his own face.

"Who knows if this will hurt either of us?" she asked, as if she had read his mind. "But I've never been cautious. Why start now?"

"Because everything is moving too fast."

" 'Too fast' is a phrase I've never understood."

He didn't know how to answer, and he didn't have time, anyway. The music grew louder. Felice moved closer as he turned toward the doorway. A woman in apricot-and-gold began to dance.

She was draped in sheer silk scarves and spangled with jewelry. Her hips and long blond hair moved in a slow sensuous rotation, and her fingers clanged tiny cymbals.

"I couldn't let you miss this," Felice said.

Gallagher leaned back and pulled her closer. The woman began to slowly weave her way between tables.

He wondered what she hadn't wanted him to miss? The food? The entertainment? Or herself in his arms in a place where romance was in the air they breathed? The belly dancer drew nearer, but only one woman claimed his attention. He could feel her breast press against his side, smell the fragrance of her perfume, hear the soft addition of her breathing to the mournful whine of exotic horns and stringed instruments.

The dancer drew nearer still. He watched the bend and provocative sway of her body, the superbly controlled play of muscles in her abdomen. If he shut his eyes he knew he would relive the bend and sway of Felice against him as they made love. Just as surely he knew that she had planned for him to relive it.

In her own beguiling way she had let him know that she was an adult; she knew exactly what she was doing.

"Let's go," he said, when the dancer had passed their table.

"She'll be back."

"And we won't be here." He stood, lifting her with him. He dropped a large bill on the table and steered her out of the room.

They didn't speak on the way to Felice's apartment. Inside she lit candles and put Gershwin on the stereo. When she turned, Gallagher was watching her. She leaned against the cabinet as he walked toward her.

He had thought that whatever they had needed to say had been said already. But now, with candlelight flickering against her skin and the smoky sound of a saxophone in the air between them, he knew it hadn't.

"I don't know what this thing between us is about," he said, his hands settling at her waist, "but what it isn't about is working so hard to make me want you."

She smiled. "It wasn't work."

"I'm not immune to you."

"No?"

"No."

"Then I don't have to spend time thinking of ways to make you want me more?"

He smiled a little. "I didn't say that."

Her hands drifted to his shoulders. "What are you saying?"

"That I'm going to carry you into your bedroom and make love to you again."

Her arms circled his neck. She moved her hips against his to the slow rhythm of Gershwin, until he lifted her in his arms.

Chapter 14

"She doesn't carry credit cards. She doesn't have a driver's license. She doesn't have a bank account or bills she has to pay. My skip tracers say she doesn't exist." Felice finished ticking off the list of dead ends on the road to tracing Sister Mary Grace. Her skip tracers, two men and a woman who spent their days wending their way through the mazes of bureaucracy to find missing persons, had spent yesterday on the mystery of Sister Mary Grace's whereabouts and turned up nothing.

Gallagher grunted. "She exists. Just not on paper."

"All we can do is keep asking people in this neighborhood if they saw a nun the night the old man says he dropped her here. How many nuns saunter down this street? Somebody must have seen her."

"One more time around this block, then we're going to have to come up with something different."

Felice swung her car into a parking spot on the curb. The section of town where Sister Mary Grace had been dropped off had very little in common with some of the multimillion-dollar homes in more exclusive sections of the city. The houses were shabbier, the yards just patches of sand and the landscaping was minimal.

Gallagher watched Felice switch off the engine. "We're still trying to get through to some of the people she worked with on Tesoro to see if they have any idea who she might have known around here."

"There wasn't anybody home at that house yesterday." Felice pointed to a ranch-style house with a yard of stones and cement and a screen door ajar. Two children's bikes flanked the driveway. "Let's start there."

Gallagher followed her up the walk. She was dressed in red this morning, a dark red summer suit that made her skin glow with good health. The glow was no illusion. He could personally vouch for her vitality. He could also vouch for his own lack of self-control.

"Do you want to do the talking, or shall I?" she asked.

He realized how few of his thoughts today had been aimed toward the search for Sister Mary Grace. "I'll flash my identification. You talk."

"I never thought a Fed would come in handy."

"You never thought you'd end up in bed with one, either."

She flashed him a come-hither smile. "Which just goes to prove that life has some interesting surprises in store."

He thought about her words as she introduced herself to a woman in her fifties who was wiping her hands on a dish towel as she came to the door. Life had pulled a few surprises on him before, but Felice was one surprise after another. He imagined that whoever grew old with her would be constantly off balance, never sure—even as the grim reaper beckoned—that Felice wasn't going to pull some stunt to keep life interesting.

His fascination with her was a surprise, too, and not one he liked.

The woman finished wiping her hand and suspiciously extended it to shake Felice's. Felice explained limited details about Sister Mary Grace. "It's important we find her," she said, ending on a pleading note. "Her life could depend on it."

"Well, I don't know." The woman sounded reluctant to get involved. "I don't pay much attention to people who go by. Especially not at night. I work hard. I'm a housekeeper up there." She pointed toward the foothills of the San Jacintos.

She lowered her voice. "Elvis visited the house where I work. On his honeymoon," she added reverently.

Like a chameleon transforming, Felice seemed to change before Gallagher's eyes. Gone was the businesslike private eye. "No-o-o...Did you get his autograph? I have a friend who went to a party..."

Gallagher listened as the two women gossiped enthusiastically about the former king of rock and roll. The woman in the doorway, graying and old before her time, came to life as she talked about the most minute details of Elvis's stay in Palm Springs. Just as he was about to break in impatiently and bring them back to the subject, Felice maneuvered her way there herself.

"You pay attention to little details," she told the woman approvingly. "You're just the kind of person we'd hoped to find. If you'd seen Sister Mary Grace, I'm sure you'd remember. Or if you hadn't seen her, you'd know who might have."

"My grandson might have." The woman looked pleased with herself. "He and my granddaughter are staying here with me for a few weeks. Sometimes it gets boring in the evening. The whole town starts to shut down in June, and there's not much for them to do. Not too many kids around."

"I'll bet they're good company for you."

"They are. But in the evening, I work sometimes, or I get tired. My grandson Bobby gets bored. So I bought him a little telescope. It's not much, but he pretends he's a spy. When there's nothing else to do, he sits at his window and writes down what he sees. Says he's going to be a policeman." Her eyes widened, and she turned to Gallagher. "Oh, I bet he'd like to meet you."

Gallagher chalked up another win for Felice. "I think we'd like to meet him."

Nine-year-old Bobby, red-haired, plump and awestruck, had seen Sister Mary Grace. She had come from that direction, he told them proudly, pointing to a service station several blocks away. She had walked slowly, like she wasn't in a hurry. He'd thought that was funny. Didn't they think so, too?

Gallagher solemnly agreed that it did seem funny.

Anyway, Bobby continued, just about the time she'd gotten close to his grandmother's house, a car had stopped and picked her up. It was a big car, long and black, like you see in the movies. Did they know what he meant?

Gallagher assured him that they did.

Gallagher and Felice left ten minutes later with the car's license number, written carefully in Bobby's rounded script.

"There are people who think Elvis performs miracles," Felice said, folding the scrap of paper and dropping it into her purse before she started the car. "What's your opinion?"

Silently Gallagher leaned over and kissed her.

At Felice's office one wheedling phone call gave her the name and address of the car's owner.

"Griff Bryant?" She balanced the receiver on her shoulder and scrawled the address. "You're sure?"

The man at the other end of the line told her that maybe she ought to get somebody she trusted to do her dirty work. She soothed him. "You know I trust you. I'm just surprised. You're my sweetie pie, Charlie. My very best."

She looked up to see Gallagher standing in her doorway. He had been in Kelley's office making his own calls. "Thanks again." She hung up. "The car belongs to Griff Bryant." When Gallagher's expression didn't change she went on. "You know, the actor? A real he-man type? His last movie was something about terrorists on a college campus. He played the part of—"

"I know who Bryant is. I already got his address." He slid a slip of paper into his pocket. "Who's Charlie the sweetie pie?"

"A great old guy with six grandkids older than Bobby. Boy, when he retires, I'll be up a creek until I can cozy up to somebody else at Motor Vehicles."

He didn't like the thought of her cozying up to anybody. And he didn't like the fact that it bothered him. Not at all. "I called Bryant's house. He's expecting me."

"Boy, what I wouldn't give for that kind of punch."

"Are you coming?"

"What do you think?" She stepped around her desk. "You don't even need to ask. I'm in this until Sister Mary Grace is found."

"Why?"

She stopped just in front of him. If a voice alone could erect walls, his had. "What kind of question is that?"

"You've done what you were hired to do. Whether you find Sister Mary Grace or you don't, you'll still get paid. You lived at the convent. You protected her. That's all that you were required to do."

"Required?"

Gallagher wasn't sure why he continued, why he couldn't stop himself. "You got into this for the money. You told me as much. Why don't you back off now? Kelley says she's been going crazy trying to do your work and hers, too. Get back to your divorces and missing persons and let us find Sister Mary Grace."

She stared at him, trying to see beyond her own hurt. It was hard, because Gallagher kept his feelings a secret. "We've been working well together. I thought we were a team."

He didn't answer; his expression didn't change.

"That's what you don't like, isn't it?" She tentatively rested her hand on his arm. "Look, I'm not asking for anything except to be included in the search. I'm not making any demands. We're good together. Let's just keep being good together until this is over with."

He didn't feel reassured. She wasn't asking for anything; in theory, he should be a happy man. Since he wasn't, some part of him was beginning to wonder if the absence of demands was the source of his frustration.

When he didn't answer, she continued. "And you can stop throwing the money up to me. I've already told Luis I don't want it."

"You've what?"

"I talked to Luis, and I told him to forget the check. I did a lousy job of protecting Sister Mary Grace. We wouldn't be looking for her now if I'd done my job better."

"Now you've really lost your mind! After all you went through, you're turning down payment? You were almost killed watching out for her!"

"What's it to you, Josiah?"

The question was an excellent one. He couldn't seem to separate or identify what he was feeling anymore. And, worse, she seemed to know it. He pulled his arm from her grasp. "If you're coming, come on." He turned and started toward the door.

"I'll drive again." She caught up with him. "I've got something to show you after we see Mr. Bryant."

Griff Bryant, dark-haired and blue-eyed, had met Sister Mary Grace on a then-peaceful Isla Tesoro while filming one in a long series of blood-and-guts thrillers. He had been impressed by her attempts to help the people of the poverty-stricken island, and they had corresponded. When she'd called him from the service-station telephone, he had been honored to have her in his Palm Springs home.

He told Gallagher and Felice as much, while leading them through a beautifully decorated and palatial house that looked curiously untouched by human hands. "Sister Mary Grace told me you might come looking for her." He waited until Felice took a seat on the terrace overlooking a tropical grotto built into his own personal hillside before he chose a chair.

"I know she wants to be alone, that she doesn't want protection, but this isn't a game. Her life has already been threatened," Felice said.

"She's not here?" Gallagher stood, looking over the grotto with his arms folded.

"No."

"Where is she?"

"I don't know."

"This is a federal investigation. We need answers."

"I've played your part. You do it better than I do." Griff stretched his arms behind his head and tilted his chair on its back legs. "I also know you'll get tougher in a minute, but it's not going to do you any good." He smiled the smile that routinely sent millions of female hearts into overdrive and aimed it straight at Felice. "I really don't know where she is."

"She left without telling you?" Felice asked.

"She left a note. You can have it if you like, but it's not going to be much help. She just said that she'd imposed on my hospitality long enough and not to worry, God would protect her."

"When did she leave?"

"She was gone when my housekeeper arrived yesterday morning. She found the note."

"Did you look for her?"

"Do you think she's playing a game?" All four legs of Griff's chair thumped to the floor, but his voice was still pleasant. "Sister Mary Grace isn't a child. If she says she needs peace and quiet, that's what she needs."

"There are men out there who would like nothing better than to give her all the peace and quiet she can handle. Eternally."

"She's aware of that." This time his smile was different, less the heart stopper's, more the real man's. "That's probably why she didn't tell me where she was going. She's afraid I'd succumb to torture."

Felice couldn't help herself. She laughed. This man was neither arrogant nor self-righteous. She guessed that here, off-camera, he was more at home with Shakespeare than with automatic weapons. "I guess that means it won't help to pull out your fingernails."

His gaze flicked down to the fingers of her left hand. "We could have dinner together, and you could try."

"I never mix business with pleasure."

"Which was going to be the pleasure, the fingernails or the dinner?"

She laughed again.

Gallagher knew that Bryant ought to be immune to beautiful women by virtue of his constant exposure. But he wasn't immune to Felice, and she was enjoying it. He took over the interview. "Do you know if anybody in the neighborhood saw her leave?"

"I haven't asked."

"We will."

"I'm sure."

"Would you give me a call if you think of anything that could help?" Felice reached inside her purse and pulled out her business card. "I know you think she has a right to do what she wants, even if it puts her in danger, but there's more involved than her need for privacy. The political and social climate on

Isla Tesoro could change for the worse if anything happened to her. She needs to understand the situation."

Griff looked at the card, then up at her. He gave a short nod, as if he were convinced. Then he smiled again. "I sometimes come up with ideas in the middle of the night. How about your home number, too?"

"I'm in the book." She stood, and so did he. She looked at Gallagher, then back to Griff. "But if you call in the middle of the night, a man might answer."

He shrugged good-naturedly. "The only time I seem to get the girl is when there's a camera rolling."

"I find that hard to worry about."

Gallagher touched her arm, and they followed Griff to the front door.

Back in the car, she pulled out onto the quiet drive that had led them up into the canyon to Griff's house. "Before we start knocking on the neighbors' doors, I wanted to show you something. Do we have time?"

"Not much."

"It won't take much." She started to wend her way expertly from drive to road. A few minutes later, on a deserted, winding stretch going up, up, up, she stopped in front of a small house almost buried in weeds. Paint peeled off the cream-colored stucco, and several windows were broken. A "for sale" sign was the brightest spot in the yard. Felice turned off the engine. "I've got the key."

"Why?"

"Because I think this is going to be mine." She got out of the car and waited for him to join her.

"This is the house you were trying to buy?"

"No. This one's half as expensive. My realtor showed it to me at first, but I wasn't interested. It needs so much work."

"It needs demolition."

"Watch what you say." She led the way down the overgrown sidewalk to the front porch. He wasn't sure, but he thought he caught a glimpse of something ominously rodent-like slinking off the front porch as they approached.

Inside, the house was in worse shape, if possible. Gallagher let Felice lead him through the rooms. They were spacious and sunlit, but the paint on the walls looked like the original, and the house was at least thirty years old. Plaster had fallen in places, and the living room ceiling was water stained.

"Under the carpet the floors are hardwood. They'll refinish beautifully. There's Mexican tile in the kitchen and bathroom, and look at all the sunshine." Felice grew more enthusiastic as they walked slowly through the house. "I'm told the fireplace works. It's real stone, Josiah. Maybe even from this area somewhere. And look." She led him to the back of the house, to a sun-flooded family room looking over a deep canyon. "Have you ever seen a more beautiful view?"

She spun around to face him. "Have you?"

He couldn't unravel the tangle of feelings inside him. "Why this house?"

"Because I need it, and it needs me. I wouldn't be buying it to impress anybody, and when I was finished doing the work on it, it would really be mine."

"You're going to do the work?"

"Why not? If I can haul manure and milk goats and grow vegetables, I can fix up this house. Oh, I know it'll take a long time, but I've got time. And when I'm done, it'll be wonderful!" When he still didn't seem impressed, she floundered a little. "It's...it's a good investment. Most of the houses up here are worth a fortune—"

He hauled her to him and kissed her until she was silent. He held her against him at last and struggled to suppress the urge to shake her.

"You think I'm crazy, don't you?"

"Felice number five," he muttered.

"What's that supposed to mean?"

He wasn't going to tell her that this last addition to her pool of personalities was the hardest to take. This woman was the one who would someday want a husband and children to make this house ring with love and laughter. Once he was gone, someone like Griff Bryant would step into her life and do the honors.

He didn't want to think of her in love and happy without him. He didn't want to think of her creating a home for someone else.

He didn't want to think. Period. But that was becoming impossible. "We'd better get back to work." He stepped away.

"You haven't told me what you think."

"You'll do what you want, no matter what."

"I'm going to buy it." She walked to the windows and stared out at the canyon. "I can't imagine living in the other place now, even if I could afford it."

"Why live in either one? Why tie yourself down?"

"I learned something at the Blessed Garden." She faced him and realized all the implications of what she was about to say. "We're always tied down, Josiah. Nobody's really free. We have obligations to each other. We just have to decide which ties we'll honor. Which ties we need."

He wondered if that was what his dissatisfaction with his own life had been all about. It was funny, but since he'd become involved with Felice, he hadn't once questioned the direction of his life. She had kept him too busy and too off kilter. He didn't want to think about that now, though. Here, in the house she was going to make into a home, he felt more off kilter than he could remember since the day Rebecca had walked out on him.

He started toward the door. "We've got people to talk to about Sister Mary Grace."

"I wonder. Do you think you'll ever be back this way?" Felice watched as he stopped in a pool of sunlight by the living room windows. For the first time she realized that she had been fooling herself to believe she could cheerfully let him walk out of her life. She took a step toward him. "I'd like to show you what I've done with this in six months or a year. I'd like you to see that I can do it."

"You'll do it, desert flower. I have no doubts."

She waited and hoped, but he added nothing. She felt a sharp stab of disappointment. "Thanks for the vote of confidence." She started toward the living room, too. She was going to call her realtor and make an offer on the house tonight, but somehow the pleasure was gone.

There was no Bobby with a spy telescope near Griff's house to give them clues about Sister Mary Grace. But there was a gardener at one of the estates down the road who remembered a taxi passing early the morning Sister Mary Grace had left Griff's. By early afternoon they had tracked down the taxi and followed the lead to first one place, then another.

The leads ended at dinnertime, at the ultimate dead end.

"Sometimes I wish I'd stayed with Spanish literature." Felice plopped down on a seat at the Palm Springs airport—Los Angeles International in miniature. "Right now I could be discussing Don Quixote instead of charging my own windmills."

"We don't have any hard evidence that Sister Mary Grace left the city."

"We don't have any evidence that she didn't, either." Felice leaned back and closed her eyes. "I guess I'm out of this now. There's nothing I can do at this point that you and your cohorts and your computers can't do a hundred times faster."

He absorbed the picture of her, black crescent eyelashes against her cheeks, hair spilling carelessly over her forehead. "I've got somebody coming over to examine manifests for every flight that's gone out of here in the last twelve hours."

"And a couple of somebodies to question every employee of every airline?"

"Yeah."

"And somebody at LAX to watch the flights to Tesoro?"

"That too."

"You never really needed me, did you?"

When he didn't answer, she opened her eyes and stared into his. "You were just trying to be sure I stayed out of trouble and didn't ruin your investigation."

"You didn't come anywhere close to ruining it. You got some good information."

"I wanted to find her. I wanted to. She might have listened to me. We were friends. She still thinks you're the handyman."

"You were doing penance for pretending you were a nun."

"Maybe." She touched his shoulder. "So what now?"

"I'm staying here to go over what I know with the men I called."

"I can have supper waiting for you."

He paused for just a second, as if he wasn't sure how to deliver the next sentence. "I'm heading back to my hotel."

He had fostered no illusions that he was going to stay with her forever, but hearing that their time together was already over was a jab at an already too vulnerable heart. She was well trained in interpreting nuance. Gallagher had just said goodbye, and tonight no fanciful seduction was going to make a difference. Her hand dropped to her lap. She took a deep breath before she spoke. "I see."

"This is a crucial time in the investigation. I'll probably be in and out all evening."

"I'm sure."

He paused again. "After she's been found, I'll be flying back to Washington."

She knew better than to argue, and she knew better than to beg. She had more pride than to make him feel sorry for her. In his own way Gallagher had been pulling away from her for the past twenty-four hours. She had never been more than a temporary pleasure in his life, and nothing she could say or do was going to change that. She could leave with grace; she could leave with dignity.

She could leave quickly.

She got to her feet. "Well, don't let me keep you." She rummaged in her purse for her car keys. Anything to keep her hands busy. "You'll let me know if you find her, won't you?"

"I'll be sure you know." Gallagher stood, too. He hadn't planned to say goodbye this way, not in the middle of an airport at the exact moment that Barker and two other agents were coming through the door. But then, plans had never had anything to do with his relationship with Felice.

"Your car's parked at my office," she said.

"I'll have somebody pick it up."

"I'd like to say it's been fun . . . but it hasn't really, has it?"

Barker was striding toward them with a curious bowlegged stride that said a lot about his weeks at the dude ranch. Gallagher bent forward and brushed a kiss across her lips. "Take care of yourself, desert flower."

"I always do."

"Yeah. I've seen that."

She wanted to say something flip, something that would leave him smiling, but for once, humor failed her. "Goodbye, Josiah. Godspeed." She turned before the last syllable had ended and started toward the door.

Barker and his men reached Gallagher a few moments later. "Don't tell me that was the nun detective."

Gallagher was still watching Felice walk away. Usually she had the sassiest, most eye-riveting walk a man could ask for. Now she walked like a woman with her soul laid bare. "No."

"No?"

He watched the automatic doors slide closed behind her. Only then did he look at Barker. "No. She's a whole lot more than that," he said.

"If the nuns at my elementary school had looked like that I'd have..." Barker stopped. "A whole lot more, or a whole lot more to you?"

Gallagher shot him a look that effectively ended that line of questioning. "We may need someone to go up into the mountains on horseback to check out some leads. You volunteering?"

Barker winced, but he knew Gallagher too well to be truly intimidated. "I heard we need someone on foot to check out leads in the desert. You volunteering?"

"If the company's right, maybe," he said enigmatically. Then he reached in his pocket and pulled out a memo pad. "Let's go over what we know together. I want to find Sister Mary Grace, and I want to find her now."

Chapter 15

"You're sure you feel like being here today?" Kelley leaned against Felice's door and observed her friend. "You haven't taken any time to recover since you got back."

"I'd rather be here than at home." Felice pushed her hair off her forehead. "And there's so much to catch up on, I can't see leaving any more of it for you. I've got an appointment this morning with some woman who wants us to look for a missing husband. Then I'm going to see Luis."

Kelley knew that Felice's search yesterday had ended at the airport, because Felice had called and given her the details the night before. "You haven't heard anything about Sister Mary Grace this morning?"

Felice shrugged. "Nothing. But I want to fill Luis in on everything we did find. He deserves that much."

"You're really not going to take his money?"

"I've already told him I don't want it." Felice looked up at her friend. "I know this leaves you high and dry, too, Kell. You've been covering for me and working too hard since I left, but I'll make it up to you."

"What about the house you wanted?"

"They've got other buyers lined up, so I was able to withdraw my offer with no problem. I'm buying a different one instead. You'll like it."

"Cheaper?"

"Much."

"I'll like it, then." Kelley pushed herself away from the door. "You know, this might not be any of my business, but I got the feeling that you and Gallagher . . ."

"Not anymore."

Kelley considered that. "I liked him."

Felice didn't look at her. "So did I."

"I wonder . . . I'm just curious. Did you tell him how you felt about him?"

This time Felice looked up. "What's that supposed to mean?"

"Seems simple enough to me."

"He's not stupid. He knows how I feel."

"How *do* you feel?"

Felice stared at her.

"Well?"

"I'm not sure." She saw that Kelley was going to wait for a better answer. "He's . . . I was . . ."

Kelley rolled her eyes.

"I think I'm in love with him," Felice said softly. "Oh, God, I think I really am, and I don't want to be."

"We can safely assume he doesn't know, since you hardly do yourself."

"What good would it do to tell him?" Felice stood and walked to the window looking out on the shopping-center courtyard. Immediately her head began to ache. She blamed the sun's glare off the concrete walkways, even though she knew better.

"What good would it do not to?" Kelley crossed the room and stood behind her. "You've always been such a self-sufficient good-time girl. How is anybody supposed to know you need them? Maybe you should tell Gallagher and find out if he needs you."

"He's leaving. For all I know he may already be gone."

"Don't tell me you don't know where to reach him. You can track anybody, anywhere."

"Except Sister Mary Grace." Felice folded her arms.

"You're not going to talk to him?"

"He made it clear at the beginning that he didn't want to get tangled up with me or anybody." She forced a laugh. "I thought that would be fine. I didn't want to get involved, either. I thought we'd just say so long and wasn't it great while it lasted?"

"You're not really the person you were before you went to the convent, are you?"

Felice turned. "Maybe I never really was that person."

"Maybe you're starting to slow down a little and figure out who you are."

"Is that good or bad? Because this person hurts."

Kelley rested her hand on Felice's shoulder in comfort. "I've always loved this person. Maybe now it's just a little easier."

"The nun's not on any of the manifests, and nobody remembers her being here." Barker delivered the bad news to Gallagher over a late morning fast-food breakfast. "Apparently she stopped dressing like a nun at some point along the way. Hundreds of middle-aged women go through that airport, and no one paid any attention to this one."

"Damn it. Somebody saw her. Somebody had to." Gallagher set his cup down too hard, and hot coffee washed over the back of his hand. He muttered another, stronger curse.

Barker handed him a wad of napkins. "You know, you don't have to stay with this. You did just what you were asked to, and a damn fine job of it. We can take over from here."

The words sounded all too familiar to Gallagher. He had said them, or something like them, to Felice yesterday. He didn't like hearing them any more than she had. Neither did he like having everything remind him of her. And since she'd walked out of the airport, everything had.

He forced himself back to the issue of Sister Mary Grace. "I'm in charge until she's found—which had better be soon."

"We've got everybody she's had contact with, everybody she knows, under surveillance. We're watching this airport and

LAX. We're still talking to anyone who might remember seeing her yesterday."

Gallagher sipped what was left of his coffee and didn't respond.

"Did you check with your detective friend this morning to see if she had any new information?" Barker asked.

Gallagher pierced him with a rapier stare.

Barker shrugged. "Would you like me to do it?"

"She's off the case."

"I've read her file. She's not the type to be off the case till it's over. She'll have her ear to the ground, no matter what she's told you." Barker looked at his watch. "In fact, she's on her way to Luis Cortez's spread just about now."

Gallagher knew there was no point in pretending he wasn't interested. "How do you know?"

"I told you we were covering everybody who knows the nun and everybody she's seen. It was a simple matter to find out Cortez's plans for the day, just so we could keep a better eye on him."

"Felice feels like she owes the guy something, even though she's not taking a cent for what she's done for him. She's probably going to tell him what little we know. It won't hurt anything."

"*If* that's why she's going."

Gallagher swished his coffee grounds. "Why else would she?"

"Maybe she's heard something."

"She'd let me know if she had."

"Would she?"

The coffee grounds settled in splotches at the bottom of his cup. He wished they were tea leaves; he wouldn't mind a quick look at his future. "I don't know. She's not predictable, that's about all you can count on with her."

"So maybe she heard something?"

"Maybe."

"Do you want me to check it out?" Barker sat back with his hands behind his head, like a man who had no intention of going anywhere.

"I'll go. I've got nothing better to do right now." Gallagher glanced up at his colleague. "Wipe that nasty little smile off your face, Barker."

"You know, you used to terrify me once upon a time."

"And I don't anymore?" His tone would have inspired terror in anyone else.

"Under the give-'em-hell boots, you've got feet of clay about this woman. I like knowing that." Barker's smile broadened. "Reminds me of Vandergriff before he went back for *his* woman. You should have watched him more carefully, Gallagher. You'd see the similarities now."

"I'm not Simon, and Felice isn't Tate. She's an impulse-driven anomaly who'd keep a man in chaos all his life. She's not thinking about marriage, and even if she were, I don't want to settle down."

"Neither did Tate and Simon. But they've been married two years, and from what I hear they're starting a family."

That was news to Gallagher. "They've got a kid on the way?"

"If it can happen to Simon, it can happen to anybody."

Gallagher narrowed his eyes. "You're enjoying this, aren't you?"

"Unprofessional, isn't it?"

"Was it the horse?"

"Was it the horse?" Barker pretended to think about it. "You mean the horse who didn't stop running around the ring until one of the cowboys came out and threw a rope over his head?"

"Yeah, that's the one."

"Or was it the time you sent me out into the wilds of Arkansas to look for Simon, and Tate knocked me out with the butt of a shotgun?"

Gallagher knew when to quit. He stood. "I'm going to Cortez's house."

"Stay in touch," Barker said. "I miss you when you're gone."

The drive out to Luis's house was just another chance for Felice to think—and she'd done plenty of that since she'd said goodbye to Gallagher. Thinking had gotten to be a habit at the Blessed Garden, and now she was afraid it was ingrained forever.

She was no longer quite the creature of impulse and action that she had once been. She doubted she would ever be as willing to jump into anything without looking carefully at it. She had learned some truths about who she really was. She didn't have to prove herself, and she didn't have to try so hard to be something other than the daughter her parents had wanted. All the myriad Felice Cristys were okay.

Although none of them felt okay at the moment.

She reached Indio and automatically made the turns that would take her to Luis's. She wasn't looking forward to confronting him in person. She was good at what she did, and she had rarely failed this dramatically. Luis had trusted her with Sister Mary Grace's life, and now Sister Mary Grace was missing.

She turned up the drive and tried to plan what she would say as she drove toward the house. No one was working in the gardens today, but she saw activity in the date groves. She parked where she'd parked before and walked through the courtyard where she'd sat and talked with Luis. He wasn't there.

Nor, as it turned out, was he inside waiting for her.

"I'm sorry, but he's gone, Miss Cristy." The same young woman who had served tea on Felice's previous visit delivered the surprise. "He asked me to tell you it was an emergency, and he couldn't get hold of you in time to stop you from coming here."

"Did he say what kind of an emergency?"

The maid shook her head.

Whether that was true or not, Felice knew she would get no further with direct questions. She relaxed her posture and gave the other woman a friendly smile. "Have you ever been stood up, umm..." She paused, as if searching for the woman's name.

"Sandy."

She snapped her fingers. "Sandy. That's right. I'm awful at names. But don't you just hate it when a man breaks a date?"

"Oh, I don't think he was breaking a date exactly, Miss Cristy."

"Felice."

The maid smiled shyly at her. "Felice."

Felice abandoned her own smile and looked wistful. "Luis is a good man, and usually so kind. I can't imagine why he would do this to me...unless there's somebody else. Maybe this is just his way of telling me..."

"Oh, no, I don't think it's anything like that," Sandy assured her. "He got a phone call. Just a little while ago. He seemed upset. He told me he had to go up into the mountains."

"Then it's just what I thought. I know he has a *friend* with a house in the mountains." Felice drew the corners of her mouth down farther.

"No, no, it's nothing like that, I'm sure. I heard him on the phone. He said he was going to take the Tramway. There's a state park at the top, isn't there? There aren't any houses."

Felice wished all her feelers ended this productively. "You're right. I must be worried for nothing."

The maid beamed. "See, I told you."

"Will you tell Luis I came? And that I'll wait for his call?"

"Of course I will," Sandy said warmly.

Felice thanked her and left. She didn't worry whether her message would be delivered or not. She was going to the top of Mount San Jacinto to find Luis herself. And she hoped she was going to find one saintly but sneaky nun emergency by his side.

The Palm Springs Aerial Tramway climbed nearly six thousand feet in fourteen minutes. The temperature dropped appreciably during the trip, so that summer clothes worn at the bottom were no longer appropriate for hiking in the thirteen-thousand-acre state park at the top.

Felice had been up the Tramway often enough to know how cool it would be on the mountain. In the parking lot she pulled on the jacket that matched her jade green dress and tied a wide silk scarf around her neck. She traded her espadrilles for canvas flats that she kept in the backseat for such an occasion.

Halfway out of the car, she realized the jacket could be camouflage for her shoulder holster and gun. She debated, then took off the jacket again and snapped the holster in place. If she could trail Sister Mary Grace to the park, so could anyone else. She had to be careful.

"I'm meeting a friend up at the top," she told the woman at the ticket booth. She gave her a conspiratorial smile "A good-looking older man with silver hair. Very elegant. Do you remember if anyone like that has come through here recently?"

"Don't know, honey." The woman handed her a ticket and change.

Fresh from her success with Sandy, Felice tried again. "You know how it is. I just wanted to know so I could pretty up down here if he's already there."

"Don't know, honey."

Felice figured that one out of two wasn't bad, and what Sandy had told her had been more important. "Thanks, honey," she said and went into the waiting room to sit until the next car arrived.

The enclosed cars that swung from steel cables as they glided toward the mountain peak were large enough for almost a hundred people, but June was an off month for tourism. During the season she was sure the room would be nearly full, but on this scorching Thursday less than a dozen wilted fellow travelers were waiting to board.

A woman with two small girls came in and sat down beside her. The younger of the two, who looked like she was about two, began to roar her displeasure and the woman shrugged apologetically. "It's the heat," she said. "That's why we're going up for the day."

Felice watched the children warily. She'd had very few experiences with them, except for several she'd been hired to track for custody cases. And then it had been their parents she had found most interesting.

Briefly she scanned the waiting room as the little girl continued to roar. A group of senior citizens with cameras and fists full of tourist brochures got up and moved to the other side of the room. Two men in sports shirts, who had come in just after the screaming child, looked at each other as if to ask whether the trip was going to be worth it.

Felice turned to the little girl. "Do you want to hear what you sound like?" She reached inside her purse and pulled out the tape recorder that she always carried to keep her log. She flicked it on and held it in front of the child, who seemed interested, but not enough to stop crying.

Felice recorded for almost half a minute, then rewound. "Let's see what you sound like." She pushed the playback button.

The little girl quieted in fascination as she listened to her own screams. The older girl, three or four, came around to Felice's side. "My turn."

Obligingly Felice let her record a song she said she'd learned in preschool. Without asking, she climbed on Felice's lap while the tape recorder rewound.

"Katie!" her mother said. "No one invited you up there."

"It's okay," Felice assured her. "You've got your hands full." She played back the song, and both children listened with the enthusiasm of opera patrons. Felice listened, too, but her mind was on the feel of the little girl against her. She was so small and so alive. She smelled like bubble gum, and her mop of curls tickled Felice's chin.

She wondered how her own child would feel against her. Gallagher's child.

Their car arrived, and everyone in the waiting room stood. The children's mother thanked Felice for helping with them, and she and the girls went to stand in line. Felice followed and took a seat inside the car beside the two men she'd noticed earlier. She spent the next fourteen minutes wondering why she had never realized that she wanted children.

At the top she disembarked with the other passengers and waved goodbye to the little girls. The air was cool and pine-scented, a different ecology altogether from the valley below. She strolled unobtrusively from one observation area to another, looking for Luis and Sister Mary Grace, but she hadn' really expected to find them in the midst of a group, and she didn't.

She weighed her choices. There were a variety of trails, all leading down and away from Mountain Station, where the Tramway ran. She tried to put herself in the place of Luis and Sister Mary Grace. They weren't here to savor the mountain air or to get their aerobic exercise. If they were here at all, it was to stroll and talk where no one would bother them. She assessed her choice of trails and started down the one that seemed most promising.

Gallagher spent just enough time with the special agent stationed across from Luis's property to find that Felice had been to Luis's and gone. Where she had gone was a question the man couldn't answer.

Next he took the same route that Felice had followed to Luis's front door and confronted the same young woman. There was no reason for him to pretend to be someone he was not. He flashed his identification and asked a few questions. Sandy told him what she had told Felice.

Back at the entrance to Luis's drive, he stopped long enough to find out why the agent hadn't noticed Luis leaving, since that was what the government was paying him to do. Why he hadn't seen Luis leave was another question the man couldn't answer. Gallagher instructed him to call for backup at the mountaintop, then headed toward the Tramway.

As he broke the speed limit he asked himself why Felice— who had probably suspected exactly what he was suspecting— hadn't called to tell him where she was going and why. He knew the answer before the question was fully formed. He had told her goodbye. Period. He had left no opening for ever seeing or hearing from her again. She was a proud, independent woman who believed in her own capabilities. She probably believed she didn't need any help, particularly not from the man who had as much as told her to get out of his life.

He didn't want her out of his life. As he drove faster, that fact, that indisputable reality, became crystal clear to him. There had been something missing, some*one* missing, from his solitary climb up the career ladder. He had been empty inside for years, and his solution had been to work harder. Somehow Rebecca, who hadn't succeeded in swallowing him whole, had tapped into all his insecurities when she'd left him. She had convinced him, without half trying, that he wasn't a man who valued relationships, wasn't a man who needed a woman and the joys living with a woman could give him.

He hadn't needed Rebecca's immature demands, it was true, but he had needed the sharing, the joys they had never found together. He still needed them, but not with Rebecca. Never with Rebecca.

He was driving like a maniac by the time the next fact crystallized. There could be three people in danger at the top of Mount San Jacinto: a distinguished, influential resident of the Coachella Valley; a nun whose courage and compassion were making waves in the world community; and one impulsive, risk-taking private investigator.

It was the private investigator for whom he was breaking the speed limit, because the private investigator was the woman he needed. The woman he loved.

Felice was almost ready to turn back and try another trail when she heard voices coming through the bushes beyond the trail's end. She stopped and listened, but the voices were a low rumble. She knew she was going to have to find her way through the dense overgrowth to trace them. She just hoped she wasn't about to uncover young lovers in their favorite trysting place.

The bushes tore at her dress and jacket, and she twisted her ankle on the rocky pathway. The voices grew louder, although she couldn't distinguish any words. When she finally emerged she was at the edge of the mountainside. Fifteen yards to her left, Luis sat on a rock with a slender, attractive woman in pale blue slacks and a matching lightweight sweater. It took Felice a moment to realize the woman was Sister Mary Grace.

The nun's hair was a strawberry blond just beginning to turn a lighter, but not unflattering shade. It fell to the collar of her sweater in natural waves. She looked like nothing more nor less than a Palm Springs matron out for the day with her favorite man.

For a moment Felice was speechless, although this was what she had hoped to find. Then she cleared her throat. "May I join the party?"

"Sister Felicia, I presume," Sister Mary Grace said. She patted the rock beside her, moving closer to Luis to make room for Felice. "Lovelier in green than in white. And more comfortable?"

Felice sat beside her. "I'm not sure what I expected, but I didn't think I'd find you looking like this."

"My order left the Middle Ages a long time ago. I wear a habit on Tesoro because it's expected by the people there, but I'm never required to wear it except for special occasions."

"Mother Jeanne never took after you with her scissors?"

"I told her I'd prefer to keep my hair longer." She smiled. "Didn't you know that having your hair chopped off wasn't mandatory at the Blessed Garden?"

Automatically Felice's hand rose to her bare neck. "I guess that was just one of the thousand and two mistakes I made while I was there."

Luis spoke. "You're a better investigator than you thought. You found us."

"I just hope I don't come up against anyone as crafty as this woman again." Felice's hand dropped to Sister Mary Grace's shoulder. "I know you didn't want anybody following you. I respect that. I really do. But there are things you don't know."

Sister Mary Grace's expression grew serious. "Luis told me about your kidnapping. I'm so very sorry—"

"It was you they thought they'd gotten, Sister. And if they had gotten you instead of me and killed you, then the political situation in Tesoro would have erupted again. You wouldn't have been a martyr. When the smoke cleared you would have been nothing more than the tool the right wing used to overthrow the moderates."

"I don't want to be a martyr or a political football. All I've ever wanted is to speak out for people who have no voice."

"You can speak more effectively alive than dead."

"I had to have some time alone to decide what was best for everybody."

"Can't you think in a safe place?" Felice asked. "I mean, I can't think so well when people are shooting at me or leaving me for dead in the desert. I can't believe it helps you, either."

"I'd prefer a safe place. But someone is always watching me in the safe places. I had to be alone to hear God's voice."

There was little Felice could say to that. She wasn't sure of everything she had learned at the Blessed Garden, but she had learned to trust the faith that led women like Sister Mary Grace to the religious life. She was touched.

She mustered what professionalism she could. "Do you think you could ask Him to continue the conversation at Luis's house? There are too many people who could be hurt if you keep making yourself a target."

"Luis?" Sister Mary Grace turned to the man beside her and took his hand. "Shall we go to your house while we make the arrangements?"

Felice interrupted. "Arrangements?"

The word was still echoing in the air when the bushes behind them rustled. Instinctively Felice's hand slipped under her jacket as she turned. The two men she had sat beside in the Tramway car were making their way toward her. She caught a flash of gold chains at the neck of one of the men's shirts, and she was on her feet starting toward them as she drew her gun.

"Get down," she shouted behind her. She couldn't look to see if her order had been obeyed. Her eyes were on the bald man whose gun was drawn now and pointed straight at her heart.

"Drop the gun, please," he said. His voice dripped with the sounds of a hot Birmingham night.

"I'd rather not," she said, making a point of where her gun was aimed.

"Do you want me to take them down first?" the other man asked, pointing *his* gun behind Felice.

She scrambled for a solution, any solution that didn't involve tossing her gun on the ground, but none appeared. She forced her clenched fingers apart, and the gun hit the dirt at her feet.

"Kick it over the side," the bald man told her.

She had the ridiculous desire to argue with him. Her revolver was a friend. She rarely wore it, even more rarely needed it—and then usually only for show. But she felt almost superstitiously attached to the little .38, and she didn't want it to spend the rest of its days on some inaccessible mountain ledge.

She pulled herself together and gave it a good, healthy shove with her foot. She would be blessed indeed if losing the revolver was the worst thing that happened to her.

She heard movement behind her, and the man turned his gun that way again. She prayed that neither Luis nor Sister Mary Grace would try anything foolish.

"If you shoot," she said, moving closer to the man so that she was more thoroughly blocking a shot to Sister Mary Grace, "someone will hear you. There's no good way to get out of here except by the Tramway or straight down the mountainside. You'll be caught before you get that far."

She took one more step until she was directly in front of the rock shielding the others. She remembered what Gallagher had said about the men pursuing Sister Mary Grace. Ex-altar boys, he had called them. Political zealots from Tesoro who were probably so torn about being sent to murder her that they were just waiting to sneak into confession when no one was looking.

These men didn't look as if they were from Tesoro, much less as if they'd ever set foot inside the door of a church. But she had to bank on the fact that nobody, nobody, was so hardened that he wouldn't feel some guilt about stalking a nun.

"Put your guns away and head out of here," she said, as calmly as she could. "Deep inside you must know that nothing good can come from killing Sister Mary Grace."

"Sister Mary Grace?" The bald man turned his head to spit; then he faced her. She saw he was grinning. "What makes you think it's Sister Mary Grace we want?"

She stared at him.

"It's you, doll," the other man said. "You with the pretty green dress and the sassy green eyes."

"What are you talking about?"

"We've come at the request of . . . a friend of yours."

"My friends don't send men with guns after me."

"Yeah, doll, probably not most of your friends. But this one, see, this friend's different. He wants you to remember him real good, and he wants us to help you."

Desperately Felice searched her mind for someone, anyone, so low class that he would have sicced these B-movie hounds from hell on her. As a private investigator, she routinely displeased somebody. Almost every time she took a case, someone was the worse for it. But she tried hard not to hurt the innocent. She turned down cases when vindictiveness or retribution were the sole motives of the person requesting her services. She refused to take cases fueled by prejudice or uncontrolled greed.

The not-so-innocent had always been fair game, though. And sometimes it was hard to tell the difference.

"Well, you've got me," she said, when no one face, no one case, would come to mind. "I don't know who your friend is, so he's going to be hard to remember."

"He says you ruined his life," the bald man said. "He doesn't have *anything* now because of you. Everything he worked for all his life is gone."

"I don't have that kind of power," Felice protested.

"You're making a big mistake," Luis said from behind her.

The bald man told him to shut up, but Luis continued to argue. Sister Mary Grace chimed in.

The diversion gave Felice a moment to think. Mentally she had already eliminated half her cases, because at least half of them had been so benign that no one lost anything.

She tried to concentrate on the other half, the custody suits, the divorce cases, the searches for debtors. More than once she'd tried to persuade clients to give up their quests for blood from a spouse or ex-spouse. Kelley was better at that than she was; Kelley was a born counselor as well as a crack shot, but Felice had done her share of counseling, too.

Silently she whizzed through case after case until the bald man spoke to her. "Your friend thinks your head is swollen," he said. "He thinks you need to be humbled."

"I've gotten so humble in the last few weeks, he wouldn't even know me."

The bald man laughed. "He'll be glad to hear it, but it won't be enough."

She knew he was waiting for her to ask. She hoped they could bargain. "And what *would* be?"

The other man answered. "Our friend says you made him lose everything. Everything."

"You're repeating yourself." She watched him raise his gun. He did it slowly, with great purpose. His hand was as steady as the proverbial rock. She knew her only chance was to duck at the exact moment he fired, to launch herself at him and knock the gun from his hand.

But as she tensed, readying herself for a last-ditch assault, she heard movement behind her again and saw the other man raise his gun and point it toward the rock. She knew that if she carried out her plan, Sister Mary Grace and Luis would surely die. She swallowed hard and thought for just the briefest moment of Gallagher and what they could have had together. Then she crossed herself and prepared to die.

"Our friend thinks you should know what it's like to lose everything, too," the bald man said.

He smiled. Then he pulled the trigger. There was an audible click. Nothing else.

"Now you know," he said. And he lowered his gun.

Chapter 16

Felice's knees began to buckle. Only the greatest effort of will kept her upright. "Who sent you?" she whispered.

"I told you. A friend of yours. Someone who thought your life ought to flash before your eyes."

The man with the gold chains turned his gun on her as she took a step toward the bald man. "That chamber wasn't loaded, doll. But it's the only one that wasn't. Mine's primed and ready to go, and my finger's all itchy."

"You bastards!"

"Hey, we could have killed you, but we didn't. You got a good scare, we get a good paycheck, your friend gets a good laugh." The man motioned to his partner, and both of them began to back toward the bushes, waving their revolvers in warning. "Don't think about following us. Somebody could get hurt."

They disappeared through the bushes. Felice sank to the rock behind her. She felt arms come around her, and she leaned against the first available shoulder, which turned out to be Luis's.

"Felice." He patted her arm. "Are you all right?"

She shook her head.

His arms tightened. She felt Sister Mary Grace's soft hand stroking her cheek, and she grasped it and held it there. She was fighting off shock and tears, and it was a moment before she could speak.

"I thought I'd bought the farm for sure this time," she gasped.

Luis was obviously chagrined. "I tried to help, we both did. I—"

"There wasn't anything you could have done," she reassured him. "I was praying you were protecting Sister Mary Grace."

"He threw himself over me," Sister Mary Grace said dryly. "A very compromising position for a nun."

"I'm so sorry," Felice said, still fighting for calm. "I didn't know. I just didn't know!"

"What in the hell's going on here? Didn't know what?"

Felice felt Luis and Sister Mary Grace draw back. She opened her eyes and saw Gallagher in front of her. The oxygen seemed to drain from her lungs. Her head spun, and tears welled in her eyes.

He took one look at her face and fell to the rock beside her to pull her into his arms. "Are you all right?" He pushed the hair off her forehead and tilted her face to his. She was the color of clouds, and her eyes sparkled like stars as tears began to spill down her cheeks.

"Will someone tell me what the hell's going on?" he snapped. "Is she all right or isn't she?"

Luis explained what had happened.

"Who were they?" Gallagher framed her face. "Come on. Help me a little here."

"I don't know who they were." She stared at him and saw something she was afraid to name in his eyes. "But they were the same men the old guy who gave Sister Mary Grace a ride told us about. I should have been suspicious when I saw them at the station. Bald. Gold chains. I should have been paying attention, but I was busy thinking about having kids...." Her voice trailed off.

"What do kids have to do with this?" Panic that she could have died made his voice sharper than he'd intended.

"Nothing." She took a deep breath and pulled away from him. She damned her overactive imagination. "Not a damn thing." She jerked her head to indicate the woman behind her. "Meet Sister Mary Grace."

Gallagher spared the nun one glance and a nod before he turned back to Felice. "Are the men connected with a case you've worked on?"

"That's all I can figure." She wiped her cheeks, furious both for crying and for believing for a moment that Gallagher really cared. "Funny, isn't it? All this time we thought it was Sister Mary Grace they wanted, and it was me."

"Then you think they're the ones who kidnapped you?"

She shrugged. "Who else? And when they didn't get a chance to deliver their little message before I threw myself out of the car, they came back to try again. Maybe they were going to leave me in the desert that night, then make a call to the authorities and tell them where I was. I don't know."

"We'll get them." He stood. "I've got to get to the station and send a message down the mountain. I've got backup coming. They'll nail these guys."

"It's not a federal case."

"We'll make it one." He got descriptions of the men from Sister Mary Grace and Luis before he told them his plans. "I want the three of you to follow me a little way. There's another path that veers off this one. I took it first. We'll go down about eighty yards to another path into the woods. You can take that and wait at the end for me. I'll come for you with a couple of my men, and we'll get you down the mountain safely."

"Those men are gone now. Aren't we safe?" Luis asked.

Gallagher shook his head. "We aren't going to make any assumptions."

Felice got to her feet. Her legs felt wobbly, but she told herself she was going to make it. She didn't look at Gallagher. "He's right, and the sooner we do it, the sooner we can get to Luis's."

"Luis's?" Gallagher asked.

"That's where they want to go. Any objections?"

He heard the ice in her voice, and knew he deserved it. Now wasn't the time to warm her up, though. Anger at him would carry her down the path and back to Luis's. Besides, this wasn't the moment to discuss their feelings for each other.

"None." He stepped through the bushes and peered up and down the path to be sure it was empty before he rejoined them. "I'm going to let you lead the way, desert flower, and I'll take up the rear."

"Don't call me that again." She moved closer to him, hands on hips. "I can barely tolerate your overbearing, macho orders as it is. I'm not now, nor have I ever been, your little bimbo." Her voice was just loud enough for him to hear. "Get out of my way and let me do my job."

He stepped aside without a word, and she checked out the path herself before she motioned for Sister Mary Grace and Luis to follow her.

The authorities swarmed through Luis's house like bees through a summer garden. They took statements from everybody and gave their own opinions freely. An expert on the Isla Tesoro political situation, who had been working closely with Gallagher's men, took Sister Mary Grace aside to acquaint her with all the new developments on the island.

Sandy served coffee and sandwiches and assured Felice she wasn't upset that she'd been tricked into telling her Luis's whereabouts. Gallagher left, and Felice tried to leave twice, but both times she was detained for more questions. The third time she was told to stay put for the rest of the day. A search was on for the men who had threatened her, and she was safer at Luis's than she would be back at her office.

By early evening the house began to clear. Questions had been answered, opinions exchanged. There were men stationed all around the perimeter of Luis's house, and the property was secure.

Felice came out to the patio behind Luis's house to say goodbye and saw Sister Mary Grace and Luis, hand in hand, walking through the gardens to his date groves.

She was exhausted and more. The hollow feeling inside her had grown until it threatened to empty her completely. Her "friend," whoever he was, had gotten exactly what he had intended. Her life *had* flashed before her eyes, then continued flashing in strobe light snatches for the rest of the afternoon.

She had seen a woman obsessed with proving herself, a woman who had sacrificed a meaningful personal life on the altar of excitement and action. She was courageous and adventurous, and there was nothing wrong with either; the world was a better place because of people just like her. But in her rush to show the world who she was and wasn't, she had shown very few people what lay in the deepest regions of her heart. Kelley and a few others knew the whole Felice. The rest of the world saw only a part.

She wondered what Gallagher had seen. He was gone again, this time walking out of her life without even a goodbye. She wished she could ask him. What had she revealed to him that had chased him away? Too much? Too little?

"She loves him."

Felice turned to see Gallagher standing behind her. He was still dressed as he had been, dark pants, lighter sports jacket. Her heart squeezed with longing.

He stared off into the distance at Sister Mary Grace and Luis. "What made her leave him?"

She turned away. "You'd have to ask her."

"When Rebecca left *me*, I asked her why. She said I wanted her to be more than she was." He laughed humorlessly. "I never figured that out. Still haven't."

"You wanted her to accept you. And you probably wanted her to be a person in her own right. Maybe she was scared."

"She got married again, two months after our divorce was final. Now she's got three little girls. Maybe she'll raise them to be people in their own right."

"We can hope." Felice stared out at the long-ago lovers. She wasn't sure where Gallagher was leading, but she did know she didn't want to talk about his ex-wife anymore. "They look deep in conversation, don't they?"

"Has she told you what she's planning to do?"

"Not yet. Has she told you?"

"No."

"She could stay here. Luis would marry her in a moment. She's served the church well in Isla Tesoro. Maybe the time's come for her to follow her heart."

"How do you suppose someone does that, desert flower."

This time she didn't balk at the nickname. "Boy, are you asking the wrong person."

"Think so?"

She didn't turn, but he sounded closer. "I don't know any more about how to do that than the man in the moon."

"I thought women came into the world knowing how."

"Which just goes to show you how little men know about women."

"Men in general, or just me?"

"You think we're all born sweet and cuddly, like your Rebecca. You think we grow up dreaming about long-stemmed roses and diamond rings, that we swoon over the first man who blinks at us and dream about leading him down the aisle. Well, it's not true. Some of us grow up wanting to discover new continents or fight side by side with Sitting Bull or play cops-and-robbers for real."

"And those women aren't interested in men?"

"Did I say that?"

"What did you say?"

"That maybe sometimes we're not born knowing how to get everything we want. That maybe we have to fight so hard just to breathe that we don't learn how to settle in with a man, how to even know when a man's the right one for us."

She felt a light pressure on her shoulders. She shrugged, but his hands grew heavier. "What brings all this on? Sister Mary Grace and Luis?"

"I thought I was going to die today."

His thumbs began a slow massage. "I would have missed you."

"Great. That helps immensely."

"I would have said to myself, the world's not the same place without Felice in it. The sun's dimmer, the night's drearier."

"Sure. I know just what you mean. I felt that way when the turtle in my fourth-grade classroom died."

He laughed, and the sound rumbled provocatively past her ear. "This would have been different."

She still didn't face him. "I keep hearing the sound of the trigger snapping. I keep waiting for the bullet to explode, to tear me apart." She took a deep, shaken breath. "But it never does, and I'm left with those moments in between and what I was thinking about you."

"You thought about me?"

"There were two little girls at the Valley Station today. One crawled up in my lap, and I realized I didn't know anything about kids. I could have had a kid by now, if I'd just thought about it."

"It takes more than thinking."

"I know what it takes. It takes what you and I did constantly for a few days. I thought about that up on that godforsaken mountain trail. We made love, Gallagher. Kids come from that. Families come from that. And it was love. I fell in love with you. You probably didn't know it, but I did."

She could feel the pressure of his hands grow lighter. His thumbs stopped their provocative massage. She could feel his withdrawal as surely as if he had announced it, but she had started something that had to be finished.

And she was going to finish it, because it took a new kind of courage to explore her feelings, and she had never been one to shy away from a challenge.

"I know you don't want to hear this," she said. "But I'm going to tell you anyway." She felt his hands leave her shoulders, but she pressed on.

"I didn't mean to fall in love with you. You're exasperating and arrogant, and sometimes you talk to me like I'm an idiot. You've never pretended you were after anything but my body. You're not husband material, and besides, I wasn't looking for a husband. But love isn't something you choose, I guess. I mean, I don't know much about it, but that much seems clear."

"Felice—"

She didn't have to be psychic to predict volumes from the way he said her name. It was Felice, not desert flower. He sounded like a man who wanted nothing more than to cut off this line of conversation.

"Look, don't worry," she said. "I'll get over you. You—"

"Save it."

She felt the wind at her back and knew he was no longer there. She whirled, eyes wide with hurt.

Gallagher was drawing his gun from under his jacket.

"What the hell are you doing?"

He grabbed her arm and jerked her behind a pillar supporting the slatted roof. "Two guys down there." He snapped his head toward the grove. "See them?"

She stared at him.

"They're heading toward Sister Mary Grace and Luis."

Felice turned her head to search for the men. "You're paranoid. Those are just two of his *palmeros*. I saw them last time I was here. They work in the groves with the dates."

"It's still hot as hell, and they're wearing windbreakers."

"Luis irrigates in the evening. They probably don't want to get wet when the sprinklers—"

Gallagher ignored her and began to weave in and out of the pillars closest to the house.

"I'm coming," she said in a loud whisper.

He waved her back. "No gun," he mouthed.

Her hand slipped under her jacket automatically, but her gun was somewhere between the top and bottom of Mount San Jacinto. She watched as he hid himself among the shrubbery. Sister Mary Grace and Luis were in an open area, just to one side of the groves. Gallagher would have to expose himself in order to protect them.

She still thought his imagination was working overtime, but she kept her eyes on the men and tried to think what she could do to assist if Gallagher were correct.

The *palmero* closer to Luis turned toward the house, as if he was checking to see whether anyone was watching. The movement could have been casual; it could have been completely innocent. But in that moment, she knew Gallagher hadn't been imagining anything. She knew the way a guilty man, a man bent on committing a crime moved. She knew the way such a man checked out his environment, because she'd paced her share of urban sidewalks and collared her share of petty criminals.

She knew this man's intentions weren't petty.

Gallagher was no longer in her range of vision. She knew she hadn't been seen, because both *palmeros* continued toward Sister Mary Grace and Luis.

Gallagher didn't have a chance. He could be Griff Bryant in one of his starring roles, with stuntmen and a host of special effects at his disposal, and he still wouldn't have a chance. Both *palmeros* were probably armed; both were probably fanatical zealots willing to lay down their lives to create chaos. When the smoke cleared, the chances were good that no one would be alive.

She didn't have a gun, and even if she had, by the time she got close enough to use it the worst could be over. It was too late to run for help, had been too late for minutes.

Wildly she looked around for anything to distract the men. Distraction could be Gallagher's badly needed cover. Her gaze landed on the gazebo. For the briefest seconds she mourned the loss of her gun. If she shot from the gazebo, her aim would be lousy, but it would confuse the men, give Gallagher time to close in. If she had a gun.

If she shot from the gazebo.

With her eyes on the men she darted from pillar to pillar. The quickest way to the gazebo and the safest was to ease herself into the pool and swim its width. She didn't want to take the time to go around it, and she didn't want her presence known. She would be seen if she ran its perimeter, but not if she swam.

Ten yards from the pool she began to crawl. The gardens surrounding it were tall enough to shield her, and at the poolside she stripped off her shoes and jacket and eased herself into the water. She swam underwater so as not to splash; then at the other side she surfaced and crawled out, careful to stay down so that she was still shielded by Luis's elaborate landscaping.

The gazebo was only yards away, but the path was not protected. She knew that if she was seen the *palmeros* would no fire at her but at Luis and Sister Mary Grace. She said a short fervent prayer that they were too absorbed in their mission to catch sight of her, and, ducking low, she began to run.

She stumbled once, but she kept herself from falling. She stood and sprinted the last few yards to the gazebo and took th steps two at a time. Praying once more, she wrenched open the cabinets just inside the door and began to flick switches.

A shout echoed from the direction of the groves. Madly her hands raced across the panel, turning knobs, pushing buttons, reversing the position of every switch. She reached the last one, then, heart in mouth, crouched in a safe corner to see what she had wrought.

Gallagher felt a jolt of adrenaline as he closed in on the *palmeros,* and a bigger jolt of terror. He'd put his body on the line for too many years not to know how stacked the odds were against him. His regrets were many, and the biggest was that he and Felice had never finished their conversation.

She loved him; she had told him so. He made a silent vow to show the same kind of emotional courage and tell her he loved her. If he ever got the chance.

The men stalking Luis and Sister Mary Grace were just ahead of him, but they were two and he was one. They were fanatics, and he knew fanatics. As he watched, one of the men drew a gun. Until that moment he'd prayed he was wrong.

If he fired, one would shoot at him while the other killed Sister Mary Grace. His only chance was to disable them both before that happened, and that was a chance in a million. There were trees between him and them. Huge, symmetrical rows of date palms. He was a good shot, but not that good.

He felt a wave of nausea. Sister Mary Grace was going to die, and probably Luis, too. He wasn't good enough to stop it. Guts had nothing to do with it. He would trade guts for a distraction. Anything.

A banshee screech shattered the deceptive silence of the gardens surrounding him. Water began to pour from sprinklers so well hidden he would never have known they were there. He was soaked immediately as Luis's gardens and groves were turned into a water park. Water sprayed in every direction, great shooting spires of it from the groves, more sedate fountains from the gardens. For a moment he couldn't see through the spray; then he spotted the four figures just ahead of him.

One of the *palmeros* had taken a direct hit. His hands were in front of him as he leaped away from the spout surging in his face. Through water-beaded eyelashes, Gallagher could see Luis standing in front of Sister Mary Grace to protect her from the water, still not aware of the greater danger.

It was all he needed. He stood and fired, wounding the *palmero* whose gun was still in his hand. Then he aimed at the second and fired, missed, then fired again. Both men were on the ground as he ran through the spray to Sister Mary Grace and Luis.

"Get down," he shouted, holding his gun in front of him with both hands. An alarm began to sound through the estate. Water trickled down his face and blinded him; the alarm deafened him. He drew closer to the men and saw one struggle to reach his gun, just inches from his hand. He shot the ground at the man's fingertips in warning. The bullet skidded crazily before it lodged in the trunk of a palm. The man lay still.

The alarm was silenced, but for a moment Gallagher's ears still rang with it. Then he heard footsteps closing in on him from all sides. Through the rainbow-hued spray he recognized his colleagues. The water shut off as suddenly as it had come on.

"So the man said, 'God, send me a miracle.' And a miracle was delivered," he muttered.

He felt a hand clap down on his shoulder. He heard Barker's voice. "You must be shaken up. I've never heard you quoting scripture."

"Writing it." Gallagher flipped the safety on his gun and stuck it in his holster. "I'm writing it."

He heard more footsteps pounding through the bushes and saw a water-soaked angel in green flying across the ground toward him.

Then she was in his arms.

Chapter 17

The next morning Felice rose long before anyone else, or so she thought. But there was a figure already standing in Luis's gazebo when, barefooted and wearing jeans and a shirt supplied by Sandy, she went to watch the sunrise.

Startled, she called the woman's name before she thought better of it. "Sister Mary Grace."

"Felice." Sister Mary Grace turned and smiled. "Come join me."

Felice held up her hands. "I wasn't following you. I promise."

"Even if you were, it wouldn't matter. I don't need to be alone anymore."

Felice took the stairs to her side and stood, looking out over the mountains. "It sounds like you've made a decision."

"Yesterday."

The previous evening had been so taken up with questions and more questions, theories and more theories, that Felice had not been able to hold a conversation with anyone. As suspected, the men who Gallagher had apprehended had been from Isla Tesoro, and he and his men had spent hours at the hospital getting information from them. As the evening had progressed, Gallagher had come and gone, and Sister Mary Grace had patiently been examined and cross-examined. Felice had given up trying to talk to anyone, but she had listened long enough to submit to Gallagher's insistence that she remain there for the night, even though, as she had politely pointed out, so far the authorities had experienced their own problems offering protection.

Now she wondered if she had the right to ask Sister Mary Grace what she was planning to do. She was no longer officially involved, and she and this woman could hardly be considered friends.

"I'm going back to Tesoro," Sister Mary Grace said, before Felice could decide how or if to broach the subject of her future. "The men who were going to kill me yesterday are in custody now. The right wing on the island seems to be disintegrating. It's doubtful that they'll have the energy or focus to keep sending assassins after me."

"But they might. These men were very clever. Impersonating Luis's *palmeros* took a lot of scheming and precision."

She shrugged. "I know. Still, the Tesoro government says that now that I've been directly threatened, they can offer me protection. I'll have a bodyguard, and I suppose I'll allow that, since my death could hurt the people I want to help."

"I don't understand." Felice watched the woman beside her and ignored the colors playing over the mountains. "Why?"

"Why am I going? Or why am I leaving Luis? You're a romantic, dear. Did you know that?"

Felice felt her cheeks grow warmer. "You love Luis."

"Yes, I do. I always have. But my first love is someone else, and my first loyalty is to His plans for me." She folded her arms and turned a little so that she could see Felice's face. "Luis understands now, I think. I can never be what he wants me to be, but he's promised to visit me on Tesoro and to write. We won't be cut off from each other again."

Felice tried to understand, but her feelings must have shown plainly in her eyes. Sister Mary Grace smiled. "This would be hard for you to understand, I suppose. Particularly..." Her voice trailed off.

"Because I'm irreverent, selfish and materialistic?"

"Don't tell me you really think of yourself that way?" Sister Mary Grace linked arms with her, as naturally as if they had always been best friends. "You're warm, concerned, caring. You spent weeks of your life at the Blessed Garden so you could protect me, and you made the very best of your time there."

She laughed as Felice began to protest. "Yes, you did. You've no potential for the religious life, but you struggled valiantly to fit in. And don't tell me you're materialistic. Luis tells me you're refusing his check."

Felice didn't want to talk about that. "A minute ago you said your decision to leave Luis would be hard for me to understand. What did you mean?"

"You're head over heels in love yourself."

Felice stared at the mountains. In the throes of dawn, they were gold and rose, and the light surrounding them seemed a promise. "I don't know that I'd say that, exactly."

"Then what would you say?"

"That I'm a fool."

There were footsteps on the stairs behind them, and Luis appeared. Sister Mary Grace held out her hand to him, and he joined them. "Couldn't you sleep?" she asked.

Luis's smile was meant only for her, and the sadness in it made Felice turn away. "I didn't want to waste any of the time left to us," he said.

Felice drew her arm from the warm clasp of Sister Mary Grace. It was time to leave. "I promised Gallagher I'd stay last night, but I didn't promise I'd stay this morning. I've got a lot I have to do."

"Will I see you again before I leave for Tesoro? I won't be going until the weekend," Sister Mary Grace said.

"I'd like that."

"Come on Friday for dinner," Luis said. He held out his hand.

Felice reached to take it and realized there was something in t. She looked closer and saw it was a check. "I told you. No."

"I really should call your mother," Luis said. "I haven't talked to dear Nita in such a long time. And I know she'd be thrilled to hear everything you've done for me."

Felice tried to imagine the effect that would have. "You're not serious."

"Take it."

Sister Mary Grace took the check instead and pressed it into Felice's palm. "There are so many ways to spend money. Good ways. Better ways." She closed Felice's fingers around it.

"And please be careful," Luis warned. "Gallagher seemed greatly concerned that you could still be in danger."

"The men who threatened me got what they wanted. They're finished with me." Felice leaned forward and kissed both their cheeks. "Friday."

When she looked back over her shoulder, Luis and Sister Mary Grace were standing quietly, arms around each other's waists, watching the sun rise.

Felice decided to wear white. The choice had been an unconscious one, although once she was wearing the simple white skirt and blouse of Mexican cotton she realized what she had done. She had chosen the closest thing she owned to a robe of the Sisters of the Garden.

Sister Felicia's robe, the robe she had worn on her desert trek, had been washed, bleached and mended as best the cleaners could manage. She had gotten it on her way back to her apartment and now it lay across the backseat of her car, waiting for her to return it.

She was going back to the convent.

She fussed over her hair and what jewelry to wear—simple gold hoops and a tiny cross that had been her grandmother's. She told herself that she had done harder things, though she couldn't think of any. When the doorbell rang, she welcomed the interruption, sure that it was Kelley, who had said she might stop by to hear all the details of yesterday's adventures before heading into the office.

The distorted, house-of-mirrors image through her peep-hole was not a woman. She opened the door to examine an altogether too appealing Gallagher.

She hoped she could still act. "I'm not going to be a prisoner," she said, fastening the last earring with studied nonchalance. "If you've come to tell me not to go anywhere today, you can forget it."

"You're free to go anywhere you want."

"Oh?"

"May I come in?"

She weighed each of his syllables, multiplied them with hope, divided them by longing, summed them up with a realistic appraisal. Gallagher had not said one word to her after the capture of the men from Tesoro. There had been mass confusion and a multitude of demands that had to be met, questions that had to be answered. But there had been seconds, even minutes when he could have told her that her own declaration of love had been heard and was returned. Instead there had been silence.

She was not going to open herself to him again.

She pretended disinterest. "No." She reached for her purse and joined him in the hallway, locking the door behind her. "I'm going out."

"Are you?" He stepped in front of her so that she was trapped between his body and the door.

"You'd be amazed what I can do with a knee and two fingers," she warned.

"You'd be amazed how well I can defend myself."

She met his eyes without looking away. "No, I wouldn't be. Your defenses are legion."

The barb didn't escape him, but he chose to ignore it. "Where are you going?"

"If it's any of your business?" She shrugged. "I'm going back to the Blessed Garden."

"Why? Planning a new career?"

"I have my reasons."

"Mind if I tag along? I'd like to check on Ralph."

"You have a car. You're a grown-up. You can go where you want."

"I want to go with you."

"I don't see why."

"Suppose I tell you in the car?"

She shrugged again, and he stepped away and followed close behind.

In the car, just outside the garage, she stopped to put the top down and flick on her radio. She chose an L.A. station famous for playing rap music without commercials and turned it to a volume that discouraged conversation.

Out on the highway, Gallagher switched off the radio, keeping his hand on the knob when she tried to turn it back on. "This is how you protect yourself? Top down? Radio loud enough to tell everybody for miles you're coming?"

She stepped down on the gas pedal. "You said I was free to go anywhere," she shouted over the wind whooshing past them. "I assume that means I don't have any reason to protect myself anymore."

"We've got the men who threatened you in custody. You'll need to go in late this afternoon and make a positive ID."

She admired their success in finding the men, but she wasn't about to tell him. "Who are they?"

"A couple of third-rate investigators who dabble in anything they can to make a little money. Want to guess who hired them?"

"The list might get tiresome."

He named the lovable husband and father in a sitcom that had been a five-year phenomenon.

She whistled sharply and forgot to be blasé. "I told you about that case when we were out in the desert. Remember? He was cheating on his wife with every female who crossed his path, but he refused to give her a divorce. So she hired me, and I got enough dirt on him to spread his name over the front page of every newspaper in the country."

"Poor guy."

"Poor guy, my foot." She slapped her palm against the steering wheel. "She wanted what she was entitled to, and that's all. He was forced to split everything down the middle without a fuss because she threatened to expose him. If she hadn't had that, she would have had to fight for every nickel.''

''Apparently he didn't see it that way. If we can prove it *was* him, maybe he'll do some jail time to change his mind.''

''He was left with millions. I know, I saw the settlement.'' She made the turn that would take them directly to the Blessed Garden. ''He said I'd taken everything from him. Everything!'' She had to swallow yesterday's fear again. ''He doesn't know what everything means. And when he sent those two goons with the gold chains to kidnap me—''

''*They* weren't your kidnappers.''

''What do you mean?''

''Just that. The kidnappers weren't the men on the mountain. Those guys were late tracing you to the Blessed Garden. The men who grabbed you were the same ones who went after Sister Mary Grace at Luis's last night. They did mistake you for her, just like we'd thought all along.''

Cold chills snaked up her spine. Late last night, staring through the darkness at nothing, she had convinced herself that she had never really been in serious danger. The men on the mountain had meant to scare her, nothing more. She had been safe. She had almost convinced herself.

Now she knew that the men who had mistakenly taken her from the convent had meant to kill her. She had almost died. ''Why didn't they kill me right away? Why did they kidnap me?''

''They were góing to demand ransom from the Isla Tesoro government, in the name of the left wing. Then, after they got their money, they were going to kill you—if you had been Sister Mary Grace.''

''When they found out I wasn't Sister Mary Grace, they would have killed me immediately.'' Suddenly death seemed much closer. She had never feared it so much, because she had never felt she had so much to lose.

''The accent,'' she said. ''The men in the car spoke a few words. One of them had an accent, but it wasn't Southern. I couldn't hear well enough to know anything for sure, and after I threw myself out of the car, I forgot."

She turned to him, and her vulnerability showed. "It must have been Spanish, but I forgot. How could I have forgotten something so important? If I'd remembered, if I'd put two and two together like I'm paid to do, we would have known yesterday that Sister Mary Grace was still in danger."

He wanted to comfort her, but he knew better than to try. He went about it the back way. "We never stopped acting like she was in danger. Besides, everything that happened was confusing. The old man with the cow told us that two sleazeballs had come asking about a nun. I guess any nun was strange enough in the middle of nowhere. He thought they meant Sister Mary Grace, since she was the one he had given the ride to, and so did we. But that time it was you they wanted. He threw them off track when he told them he'd taken her into Los Angeles to catch a bus to San Diego. That's why they didn't find you until yesterday. They had traced you to the Blessed Garden, then they were thrown off course until they backtracked."

"Two nuns. Two different sets of creeps."

"Both in custody," he reminded her. "You're safe now."

"And Sister Mary Grace?"

"She lives a charmed life. We've been promised she'll be protected." He hesitated. "We can even hope she will be."

"Nothing's for sure, is it?"

"Some things are," he said mysteriously. He settled back against his seat to close his eyes.

She drove the rest of the way in silence, overloaded with emotions, not the least of which was love for the man beside her. But once again he had said nothing about their relationship. She had barely found the strength to be honest with him once. She could not find it again.

At the gates to the Blessed Garden she had the urge to turn and start back toward Palm Springs, but she knew this was one last thing she had to see through. She got out of her car and took the robe in her arms. Gallagher got out with her.

She rang the bell and waited for someone to answer. Sister Faith gasped when she saw her, then clamped her lips together. Felice got the distinct impression it was to discipline a smile.

"Sister Faith," she said humbly, "would it be possible to see Mother Jeanne?"

Sister Faith let them in without a word. Gallagher took Felice's arm at the front door. "I'm going to find Ralph."

"You're not coming?"

"This one's yours, desert flower."

Felice followed Sister Faith through the Blessed Garden's hallways. After a second she realized she was being allowed into the interior of the convent, where visitors never went. "I don't want any special privileges," she said, her voice hushed. "I could wait in the visitors' parlor."

"And what will you see in this hall that you didn't see every day for weeks?" Sister Faith asked.

"I never wanted to pry or hurt anyone."

Sister Faith didn't reply. They passed other sisters, women who Felice realized she would never be able to chat with or work with again. She felt a distinct sense of loss.

Sister Faith left her at the door to Mother Jeanne's office. She took a deep breath before she knocked. She hesitated, even after Mother Jeanne's response, but finally she opened the door.

"Mother Jeanne?"

Mother Jeanne looked up. Slowly she removed her wire-rimmed spectacles. Even more slowly she shook her head. "You have courage. I'll give you that, child."

"May we talk?"

"Have we anything to talk about?"

Felice entered the office and closed the door behind her. "I came to return my robe. It...it's not in the best of shape." She laid the robe across a chair.

"I understand that you weren't in the best of shape when you were last wearing it, either."

"I'm fine. I . . ." She stopped. "You know, it's no easier being in here when I'm not a nun than when I was."

"You never were a nun."

"I know you're not going to understand this, but I was on my own kind of quest while I was here." Felice walked around the room, examining the items on the bookshelves lining the walls. It was easier than facing Mother Jeanne. "I came to protect one of your sisters. I came under false pretenses because that was the only way I could do it, but I never liked the lies I had to tell. I started to feel like I was part of something while I was here, almost like you were my family. I didn't want to lie, but I didn't want Sister Mary Grace to be hurt or killed, either. I had to make a choice, and I'd make the same one again."

"Would you?"

Felice faced her. "Yes. Look, I could never live the religious life. Both of us know that."

"I'll agree."

"But I have my own talents and abilities, and while I was here I was putting them to work for..." She swallowed, because the words didn't want to come out of her throat. "For a greater good."

"Surprises you, doesn't it?" Mother Jeanne sat back. "Why *are* you here?"

"To ask for your forgiveness. To tell you I'm sorry I had to breach your trust." Felice reached in her purse and pulled out Luis's check, which she had endorsed. "To give you this." She stepped forward and put the check on Mother Jeanne's desk.

Mother Jeanne put her spectacles back on and squinted over the numbers. "Am I counting these zeros right?"

"Probably."

She took off her spectacles again. "A bribe?"

"The church doesn't sell indulgences anymore, does it?"

"Just so you know, Father Melrose and I have discussed your presence here, and we've decided that no one higher in authority ever has to find out. You're in no danger of the church taking action against you."

Felice shook her head. "Thanks. But that's not what this is about. I just want you to have it. I know it will help." She managed a joke. "Maybe you can even get rid of the goats."

Mother Jeanne folded the check and slipped it in her desk drawer. "We'll keep the goats, thank you, but we might get a new air conditioner."

Felice turned to go.

"You should know one more thing," Mother Jeanne said sternly. Felice turned back, expecting the worst. Then the mother superior smiled, and her voice gentled. "All the sisters agree, *Sister* Felicia. The house seems emptier without you."

"So you're feeling better?" Gallagher asked Ralph.

"Don't need you. Kin do everything myself."

"I'm not here to take your job," Gallagher assured him. "I'm working somewhere else now."

"No life for a young man here." Ralph looked up from the old plow he was coating with oil. "Need a wife and kids. I know."

Gallagher remembered Ralph's life story, but he also knew an opening when he heard one. "Did you ever have a wife, Ralph?"

"Did. Let her go without a fight. A fool."

Gallagher was sure he didn't mean the fool had been his wife. He was deeply moved. In his own odd way, Ralph was reaching out to him, trying to be sure Gallagher didn't follow in his footsteps. "It's hard to tell a woman you love her, need her."

"You don't do it, she has to. Humiliation. That's what that is. Women don't like it."

"I'll remember."

"Good." Ralph stood and held out an oil-coated hand. "Good luck."

Gallagher grasped his hand firmly. "Father Melrose will know how to get hold of me if you ever need anything."

"Won't."

Gallagher smiled. "Well, I might need you, so let's stay in touch."

Ralph's smile was missing three teeth and decidedly out of practice. But it was genuine.

* * *

Felice put the top up and left the radio off for the trip back to Palm Springs. Still, they were halfway there before either of them spoke.

"I quit my job," Gallagher said.

Felice swerved, and for a moment she had to concentrate on staying on the highway. "You what?"

"I quit. Well, that's not quite true. I asked for a demotion. I'll be narrowing my scope a little. Having more fun."

"What does that mean, exactly? Or shouldn't I ask?"

"Less paper pushing, more fieldwork." He paused. "A hotter, drier climate."

"Am I supposed to guess? Or is this just your typical evasive maneuvering."

"Can you use a friend in the local FBI office?"

Driving seemed to be getting more and more difficult. Felice realized her pulse was racing as fast as the car. "If there was such a thing."

"There might be. Who knows?"

"Look, even if you were *head* of the local office, you wouldn't give me information." She glanced at him and saw that she had scored a hit. She pushed on. "Not even if we were lovers. Not even if we were married and I was the mother of your children!"

"Interesting you should put it that way."

"That was hypothetical."

"I'm going to have to look for a house. I've seen one I liked. It's up in the mountains. Needs a lot of work, though, so I think I can get a good deal on it, though a local woman may have made an offer on it."

"Josiah, what are you trying to say?"

Minutes passed before he spoke. "Ralph had some interesting things to tell me."

"Impossible."

"He was married once, but you probably already know that. He told me he should have fought harder to keep that marriage alive."

She managed something appropriately sympathetic.

"I said that telling a woman you love her and need her is hard. I was trying to show him I understood," Gallagher continued.

"Of course you were." Her gaze flicked to the speedometer, and her foot leapt to the brake.

"He said that women don't like to be the ones to tell a man they love him. He said it was humiliating."

"A big word for Ralph. He must have been moved."

"I was moved."

She waited. The silence grew longer and longer. "Well?" she said at last, louder than she'd intended.

"I'm sure Ralph thinks a man should ask a woman to marry him, too. To save her the humiliation. If we were to fall in love, for instance, I'd have to be the one to ask you to marry me."

"Well, just suppose we did fall in love. Would you be the one to do the asking?"

"I don't know. A little humiliation might be good for you."

She told him what she thought of that in one word.

He winced at her language and touched her arm. "Would you have the courage to ask me?"

"Any man who waits for me to go down on my knees is going to have to wait forever!"

"I guess I would have to be the one to ask, then."

She glanced at him. He had shut his eyes and appeared to be resting. "*If* we'd fallen in love," she said sharply.

"We have."

She drew a deep breath. "Have we?"

"Yeah." He sounded unconcerned.

"And *if* we were even *thinking* about marriage."

"We are."

"Are we?"

"Yeah."

She edged the car to the side of the highway, applying the brake judiciously. "And *if* you had more than about a minute to live!"

He opened his eyes in time to watch the car glide to a stop. "I've got years. With you, I hope." He turned a little and held out his arms.

She went into them, and there on the side of the highway, she made sure that she had understood him.

There had been no mistake.

*   *   *   *   *

SILHOUETTE·INTIMATE·MOMENTS®

COMING NEXT MONTH

#405 PROBABLE CAUSE—Marilyn Pappano

Strictly-by-the-book FBI agent Thad McNally had never gotten over his love for Lindsey Phillips. So when the case that had torn them apart was reopened, he didn't hesitate—he went to see her. But things got complicated when he realized that her life—as well as their love—was in danger.

#406 THE MAN NEXT DOOR—Alexandra Sellers

Hot on the trail of an international smuggling ring, police officer Sunny Delancey's low profile was nearly compromised when a mischievous cat got her entangled with the infamous Jock Prentiss. Yet being front-page news proved to be an advantage Sunny couldn't pass up, especially since being considered this hunk's latest lover was no hardship!

#407 TAKING SIDES—Lucy Hamilton

Determined to clear her father's reputation, faithful daughter Hope Carruthers confronted Sean Boudreaux, the only man who could set the record straight. Yet when searching for the truth demanded working closely with sexy Sean, Hope's heart discovered a different sort of truth altogether.

#408 ANGEL ON MY SHOULDER—Ann Williams

Cynical Will Alexander had no idea who the cupcake with the big blue eyes was—she claimed to be Cassandra, his guardian angel—but there was no way *anyone*, not even a woman as enticing as Cassandra, would stop him from getting revenge against his enemy. But he hadn't counted on Cassandra's heavenly means of persuasion....

AVAILABLE THIS MONTH:

Take 4 bestselling love stories FREE

Plus get a FREE surprise gift!

Special Limited-time Offer

Mail to
Silhouette Reader Service™
3010 Walden Avenue
P.O. Box 1867
Buffalo, N.Y. 14269-1867

YES! Please send me 4 free Silhouette Intimate Moments® novels and my free surprise gift. Then send me 4 brand-new novels every month, which I will receive months before they appear in bookstores. Bill me at the low price of $2.92 each—a savings of 33¢ apiece off cover prices. There are no shipping, handling or other hidden costs. I understand that accepting the books and gift places me under no obligation ever to buy any books. I can always return a shipment and cancel at any time. Even if I never buy another book from Silhouette, the 4 free books and the surprise gift are mine to keep forever.

240 BPA AC9Q

Name	(PLEASE PRINT)	
Address		Apt. No.
City	State	Zip

This offer is limited to one order per household and not valid to present Silhouette Intimate Moments® subscribers. Terms and prices are subject to change. Sales tax applicable in N.Y.

MOM-BPA20R   © 1990 Harlequin Enterprises Limited

SIX WILDLY SEXY HEROES FROM
SIX SENSATIONAL COUNTRIES
MAN OF THE WORLD
ONLY IN

® SILHOUETTE®
Desire™

Have you ever longed to visit another country and meet your
own special hero? Or maybe you think happiness can be found
in your own backyard. No matter what, MAN OF THE WORLD is
sure to fulfill your deepest desires. From Europe to the U.S.A.,
from Australia to the hot desert sands, when you open the
covers of a MAN OF THE WORLD book, you'll find the man of
your dreams waiting for you.

Travel to . . .

Australia in Linda Lael Miller's WILD ABOUT HARRY
England in Kathleen Korbel's A FINE MADNESS
Italy in Lucy Gordon's ON HIS HONOR
The kingdom of Rashdani in Barbara Faith's
   LION OF THE DESERT
Austria in Jennifer Greene's FALCONER
The United States in BJ James's SLADE'S WOMAN

MAN OF THE WORLD . . . available in October,
only in Silhouette Desire!

SDMOW

WRITTEN IN THE STARS

STUNG BY LOVE

Will Susannah Dushay pay the price for sexy Scorpio Jake Taggart's revenge on her family in Ginna Gray's STING OF THE SCORPION, November's WRITTEN IN THE STARS?

Susannah only knew that Jake was her new employer and that he and his offer— *demand*—of marriage were difficult to resist. What would happen when she discovered the truth?

Find out in STING OF THE SCORPION by Ginna Gray... coming from Silhouette Romance this November. It's WRITTEN IN THE STARS!

Available in November at your favorite retail outlet, or order your copy now by sending your name, address, zip or postal code, along with a check or money order for $2.59 (please do not send cash), plus 75¢ postage and handling ($1.00 in Canada) for each book ordered, payable to Silhouette Reader Service to:

In the U.S.
3010 Walden Avenue
P.O. Box 1396
Buffalo, NY 14269-1396

In Canada
P.O. Box 609
Fort Erie, Ontario
L2A 5X3

Please specify book title with your order.
Canadian residents add applicable federal and provincial taxes.

NOVSTAR

Silhouette Romance®

FASHION
A WHOLE NEW YOU
WIN
CARS, TRIPS, CASH!

SILHOUETTE®
OFFICIAL SWEEPSTAKES
RULES

NO PURCHASE NECESSARY

1. To enter, complete an Official Entry Form or 3" × 5" index card by hand-printing, in plain block letters, your complete name, address, phone number and age, and mailing it to: Silhouette Fashion A Whole New You Sweepstakes, P.O. Box 9056, Buffalo, NY 14269-9056.

   No responsibility is assumed for lost, late or misdirected mail. Entries must be sent separately with first class postage affixed, and be received no later than December 31, 1991 for eligibility.

2. Winners will be selected by D.L. Blair, Inc., an independent judging organization whose decisions are final, in random drawings to be held on January 30, 1992 in Blair, NE at 10:00 a.m. from among all eligible entries received.

3. The prizes to be awarded and their approximate retail values are as follows: Grand Prize — A brand-new Ford Explorer 4×4 plus a trip for two (2) to Hawaii, including round-trip air transportation, six (6) nights hotel accommodation, a $1,400 meal/spending money stipend and $2,000 cash toward a new fashion wardrobe (approximate value: $28,000) or $15,000 cash; two (2) Second Prizes — A trip to Hawaii, including round-trip air transportation, six (6) nights hotel accommodation, a $1,400 meal/spending money stipend and $2,000 cash toward a new fashion wardrobe (approximate value: $11,000) or $5,000 cash; three (3) Third Prizes — $2,000 cash toward a new fashion wardrobe. All prizes are valued in U.S. currency. Travel award air transportation is from the commercial airport nearest winner's home. Travel is subject to space and accommodation availability, and must be completed by June 30, 1993. Sweepstakes offer is open to residents of the U.S. and Canada who are 21 years of age or older as of December 31, 1991, except residents of Puerto Rico, employees and immediate family members of Torstar Corp., its affiliates, subsidiaries, and all agencies, entities and persons connected with the use, marketing, or conduct of this sweepstakes. All federal, state, provincial, municipal and local laws apply. Offer void wherever prohibited by law. Taxes and/or duties, applicable registration and licensing fees, are the sole responsibility of the winners. Any litigation within the province of Quebec respecting the conduct and awarding of a prize may be submitted to the Régie des loteries et courses du Québec. All prizes will be awarded; winners will be notified by mail. No substitution of prizes is permitted.

4. Potential winners must sign and return any required Affidavit of Eligibility/Release of Liability within 30 days of notification. In the event of noncompliance within this time period, the prize may be awarded to an alternate winner. Any prize or prize notification returned as undeliverable may result in the awarding of that prize to an alternate winner. By acceptance of their prize, winners consent to use of their names, photographs or their likenesses for purposes of advertising, trade and promotion on behalf of Torstar Corp. without further compensation. Canadian winners must correctly answer a time-limited arithmetical question in order to be awarded a prize.

5. For a list of winners (available after 3/31/92), send a separate stamped, self-addressed envelope to: Silhouette Fashion A Whole New You Sweepstakes, P.O. Box 4685, Blair, NE 68009.

PREMIUM OFFER TERMS

To receive your gift, complete the Offer Certificate according to directions. Be certain to enclose the required number of "Fashion A Whole New You" proofs of product purchase (which are found on the last page of every specially marked "Fashion A Whole New You" Silhouette or Harlequin romance novel). Requests must be received no later than December 31, 1991. Limit: four (4) gifts per name, family, group, organization or address. Items depicted are for illustrative purposes only and may not be exactly as shown. Please allow 6 to 8 weeks for receipt of order. Offer good while quantities of gifts last. In the event an ordered gift is no longer available, you will receive a free, previously unpublished Silhouette or Harlequin book for every proof of purchase you have submitted with your request, plus a refund of the postage and handling charge you have included. Offer good in the U.S. and Canada only.

SLFW-SWPR

SILHOUETTE® OFFICIAL SWEEPSTAKES ENTRY FORM

4-FWSIS-3

Complete and return this Entry Form immediately – the more entries you submit, the better your chances of winning!

- Entries must be received by December 31, 1991.
- A Random draw will take place on January 30, 1992.
- No purchase necessary.

Yes, I want to win a FASHION A WHOLE NEW YOU Sensuous and Adventurous prize from Silhouette:

Name _____ Telephone _____ Age _____

Address _____

City _____ State _____ Zip _____

Return Entries to: Silhouette FASHION A WHOLE NEW YOU,
P.O. Box 9056, Buffalo, NY 14269-9056 © 1991 Harlequin Enterprises Limited

PREMIUM OFFER

To receive your free gift, send us the required number of proofs-of-purchase from any specially marked FASHION A WHOLE NEW YOU Silhouette or Harlequin Book with the Offer Certificate properly completed, plus a check or money order (do not send cash) to cover postage and handling payable to Silhouette FASHION A WHOLE NEW YOU Offer. We will send you the specified gift.

OFFER CERTIFICATE

Item	A. SENSUAL DESIGNER VANITY BOX COLLECTION (set of 4) (Suggested Retail Price $60.00)	B. ADVENTUROUS TRAVEL COSMETIC CASE SET (set of 3) (Suggested Retail Price $25.00)
# of proofs-of-purchase	18	12
Postage and Handling	$3.50	$2.95
Check one	☐	☐

Name _____

Address _____

City _____ State _____ Zip _____

Mail this certificate, designated number of proofs-of-purchase and check or money order for postage and handling to: Silhouette FASHION A WHOLE NEW YOU Gift Offer, P.O. Box 9057, Buffalo, NY 14269-9057. Requests must be received by December 31, 1991.

ONE PROOF-OF-PURCHASE

4-FWSIP-3

To collect your fabulous free gift you must include the necessary number of proofs-of-purchase with a properly completed Offer Certificate.

© 1991 Harlequin Enterprises Limited

See previous page for details.